For Mandy and Heather

CHAPTER
ONE

London, 15 May 1953

It was raining when Max came out of the news cinema but even this could not dent his good spirits. He simply adjusted his trilby and kept his head down as he crossed Piccadilly Circus. Rain in the town was not the same as rain in the provinces: memories of sleet-washed seaside promenades, of deckchairs sodden and flapping in the wind, of Sunday afternoons so grey and endless that they seemed like a foretaste of purgatory. But in London the red buses were still running, people were still darting through the traffic and somewhere — the Theatre Royal, Drury Lane to be exact — his name was spelled out in lights.

LONDON PREPARES FOR CORONATION. That was the headline on the newsstand and variations of it had been appearing all week. The newsreel he had just seen had been full of it: the processional route to include twenty-six miles of specially built stands, the flowers being grown, the dresses being made. All this optimism, all this romanticism, it was very un-English. Max thought he actually preferred it when the country was stuck in post-war austerity gloom. As anyone in show

1

business would tell you: when people are depressed, the theatres are full.

Not that he could complain at the moment. He had a two-week run at the Theatre Royal, a Number One. Gigs like this were rare nowadays. Variety was dying. The old seaside theatres were closing and the pros were retiring or living out half-lives as dance professionals or bingo callers. "And it's hard work being a bingo caller," The Great Diablo assured him, "you have to be bally good at maths." Drinking whisky from tooth mugs late at night in their digs, the pros searched for a culprit, looking for someone to blame for the collapse of their world. Was it that the British people had changed? They had unexpectedly turned their backs on Churchill and voted in a socialist government (though the old boy was back in again now). Were they simply turning their backs on the old entertainers and looking for something new? Or was it the new NAAFI performers, fresh from entertaining the troops, with their incomprehensible jokes and strange surreal humour? Max had his own *bête noire* in this respect: Tommy Cooper, aka Cooper the Trooper, a magician who mumbled and stumbled his way around the stage and — what's more — deliberately got the tricks wrong. Yet people loved Tommy Cooper, more than they loved smooth, well-executed stage tricks, the kind that had made Max Mephisto a household name before the war.

But, in his heart, even as he knocked back the mugs of whisky, Max knew the real culprit. It was the enemy lurking in sitting rooms around the land. It was the smug grey box that had hypnotised America — Max's

2

old colleague Tony "The Mind" Mulholland couldn't have done it better — and was on its way to brainwashing Britain. Television. According to today's newsreel more than half the homes in the country had purchased a set in order to watch the coronation. And television would eventually kill variety stone dead. Why go out to a theatre when you could stay in your armchair watching those flickering little figures? Comedians would be all right. They could go on the wireless or on the evil box itself. But magicians were done for. Who would watch a magic trick on television? You needed to be there, eyes fixed on the cabinet, seeing the swords splinter the wood, wondering how the girl could possibly survive but somehow knowing that she would. You needed to have colour, music, lights and two thousand people in the audience. None of that was possible on a tiny black and white screen. No, magicians would vanish as surely as the girl disappearing into the cabinet. Abracadabra. Goodbye.

But, in the meantime, Max was halfway through a two-week run in London, playing to full houses every night. He owed his good fortune to a successful pantomime in Brighton two years ago. The producer, Bert Billingham, owned a string of theatres and he had been so impressed by Max's portrayal of Abanazar in *Aladdin* that he had immediately booked him for a tour of Number Ones, the top music hall venues. Now Max was enjoying a resurgence in popularity that had culminated in the Theatre Royal, Drury Lane. No, he couldn't really complain.

The rain had almost stopped. Max strolled past the Criterion and the Cafe de Paris, thinking of leisurely pre-war days, of champagne and showgirls and dinner-jacketed audiences rising to applaud him. The Cafe de Paris had suffered a direct hit during the Blitz, Ken "Snakehips" Johnson and his band dying as they had lived, performing on the stage. But, like so much else, the club had survived and reinvented itself and now the billboards were announcing a new band, live that evening. One of the new comedians too, Spike Milligan. Perhaps this was a sign that Max also could adapt to the post-war world. But, if he wasn't a magician, what else could he do?

At Charing Cross Road he found a small but excited crowd outside a news theatre. They were queuing, an elderly woman told him, to watch a film about the Queen. It was called *Happy and Glorious* and was due to start at six. Max looked at his watch. It was five o'clock. He raised his hat and made his way towards Trafalgar Square and the Strand.

He was staying at the Strand Palace Hotel. "If you stayed at cheaper hotels," his friend Edgar told him, "you wouldn't ever have to worry about money again." But Max had had his fill of cheap hotels, seaside digs with moustachioed landladies, soot-stained terraces in the north, faded stuccoed splendour in Bristol, Glasgow and Edinburgh. When he was in London and he could afford it, he stayed at the Strand Palace.

He stepped into the art deco lobby feeling, as he always did, that he was on board an ocean liner. Maybe he should do a transatlantic trip, performing card tricks

4

at the captain's table, entertaining bored widows as part of the cabaret. On second thoughts, maybe not.

"Mr Mephisto?" The commissionaire was approaching him, bearing an envelope on a silver salver. "A gentleman called for you this afternoon."

A gentleman. That must mean it wasn't one of the pros on the bill with him. Mildly interested, Max opened the envelope and found a note.

Can you please telephone me on the following number as soon as possible? It is a matter of the greatest urgency. There was a card too. Embossed. *General D.N. Petre DSO.*

It took a lot to surprise Max but, yes, he was surprised.

DI Edgar Stephens got the call at work. It had been a rather trying day. His team were investigating the death of Madame Zabini (real name: Doreen Barton), a gypsy fortune-teller whose body had been washed up near the Palace Pier two days ago. It was impossible to tell from the post-mortem whether Doreen had been pushed or whether she'd jumped. Her gypsy caravan was actually on the pier itself so, presumably, it would have been easy for her to climb onto the railing and jump to her death. But why? Her colleagues and family were unanimous in describing Doreen as a kind, contented woman, "salt of the earth", according to the pier's entertainment manager Lou Abrahams.

"You'd think, being psychic, she'd know if someone was going to do her in," said DS Bob Willis.

5

" 'Do her in'," repeated DS Emma Holmes. "Are you trying to sound like a member of a razor gang?"

The razor gangs were hoodlums who had terrorised Brighton in the thirties and forties. Based mainly at the racecourse, they were famous for racketeering and organised violence. In recent years, though, there were signs that the gangs were losing their influence, or that the police were winning the battle against them. Edgar inclined to the former view, his boss Frank Hodges to the latter.

There was no sign that Madame Zabini had been the victim of a gang. Her sad, bloated body showed no sign of razor cuts or violence of any kind. Had Doreen, who "liked a tipple" according to her daughter-in-law, simply had one too many and fallen into the sea? Edgar disliked unanswered questions but the family were pressing for a "proper gypsy funeral" so he ought to conclude the investigation. He was just reading through the reports when the telephone rang.

"DI Stephens? It's Petre here, General Petre."

The voice sounded as if Edgar should recognise it and, for a moment, he was swept back to the chaotic days at the start of the war when everyone seemed to have a job and a rank and licence to tell him what to do.

"I'm investigating a matter of gravest national importance," the voice continued, "and it's imperative I talk to you."

"To me?" That was the best that Edgar could manage.

"You're the Edgar Stephens who served in Horace Gormley's lot during the war? The so-called Magic Men?"

"Yes."

"Then it's you I need to talk to. I've contacted Mephisto as well."

"You've contacted *Max?*"

"Yes. Dashed inconvenient, he's doing some sort of show tonight and apparently it can't be put off. He's meeting me here at eleven o'clock."

"Eleven o'clock tonight?"

"Yes." Impatiently. "Eleven p.m. at the briefing rooms, number twelve, Whitehall. Ask for me."

Edgar was about to ask how he could get to London at eleven o'clock without a car but he suspected that General Petre was not one for the minutiae of life. Besides, he was almost bursting with curiosity.

"I'll be there," he said.

CHAPTER
TWO

Edgar set off for London that evening with a feeling of excitement which, though he hated to admit it, reminded him of the war. He didn't want to turn into one of those bores who was always talking nostalgically about "their" war but there was no denying that the prospect of imminent death did tend to throw the rest of your life into glorious Technicolor. Edgar had been called up in 1939, only two terms into enjoying his hard-won place at Oxford. In 1940, he had been sent to Norway as part of the Allied Expeditionary Force. That campaign — the cold, the exhaustion, the constant sense of failure and mismanagement — was still capable of resurfacing in his dreams. He lost a toe in Norway as well as most of his faith in the British army. And it was when he was recuperating that he was recruited into the Magic Men, a top-secret espionage unit. Or that was how it had been sold to him by the senior recruiting officer, at any rate. He had been sent to Inverness and there he had met Max and Diablo, had his heart broken and the rest of his illusions destroyed. Ironical really, because illusion had been the sole business of the Magic Men.

THE BLOOD CARD

ELLY GRIFFITHS

ISIS
LARGE
PRINT

First published in Great Britain 2016
by
Quercus

First Isis Edition
published 2019
by arrangement with
Hachette UK

A catalogue record for this book is available
from the British Library.

ISBN 978–1–78541–789–4 (hb)
ISBN 978–1–78541–795–5 (pb)

Published by
F. A. Thorpe (Publishing)
Anstey, Leicestershire

Set by Words & Graphics Ltd.
Anstey, Leicestershire
Printed and bound in Great Britain by
TJ Books Limited, Padstow, Cornwall

THE BLOOD CARD

Elizabeth's coronation is looming, but the murder
of their wartime commander, Colonel Cartwright,

sp   ens and
m   eaturing
an   Colonel
C   ng card,
th   is busy
re   variety
sh   on the
tr   provide
th   nds the
cl   , which
le   ent on
pi   on day.
N   foil the
pi   rds . . .

SPECIAL MESSAGE TO READERS

THE ULVERSCROFT FOUNDATION
(registered UK charity number 264873)
was established in 1972 to provide funds for
research, diagnosis and treatment of eye diseases.
Examples of major projects funded by
the Ulverscroft Foundation are:-

- The Children's Eye Unit at Moorfields Eye Hospital, London
- The Ulverscroft Children's Eye Unit at Great Ormond Street Hospital for Sick Children
- Funding research into eye diseases and treatment at the Department of Ophthalmology, University of Leicester
- The Ulverscroft Vision Research Group, Institute of Child Health
- Twin operating theatres at the Western Ophthalmic Hospital, London
- The Chair of Ophthalmology at the Royal Australian College of Ophthalmologists

You can help further the work of the Foundation
by making a donation or leaving a legacy.
Every contribution is gratefully received. If you
would like to help support the Foundation or
require further information, please contact:

THE ULVERSCROFT FOUNDATION
The Green, Bradgate Road, Anstey
Leicester LE7 7FU, England
Tel: (0116) 236 4325

website: www.foundation.ulverscroft.com

Driving to London along the dark, deserted roads also reminded him of the war years when — if you were lucky enough to get hold of a staff car — the streets were yours. Now it seemed as if half the world had a car. On sunny weekends the roads into Brighton were packed with them, nose to nose, bumper to bumper, entire families squashed inside, hot and excited. His own parents had never owned a car and his mother still saw driving as something slightly ostentatious, associated in her mind with Edgar's flash Uncle Charlie and his purple Rolls Royce. Didn't stop her making Edgar feel a failure for not having a car of his own though.

But feeling disappointed was Rose's default position. Edgar didn't know if it had begun with the death of Jonathan, Edgar's younger brother, at Dunkirk. Rose had been devastated by his death; Jonathan was her favourite but then he was everyone's favourite, including Edgar's. No, Edgar thought that the disappointment was always there. The weather, the butcher's cuts, the spring flowers; they were never quite what Rose wanted them to be. Her remaining children, Lucy and Edgar, were no exception.

Edgar drove past Buckingham Palace and down the Mall feeling as if he was the only man left alive in London. What was going on inside the palace, he wondered? Frantic preparations for next month's coronation? His mother was expecting him to spend the day with her and to attend a street party, something which in any other circumstances she would consider unspeakably vulgar. He felt a moment's sympathy for the young Queen preparing, as she was, for a lifetime of doing things she didn't want to do. On VE night the crowds had gathered outside the palace and shouted for the King and for Churchill. Edgar hadn't been there. He had been glad that the war was over but, with his brother and a woman he'd loved dead, a party didn't seem exactly appropriate. He had got drunk with Max in a pub in Golders Green accompanied by two German-Jewish violinists who hadn't really felt like celebrating either.

As he neared Trafalgar Square he could see taxis and buses — signs that the West End was still alive and kicking — but as he turned down Whitehall the wide road was dark and silent. He could see a policeman standing outside Downing Street but otherwise the centre of government was as sleepy as a Sussex village. Even so, Edgar felt another twinge of excitement at the thought that he was entering a world where momentous decisions were made and people's lives changed for ever. It was a change from investigating the death of a drunken gypsy woman, that was for sure. Edgar found number twelve (with difficulty because the solid town houses did not display anything as common as numbers) and parked outside. As he stood looking up at the shuttered windows in front of him, a taxi drew up and Max got out.

"Hi, Ed," said Max, as if they had just seen each other yesterday. In fact, it was three months since they had last met. Max was in his stage clothes, dinner jacket and untied bow tie. His white teeth gleamed in the darkness and Edgar was pretty sure that he was still wearing greasepaint.

"Hallo, Max. What do you make of all this?"

"It's a mystery." Max got out his cigarette case. "I know how you like mysteries."

Edgar ignored this. "Did you get the same message? About the Magic Men and Major Gormley?"

Max took a long pull of his cigarette. For a moment his head was wreathed in smoke, like a stage effect.

"That was the gist of it," he said. "I spoke to someone called Petre. Have you ever heard of him?"

"No."

"Gormley's dead, isn't he?"

"Yes. He died about a year ago. A stroke, apparently."

"Well," said Max, "we'd better find out some more." He spoke casually but, Edgar knew that he too was excited by the strange summons, perhaps remembering his own army days. Max's military career was still shrouded in secrecy but Edgar knew that he'd seen action in North Africa as well as masterminding the Magic Men operation which, even if it was ultimately a failure, certainly had its moments of glory.

Edgar didn't know what he expected: the door to be opened by a liveried butler or to creak open on its own. Instead their knock was answered quickly by a tall man in military uniform who introduced himself as General Petre.

"Edgar Stephens." Edgar resisted the temptation to salute.

"Max Mephisto." Max made a small, semi-ironical bow.

"I know who you are," said the general unexpectedly. "Saw you once at the Chiswick Empire. Did a hell of a trick with a levitating table. The gel disappeared and turned up again on the balcony. No idea how you did it."

He looked at Max as if expecting him to come up with the trick. Edgar smiled to himself. Max had sometimes condescended to explain his illusions to Edgar but he would never divulge the secrets to a stranger.

"I'm glad you enjoyed it," he said politely.

The general shot him a look under bushy white eyebrows and ushered them through a marbled hall and into an empty office.

"Take a seat."

They did so. Edgar, looking for clues, was disappointed. Apart from a map of Europe on the wall there was nothing to suggest that this was anything other than a small, commercial office. The desk was empty apart from a telephone and an in-tray containing a solitary sheet of paper. Edgar craned his neck to look at it. Max saw what he was doing and smiled. He, on the other hand, seemed to display no curiosity about his surroundings at all.

The general sat opposite them. "You'll be wondering why I asked you to come here," he said.

Edgar assumed that this was a rhetorical question but Max answered, "We were a trifle intrigued, yes."

The white eyebrows rose again at the word "intrigued" but General Petre continued in the same brusque tone, "I understand you both knew Peter Cartwright."

The "Peter" threw Edgar at first but then he remembered: a train journey, a cryptic crossword and a tall, distinguished man saying, "Have you ever thought about the Secret Service?" Colonel Cartwright had been the officer who had recruited him into the Magic Men. Edgar could see him now: a soldier of the old school, upright, patrician, utterly incorruptible. He'd won the VC in the first war, Edgar seemed to remember.

Max said, "Knew?"

"What?" The general's eyebrows now seemed permanently suspended in the air.

"You used the past tense. Is Cartwright dead?"

Max had put his finger on the salient point while Edgar was still wandering off down memory lane. Not for the first time he wondered which of them was the real detective.

"Yes, Cartwright's dead," said Petre. "Murdered."

"Murdered?" Edgar sounded more shocked than he'd intended.

"Well he was found last night with a bloody great knife stuck in his chest so I'd say he was murdered, yes." The general's irony was as unsubtle as his eyebrow work. "That's why I wanted to see you two so urgently."

The connection wasn't at all clear to Edgar. He waited for Petre to say more and, with a sigh that seemed to imply that these were not words that he'd ever thought he'd have to say, the general continued, "There were things . . . things in the room that seemed to point to a . . . well, to a *magic* connection. That's why I called you in."

Now Edgar really was amazed. "Magic?"

"Why don't I take you to see the room," said the general. "Then you can see for yourselves,"

"Seeing is believing, after all," said Max.

The general shot him a distinctly unfriendly look.

Colonel Cartwright had lived in Kensington Square. They drove there in an official car, gliding almost soundlessly through the empty streets. It was midnight when they reached the square, the tall houses dark except for a light outside one block of flats, Abbot's Court, where a policeman was shining his torch. In silence, Max and Edgar followed Petre up the stairs. "Can't use the lift, too noisy," he explained. Despite his grey hair the general climbed easily, taking the stairs two at a time. Edgar, who thought himself fairly fit from the hills in Brighton, was annoyed to find himself out of breath by the time they reached the third floor. Max, who did no exercise apart from lighting cigarettes, seemed to be breathing completely normally.

Petre took out a key and let them in. Inside, the flat had the high ceilings and black and white tiles that Edgar associated with apartments belonging to titled old ladies in Hove. They passed through a sitting room which showed signs of disturbance, tables knocked over and a velvet curtain hanging from its pole as if someone had grabbed it as they fell. Petre didn't allow them long to look around. He crossed the corridor (chandelier, more chequered tiles), opened another door and switched on the light.

The room was dominated by a huge double bed. Edgar's eyes were drawn immediately to the blood stain on the white eiderdown. If Cartwright had fought with his assailant in the sitting room, how come the blood was here?

"That was how he was found," said Petre. "His body was here on the bed but, as you saw, there had obviously been some sort of altercation in the other room. Cartwright wasn't the sort of man to go down without a fight. He had stab wounds on his hands as if he'd tried to defend himself."

Max crossed over to the bed and bent to examine something. Edgar, following him, saw that what he had taken to be a large spot of blood was actually a playing card. Red on white. The ace of hearts.

"The card was found on the body," said Petre. "Body laid out on the bed, knife still in chest. This card was next to the knife."

"The blood card," said Max.

Petre turned to stare at him. "What did you say?"

"The ace of hearts," said Max. "Magicians call it the blood card."

CHAPTER
THREE

"The blood card." The general's face was in shadow but his voice sounded odd, strained and fearful, nothing like his normal parade-ground rasp.

Max shrugged. "It's just a superstition, that's all."

"Did anyone take a photograph of the room as it was when the crime was discovered?" asked Edgar.

"Of course not." The general seemed to have recovered his scornful tones. "They had better things to do than take *photographs*."

But it had occurred to Edgar that, if the playing card had been left as a message, then perhaps there were other messages hidden around the room, clues that the police and ambulance men could have destroyed as they rampaged through the flat.

"What else was here?" he asked. "You said there were several things that pointed to a magic connection."

"I found this in his bedside cabinet," said Petre. He produced a scrap of paper from an inside pocket and handed it to Edgar. It looked as if it had been ripped from a newspaper. Edgar went over to the bedside table and turned on the Tiffany lamp. The blue and green glass reflected eerily on the page.

16

Woman Faints at Mind-Reading Exhibition

Mrs Velma Edwards, 58, was taken to hospital after fainting at a mind-reading exhibition given by the celebrated mesmerist William "Wild Bill" Hitchcock at the Albany state fair. "It was his eyes," Mrs Edwards told . . .

The rest of the article was missing but in the margin someone using a blue fountain pen had written *HEmlock 5-1212*. Edgar turned the scrap of paper over but the back only contained some sentences about a game Edgar guessed to be baseball.

Max looked over Edgar's shoulder. "What's this? A phone number?"

"An American phone number," said Petre, with a certain amount of distaste. "Apparently it refers to a district in New York State, as opposed to the city."

"And do you know anything about this William Hitchcock?"

"According to this he's a small-time magician. He does a mesmerist act at state fairs and the like. Nothing very exceptional."

Except that he made Mrs Velma Edwards faint dead away, thought Edgar. Aloud he said, "Was that all? Just this scrap from the paper?"

"This was in the drawer with it," said Petre. He reached into his pocket and Edgar wondered what else was going to emerge. A white rabbit? A pair of doves? Instead the general unfolded and held out a piece of paper revealing red and blue lettering. Edgar looked at it curiously. It was a playbill, a flyer, the sort he had seen hundreds of times before, usually with Max's name emblazoned across the top.

This time the name he recognised was halfway down the cast list.

Tony "The Mind" Mulholland. He knows what you're thinking before you do.

The bill was from the Liverpool Empire, dated May 1939.

Max was still reading over Edgar's shoulder. "Tony! Why would Colonel Cartwright have one of his playbills? From before the war too."

"That's what I was hoping you might tell me," said the general. "Is this Mulholland still around?"

Edgar and Max exchanged glances. "Tony died three years ago," said Edgar. "He was murdered. Did you ever hear about the Zig Zag Girl case? The Conjurer Killer?"

"Was he involved in that affair? I remember reading about it."

"Tony was one of the victims, yes."

"Was he one of your lot in the war? The Magic Men?"

"Yes," said Edgar. "He was." As he said this, he could see Tony sitting at the bar in the Caledonian, wearing his pinstriped spiv's suit. Heard his voice too, as loud and clear as if it was transmitted by radio waves: *I was only the top of the bill at the Liverpool Empire.* Well, he hadn't been top of the bill, not by a long chalk. Judging by the size of the names on the piece of paper in his hand, the top of the bill had been a double act

18

called Roman and Renée. Where were they now, he wondered?

"Have the police seen this?" he asked.

Petre hesitated for a moment before replying. "I did a quick search of the room before they arrived. There were reasons why I felt it better that the police did not know about the possible . . . theatrical connection. That's why I contacted you."

That seemed to leave a hell of a lot of questions unanswered, thought Edgar. Specifically, what did the general mean by "theatrical connection"? And why was General Petre consulting an obscure detective inspector from Brighton rather than Scotland Yard? More to the point, why involve Max, who was now examining the playbill with a rather sardonic expression on his face?

"I suppose I'd better explain," said the general. "Let's go into the sitting room. This room gives me the heebie-jeebies."

Max headed to the door but Edgar stayed to look around one more time. As he bent to turn off the bedside light, he caught sight of something white under the bed, half hidden by the eiderdown. He pulled it out. It was the *Evening Standard* from two days ago, folded over at the cryptic crossword. Half the clues had been filled in, using the blue fountain pen that had scribbled down the phone number. Edgar took the page with the crossword and put it in his pocket.

In the sitting room General Petre turned on the centre light, as if determined to chase away the shadow of death. Then he sat heavily on the sofa without

19

bothering to right the coffee table which lay on its side in front of him. Max and Edgar took armchairs on either side of the general. Edgar put the table on its feet; it was a flimsy wooden affair with a carved top, rather oriental in appearance. Edgar had noticed a few other Chinese objects around the room. Had Cartwright served in the East? Well, maybe they were about to find out.

But the general's opening line surprised them both. "As you know, it's the coronation in two weeks' time."

Edgar stared at him. Was there anyone in the country who didn't know? The papers had been full of nothing else for weeks. Sweets were going to be taken off ration to celebrate. His sergeant, Bob Willis, was counting down the days.

"For some time MI6 has been aware that there are certain anarchist groups who would like to . . . well, *disrupt* the occasion. Peter Cartwright was on the trail of one such group. The day before he died he telephoned me to tell me that he thought he'd made a breakthrough. We made an arrangement to meet at number twelve the next day. When he didn't arrive, I came round here, found the sitting room disturbed and Cartwright on the bed, dead. As soon as I saw the card I thought of the Magic Men. Then, when I saw the playbill, I knew there must be a connection. I did some digging, found out that Stephens had joined the force, so I contacted you. I asked Mephisto because Cartwright always spoke so highly of him. I thought you might be able to help me make sense of it all."

Cartwright had been a fan, Edgar remembered, and it sounded as though General Petre was one too. Still, that didn't altogether explain why they had been summoned to London in the middle of the night.

"But why me?" said Edgar. "Surely Scotland Yard are the ones to handle it?"

Petre took out a large white handkerchief and unfolded it so slowly and deliberately that Edgar thought, for one wild moment, that he was about to perform a magic trick. Instead he wiped his brow and then carefully refolded the handkerchief. But Edgar knew that the white linen square was performing the same role as the magician's cape; the general was buying time.

"In situations like this," he said at last, "you have to be very careful who knows what. For security reasons, you understand. The fewer people that know about this American angle the better."

"So do you think that the cutting about the American mesmerist had something to do with why Colonel Cartwright was murdered?" Edgar had to fight to stop the incredulity creeping into his voice.

"It's a line of enquiry," said Petre, "and one that I want you and Mephisto to follow, discreetly, mind you. After all, presumably Mephisto can use his show business contacts." He said this as though he was referring to the mafia. Which, after all, maybe he was.

"I don't have many contacts in America," said Max.

"It may be nothing," Petre continued, although the late-night trip, the ransacked room and the bloodstained bed hadn't exactly felt like nothing, "but the playing card, the cutting and the playbill do point to a theatrical connection. That's what I want you two to investigate. You'll report directly to me. The password is Lorgnette."

Edgar thought long and hard afterwards about the meaning of the password but, to his disappointment, he was to find out that all MI6 code words were picked at random from the shorter Collins dictionary.

The general dropped them back at Whitehall. It was nearly two o'clock in the morning but somehow the thought of trundling tamely back to Brighton didn't appeal to Edgar. It was Saturday tomorrow (today!) and there was no reason for him to go into work. So, when Max mentioned that he knew an all-night cafe in Covent Garden, Edgar offered to drive them both there and, after another glide through the dark streets, they found themselves eating bacon and eggs as the market traders set up their stalls outside.

"I thought you never ate breakfast," said Edgar, taking a swig of dark brown tea.

"This isn't breakfast," said Max. "It doesn't count if I haven't been to sleep."

"Of course, you're always awake at two a.m.," said Edgar. "It's an unusual experience for me."

"That was when I was young," said Max. "These days I'm asleep by midnight. Alone."

Edgar said nothing. He knew that Max had what he called an "understanding" with a Brighton landlady called Joyce Markham (Mrs M), but he didn't know how this relationship operated when the two were

22

apart. Edgar didn't really want to talk about love affairs with Max for the very good reason that he, Edgar, was planning to marry Max's daughter, Ruby. Max didn't exactly disapprove — he didn't really have the moral high ground when it came to love affairs — but Edgar thought that it was safest to keep off the subject for now.

Luckily, Max's thoughts were still on Colonel Cartwright.

"So who's going to make the trunk call, you or me?"

"It had better be you. If I telephone it'll become official police business. You can find some show business excuse."

"Help! I need a mind reader urgently."

"That sort of thing."

Edgar took a last delicious mouthful of fried bread. "What do you make of it, Max? The ace of hearts and all that. What did you call it? The blood card?"

Max sighed and pushed his food away. There was still some bacon left on his plate, Edgar had to stop himself eating it.

"The ace is the highest card," said Max, "so some people say it's lucky but it's also unlucky. An ace is the highest score and the lowest. If the ace is high it scores eleven. K is the eleventh letter of the alphabet, so ace means kill."

"Is the ace of hearts particularly unlucky?"

"No. It's the ace of spades that's known as the death card, supposedly because an ace of spades was found in Wild Bill Hickok's hand when he was shot during a card game."

"Wild Bill Hickok?"

"I thought of that immediately. Wild Bill Hitchcock of Albany must be a fan."

"Then why not an ace of spades?"

"The ace of hearts is the magician's favourite card. When you do a trick, you usually end up with the ace of hearts because it's showy. When you ask people to think of a card, any card, it's usually the ace of hearts. That's why it's the blood card, because it's the most important."

"Is that the only reason?"

Max sighed again. "There's a card trick that involves blood coming out of the ace of hearts. It's a variation on the Whispering Queen."

"The Whispering Queen?"

"It's very simple. Look." Max took a deck of cards from his pocket. Edgar had long ago stopped being surprised at the way Max could summon playing cards from anywhere. He remembered the first time he saw Max, on Inverness station, the way the magician had shuffled the cards in his hand without looking at them once.

"Pick a card." Max was grinning at him.

Edgar took a card, hardly thinking about it. He had given up trying to second-guess Max in this kind of trick. Three of diamonds. He put the card back, face down. Max shuffled and reshuffled. Then, from the centre of the pack, he took the queen of hearts.

"The queen is going to whisper to me," he said, "tell me what to do. Of course you'd make a lot more of this on stage. What are you saying, Your Majesty? Cut the cards again, Your Majesty? Of course." He cut the cards once and again, separating them until just one card lay on the table between their egg-smeared plates.

"Now I'm going to slide the queen under the card so she can see it." He did so, then held the card to his ear again. "The queen tells me your card is the three of diamonds. Is that right?"

"No," said Edgar.

"Crap. You know it is."

"OK. It is."

"Now, if I was playing the blood card, I'd say that the queen represented the girl who broke my heart. I'd take the ace of hearts and put a pin through the card. Then, I'd make you pick out the ace of hearts and, when it was in your hand, I'd make it bleed."

"How the hell would you do that?"

"It's the easiest thing in the world. Blood capsule in your hand. But if you want to take it further, you can make the punter himself bleed. All you have to do is get him to hold the card to his chest. Then, when he takes it away, it looks as though he's been stabbed in the heart."

Edgar stared at him.

"It's a nasty little trick," said Max, "totally lacking in finesse. I never do it."

"Did Tony perform that trick?"

Max looked up as he passed the cards from hand to hand. "Yes," he said. "It was one of his favourites."

When they left the cafe, the stallholders were unloading fruit and vegetables from cars and lorries and even from a couple of horse-drawn carts. Trolleys were being trundled to and fro, sacks of potatoes, wooden crates of apples and pears. There was a brazier at one end of the covered market and some traders were gathered around it drinking mugs of tea. Edgar thought it looked rather convivial but Max shivered as they passed. "What a life."

"Looks all right to me."

"Getting up at two a.m. to dig potatoes out of a frozen field. No thanks."

Max always claimed to hate the outdoors. Edgar thought that this was because his father, Lord Alastair Massingham, was a typical hunting and shooting aristocrat. Max had escaped the landed gentry to join the secret world of the theatre, a life without mornings, two shows a night, a different town every Sunday. Along the way he had shed his title and become Max Mephisto. Pursuing his own train of thought Edgar asked Max if he'd seen his father recently.

"Not for over a year, thank God."

"Ruby says he's coming to the wedding."

Max stopped by the opera house steps to light a cigarette. In the darkness his face was hard to read. "So you're still getting married then?"

"Yes," said Edgar. "I'm hoping we'll be married by the end of the year."

CHAPTER
FOUR

Max reached the Strand Palace Hotel just as the boot boys were scurrying along the passages delivering freshly polished footwear. The night porter was still at the desk. Max was tempted to ask for a black coffee but he knew that would stop him sleeping and he wanted to get in a few hours before the Saturday matinee. When he got to his room he hung a do-not-disturb sign on the door, undressed (hanging up his suit carefully because he'd have to wear it again on stage), put on a dressing gown and ran a bath. As he waited for it to fill — it was one of those huge old-fashioned tubs that took for ever — he thought about the events of the night.

Max had always liked Colonel Cartwright. He remembered the first time they had met, in an army camp in Cairo. Max had been seconded to a camouflage unit and was working on creating dummy tanks that would convince Rommel, currently camped only a few miles outside the city, that the British army was bristling with reinforcements. Max was in the repair shed putting the finishing touches to a Matilda tank.

"Do you really think that'll take Rommel in?" asked a voice behind him.

"From the air it will," Max answered. He didn't look round, he was used to his work being questioned and criticised by anonymous members of the armed forces.

"It's all in the shadows," piped up Stan Parks (aka The Great Diablo) who was at work on the undercarriage.

"And in the colour," added Max. "We use camel dung." This was true.

Colonel Cartwright had walked into the shed and inspected the tank from all angles.

"What's the chassis?" he asked.

"A truck," said Max.

"Trucks don't move like tanks."

Max remembered turning to face the colonel, a tall figure in battle fatigues. "The thing is," he said, "our tanks will be with the real thing. That's the best way to disguise the fake card, put it in the middle of the pack. We'll have real tanks at the beginning and end of the cavalcade."

"So it's a card trick then?"

"All tricks are the same," Max had said. "You have to make the punter — in this case Rommel — look where you want them to look. Misdirection. Our only chance of victory is in surprise. These little fellows —" he gestured at the disguised truck — "might just give us time to spring a surprise."

Cartwright had left then and Max didn't know if he ever got to see the Western Desert Force spring their surprise. But, a month later, Max received a summons to join a secret unit based in Inverness. "The aim," Cartwright explained to him over dinner at his London club (a London so bruised and battered as to be almost unrecognisable), "is to convince the Germans in Norway that we're ready to invade. The only problem is that we've got no troops and no armaments. So we need a bit of — what did you call it? — misdirection."

So Max, accompanied by a thoroughly overexcited Diablo, had travelled to Scotland to set up the Magic Men. And now Cartwright was dead, killed with a playing card left next to his heart.

After his bath, Max lay on the bed waiting for sleep. Outside he could hear London waking up but he'd always found the sounds of the city soothing rather than otherwise. He had asked to be called at midday. The matinee was at two and he could make the call to Albany before the evening show; he calculated that it should be midday in America then. He'd never been to America but suddenly he longed to be in the New York that he had only seen in films. Now that was a city, if you like. He wondered about the mesmerist, William Hitchcock, the man who had copied the name of an outlaw killed with cards in his hand. He thought of Tony Mulholland, whom he had disliked intensely. What linked the two men who claimed to be able to read minds to the death of a senior army officer? He thought of the room in the Kensington flat, the upturned tables, the curtain pulled from its pole. It was carefully staged, perhaps too carefully. Was it misdirection? What did the killer not want them to see?

He sighed, got up and drank some water from his tooth glass. Why couldn't he sleep? Was it the thought of the man he had admired being brutally murdered?

Was it the crime scene, the clues so carefully displayed? No, not if he was honest. It was the thought of Edgar and Ruby getting married. He realised that he wasn't in any position to object. He had only found out that Ruby was his daughter three years ago and, though he had tried his hardest, he wasn't sure that the heavy father was a role that he was born to play. He was surprised at the wave of love and protectiveness that overcame him when he learnt that his lovely assistant was, in fact, his lovely daughter. But Ruby was a modern girl who would not brook any interference from him. Besides, she had a stepfather who, much as Max hated to admit it, had fulfilled the paternal role perfectly adequately for twenty-three years. She wasn't going to start taking advice from a showbiz roué who had seduced her mother and then vanished into the ether. And, anyway, what advice did Max want to give? He couldn't advise her not to marry Edgar, who was a good and decent man. No, when Max thought of Ruby and Edgar together, it wasn't Ruby that he worried about. It was Edgar.

Edgar had no such trouble with sleep. The roads were clear and he was back in Brighton by five a.m., driving along the seafront as the fishermen were pulling their boats onto the beach. He drove up Albion Hill to his lodgings on one of Brighton's most vertiginous streets. The house was silent. He let himself into his flat, took off his jacket and shoes, lay on the bed and was asleep in seconds.

It was afternoon when he woke up. He could hear the seagulls outside and the cars labouring up the hill. He lay there, looking at the crack in the ceiling and wondering if it was getting wider. The flat was not the most salubrious of dwellings, the rooms were both cold and damp and there was a strange smell, winter and summer, that never seemed to go away no matter how often he opened the windows. At one time Edgar had thought about getting new lodgings, in Hove perhaps or in one of the nicer Brighton mews, but somehow he had never got round to it. Ruby didn't seem to mind the flat, the few times she had been there. She wasn't the sort of woman who had the urge to rearrange her surroundings. She had cooked meals in his tiny kitchen and slept in his bed. Ruby was a show-business girl through and through, digs were just digs to her. Nevertheless, Edgar would have to find them somewhere else to live when they were married.

The tiny bedroom window showed only the sliver of back garden. He went into the sitting room and looked out. He could see the green and white buses trundling to and fro along the terraces that led to the sea, like one of those games on the pier where you put your penny in the slot and watched it roll backwards and forwards along the painted slats. The sea was a line of blue against the horizon, the sun high and pale. It was just after two o'clock. Ruby would be on stage now. She was appearing in a show in Bournemouth. He would try to ring her in her lodgings later but it was difficult with two shows a night. He was seeing her tomorrow though. Sunday, changeover day, was the chance for a snatched few hours before Ruby was off to her next gig. Worthing, Blackpool, Scarborough. Ruby was determined to make it as a magician despite the fact that there hadn't been a woman conjurer since Eusapia Palladino in the 1890s. Ruby had the advantage of being Max Mephisto's daughter but also the disadvantage of being so pretty that directors only saw her as an ingénue or chorus girl. But she'd had a few bookings for her magic act and, whenever Edgar watched her, she seemed disconcertingly poised and skilled on stage. She would make it to the top, he was sure of it.

He went into the kitchen in search of food. Stale bread and fish paste seemed to be about the sum of it. He put two slices of bread onto the grill and made himself some black tea. He didn't have a refrigerator so there was never any milk. Was she really going to marry him, the glamorous starlet who had men queuing for her at the stage door? In some moods, she said she would. She had made that comment about her grandfather coming to the wedding, after all. In some moods she told Edgar that she loved him. In others she talked only about her career, her future on films and TV, the days when she'd be bigger than her errant father, called by some people the greatest magician in the world.

It must be difficult for Max to see his daughter being courted by his best friend. But he'd have to get used to it, Edgar told himself, scraping mould off the toast crust, once he and Ruby were married. Edgar wanted to marry Ruby more than anything in the world but at times it was hard to believe it would ever happen. He had proposed to her on the night they first slept together, a night branded on his soul. "You don't have to marry me," Ruby had said, innocently tousled in one of his old shirts. "I want to," Edgar had assured her and he had repeated this desire many times over the last two years. He had given her a ring which she wore on a chain around her neck. One day she'd put it on her finger.

What would Ruby say if she knew about the strange trip to London and about the man found dead with a playing card on his chest? She'd have a theory — she was an expert on card tricks — but he always tried not to tell her too much about his working life. He wanted to shield her from the sordidness of crime and from the sheer mind-numbing slog of police work. He didn't talk about Ruby at work either. He'd never even told Bob or Emma that he was engaged, though somehow they knew.

He wondered if Max had managed to call the strange foreign-looking number. What if Wild Bill himself had answered? And what was the link with Tony Mulholland, the man murdered on Edgar's own patch, just a mile or so from this flat? He felt the same rush of excitement that had surged through him as he had driven past the dark offices in Whitehall. He knew that he would telephone Max, as well as Ruby, before the evening was out.

Edgar went back into the sitting room with his toast. He was just looking for yesterday's cryptic crossword when he remembered the half-finished crossword taken from Colonel Cartwright's bedroom. He found it in his overcoat pocket and flattened it out on the table in front of him. Cartwright had filled in the answers with the same blue pen that had jotted down Bill Hitchcock's telephone number. He had got half the clues. He was stronger on conundrums than anagrams. Edgar filled in one of these almost without thinking (orchestra = carthorse) and tried to puzzle out the others. Cartwright had done some workings of his own in the margins and seeing the letters and the spaces made Edgar feel suddenly close to his old commanding officer, who had shared his passion for word games. Edgar too liked the *Evening Standard* cryptic crossword but he would have thought that Colonel Cartwright was more of a *Times* or *Telegraph* man. Had Cartwright been interrupted in the middle of the crossword? No, it had been found by his bed and Cartwright was disturbed in the sitting room. He, too, had left the crossword as a treat for the end of the day.

Number of people in theatre (12).

Theatre could mean operating as well as dramatic. Number could also mean "one who numbs". Edgar wrote "anaesthetist" in careful capitals. As he did so he noticed that Cartwright's scribbles were not just random letters. Reading downwards he read "Max" and across "Edgar", the two names sharing the "a". "Tony" and "Diablo" had been crossed in the same way. Whatever had been going on in Colonel Cartwright's life, it was clear that the Magic Men were uppermost in his mind.

The matinee went well. It was a different audience in the afternoons, more families, fewer couples. Max

34

edited out some of his more risqué lines and made more of his show-stopper trick which involved a white fluffy dog borrowed from the stage manager. The dog, whose name was Alfie, was one of the best assistants Max had ever had — the best since Ruby, in fact. With Alfie on stage, tail wagging, head cocked hopefully, there was no way that the audience was going to notice Max's sleight of hand with the false-bottomed box. When Alfie trotted into the box there was an audible sigh from the audience and, when the dog reappeared just behind Max (cue double take), the laughter was warmer and more affectionate than any Max had ever experienced. At the stage door, several of the younger fans requested an audience with the canine star.

"I'm sorry, he has to rest before the next show," said Max, "he's very temperamental. He's sulking because my dressing room is bigger."

He had asked the theatre manager, Dan Napier, if he could make a trunk call from his office. "I'll reimburse you of course." Dan had waved this aside, impressed by his star's profligate habits. Max sat at Dan's desk and dialled the number that had been written on the newspaper cutting. Even at the Theatre Royal, Drury Lane, the manager's room was an unimpressive place, an airless cubbyhole filled with broken seats and forgotten billboards. Would he end up here, thought Max, listening to the telephone exchange clicking away, a name on an advertising board for a forgotten show? Max Mephisto, twice nightly. He thought about the playbill that had been found in Peter Cartwright's bedroom. Tony "The Mind" Mulholland. Why had the colonel kept it all those years?

"Hello?" The voice gave Max a shock. An American accent, so loud and clear that the speaker could be in the same room.

"Hallo. Is that Bill Hitchcock?"

"This is he." Another shock. Could it really be that easy? Hitchcock sounded older than he had expected and more hesitant.

"This is Max Mephisto, calling from London."

An intake of breath. "Max Mephisto?" Max couldn't help being pleased that his fame had obviously crossed the Atlantic.

"I served in the army with Tony Mulholland. I believe you knew Tony?"

This was a shot in the dark but Hitchcock replied, still warily, "Yes, I knew Tony."

Max noted the past tense.

"I'm planning a memorial concert for him." This was the line he and Edgar had agreed. "All his old friends and fellow professionals. Would you be interested? Do you ever come to England?"

Another pause. "I don't think so . . . My health isn't so good. And I wouldn't have said I was a friend of Tony's exactly . . ."

Who would? thought Max. Hitchcock sounded believable enough but Max would have to be looking at the man to know if he was lying. Then it would be easy.

"How did you know Tony?" he asked.

"He came over to the States a few years ago. We did a couple of shows together. He was a smart cookie."

"You're a mesmerist, I believe?"

"Yes." Hitchcock sounded pleased, as Max had been a few moments before, to know that his reputation had preceded him. "I come from a long line of seers and mystics. I do a mind-reading act that would blow you away. Why, I could tell you what you're thinking now, Mr Mephisto."

"What am I thinking?"

"You're thinking, why did Colonel Peter Cartwright have a newspaper cutting with my name on it?"

Max took a deep breath, wasting several expensive seconds. "We need to talk about Colonel Cartwright."

CHAPTER
FIVE

"You talk, Mr Mephisto," said the amused American voice, "I'm listening."

"How do you know Colonel Cartwright?"

"I think I might leave that to you to find out. You're a magician, after all. Though not a mind reader like poor Tony."

"Let's start with Tony, then. How well did you know him?"

"Not very well. As I say, we did a few shows together a couple of years back. He didn't impress me much. He had a few obvious tricks and an effective stage manner but he hadn't got the true gift."

"And you have?"

"It's in the blood, Mr Mephisto, it's in the blood. I know what you're thinking right this minute."

"You've tried that one before."

"These things always go in threes, you know that. Right now you're thinking — how does this American idiot know about the newspaper cutting? Why don't you ask your old colonel?"

"Well, that would be slightly difficult," said Max. "Considering that he's dead."

Now it seemed that Max had succeeded in silencing Wild Bill Hitchcock. There was a long pause probably costing Dan Napier several pounds.

Eventually Hitchcock said, his voice considerably sharper and less amused, "Dead? Do you mean that he was killed?"

This was interesting. "Why would you say that, Mr Hitchcock?"

"These are dark times," said Hitchcock. "Dark times indeed."

"It seems so," said Max. "Why don't you tell me everything that you know about Colonel Cartwright?"

"I can't do that." Hitchcock seemed to be recovering some of his poise. "You'll just have to work it out for yourself."

"The police may well be in contact with you," said Max, more to scare the man than anything.

"Always happy to help a British policeman. And, if I may give you one piece of advice, Mr Mephisto?"

"Yes?"

"Proceed with hesitation. Goodbye, Mr Mephisto."

Max was left listening to the humming of the wires.

Dan, who must have been listening outside the door, put his head round.

"Everything OK, Max?"

"Yes. Sorry that took so long."

"That's all right. Actually I came to tell you that you've got a visitor."

"A visitor?" For a moment Max thought it was General Petre, come to offer him another top-secret assignment. What was that password again? He realised that Dan was still talking.

". . . recognised him at once. Offered to show him to your dressing room but he wanted to wait in the auditorium."

"Recognised who?" Max was conscious of the conversation slipping away from him, Bill Hitchcock's contemptuous transatlantic tones still ringing in his ear. *I think I might leave that to you to find out. You're a magician, after all.*

"Joe Passolini." Dan's voice was reverent. "The agent."

Now Max was alert all right, thoughts of General Petre and Bill Hitchcock banished from his mind. Joe Passolini was one of the new breed of theatrical agents, young men making their way in show business. Not for their artistes an endless procession of weekly Number Three venues with the occasional pantomime as a treat in December. Men like Joe Passolini talked about films, the wireless, even television. Max, who hadn't had an agent since Ted Solomon dropped down dead backstage at the Majestic in 1933, was prepared to do business.

Joe Passolini was sitting in the second row of the stalls. He was a thin young man of about twenty-five with a prominent nose and surprisingly soulful brown eyes. He was wearing a trench coat and carrying a soft-brimmed hat. There was a faint suggestion of American gumshoe about him. Not accidental, Max was sure.

40

Passolini stood up as Max approached. "Max Mephisto. This is an honour."

Max bowed slightly. No point in being too humble, after all.

"I'm Joe Passolini, theatrical agent. Have you got a few minutes?"

"Of course." Max sat down next to Joe Passolini. The stage loomed above them, safety curtain down, spirit lights covered.

"I love these old theatres," said Passolini, gesturing up at the gilded ceiling, the boxes shadowy with red velvet. "All that history, all those stories."

"This one's meant to be haunted by the ghost of Grimaldi. The famous clown," Max added, in case Passolini's theatrical enthusiasm didn't stretch that far back.

"I know who he was," said the agent. His voice was part London market-stall, part New York gangster. "Joseph Grimaldi, the father of clowns. He's why we call clowns Joeys. And he had something in common with you and me."

"What's that?"

"He was of Italian descent. Just like us."

Max was surprised. Although it was not exactly secret, very few people knew that his mother was an Italian opera singer. She had died when Max was six.

"My parents emigrated to England after the First World War," said Passolini, "and in the Second World War they were interned as enemy aliens for their trouble. My mother was released after a few months but Pa was in for the duration, though it's hard to see a

41

fifty-year-old baker as being much of a threat to the allied war effort." He had an odd way of speaking, half formal, half cockney.

"Do you speak Italian?" asked Max. His mother had taught him and, for years, he used to practise the language in secret so as not to lose this link with her. He was pretty rusty now though.

Passolini grinned. "I speak fluent Sicilian but not a word of Italian. So, tell me the story about Grimaldi."

"This was a famous venue for him," said Max. "He's meant to appear at the back of the stalls whenever a show's set for a long run."

"Has he appeared in this run?"

"Not yet."

"That's because the days of fortnightly variety are over," said Passolini. "This sort of show is dead and buried. Thought you were very good, by the way. I liked the bit with the dog."

"Thank you."

"Now, Max. Can I call you Max? I've got an offer for you. Have you ever thought about television?"

"I've thought about it."

"Max." Passolini leant forward, his eyes very large and sincere. "In two weeks' time London will be staging the biggest show on earth." He paused, as if waiting for Max to comment and, when he didn't, continued in a faintly disappointed tone. "The coronation, Max. The whole country will be watching. And do you know where they will be watching?"

"In their own drawing rooms?"

"Exactly." Passolini leant back, delighted with this answer. "On television. And, after our lovely Queen has been crowned, do you know what they'll be watching?"

Max didn't.

"They'll be watching *Those Were the Days*. The greatest variety show ever. And what does the greatest variety show need? The greatest magician."

"On television?"

"Yes. I know what you're going to say. Magic won't work on television. But this way it will. The camera won't be looking over your shoulder. You'll be up on stage, you'll be able to use all the old tricks. It's going back to the good old days of music hall. Everyone will be dressed up, the audience too."

"Sounds like hell."

"Come on. You can't tell me that you've never wished you were born fifty years earlier. The days of Max Miller and Vesta Tilley. The days when music hall stars were gods."

Max was silent. He had, of course.

"The thing is, this show, it'll be like being in the theatre. It'll be like sitting here in the Theatre Royal, Drury Lane, watching you, Max Mephisto, on the stage."

"What's to stop them coming to see me here?"

"Because they won't, Max." Passolini was suddenly businesslike. He stood up, gangster hat in hand. "Soon people won't go outside for entertainment. They'll expect it at home in their front room, or drawing room, according to you. How many people can you fit in this place if it's full?"

Max shrugged. "About two thousand."

"If you do this show, millions of people will watch it. Millions. Think about that, Max."

Max thought about it. Did he want to sell his soul to television? Joe watched him, Mephistopheles in a trench coat, his shadow monstrous on the empty stage.

By five o'clock Edgar could stand it no longer. He rang the Strand Palace to be told that Mr Mephisto was not in his room. Then he telephoned the Theatre Royal and asked to leave a message for Max. "Can you ask him to telephone me as soon as he gets in? When are you expecting him?"

"Curtain up is at seven-thirty, sir. Mr Mephisto normally gets here about seven."

Trust Max to cut it fine. "Can you ask him to ring me?" said Edgar again. "It's rather urgent."

Max telephoned at five to seven.

"What's up, Ed?"

Edgar wanted to hit him. "You know bloody well what's up. Did you speak to Bill Hitchcock?"

"Yes."

"Then why didn't you ring me?"

"I'm sorry, Ed." Max sounded amused. "I've been having a drink with an extraordinary man called Joe Passolini."

"I don't care about Joe Whatshisname. What did Hitchcock say?"

"Well, he was rather extraordinary too. For one thing, he knew that I was ringing about Colonel

44

Cartwright. And he knew that Cartwright had a newspaper,cutting with his name on."

"Good God. How could he have known that?"

"He's a seer, he told me. From a long line of seers and mystics."

"Did he know that Cartwright was dead then?"

"No. That seemed to come as quite a surprise."

"Did he say anything more?"

"No. He said he'd leave me to work it out for myself."

"Was that all?"

"One more rather cryptic thing. He said to proceed 'with hesitation'. He said it as if it should mean something."

Edgar was silent. The word "cryptic" had triggered something in his brain.

"Are you still there, Ed?"

"Yes. Max, do you think this Hitchcock is a crossword fan?"

"I've no idea. Why?"

"In cryptic crosswords, 'with hesitation' always means 'er'. ER. What else does that stand for?"

"I'm sure you're going to tell me."

"Elizabeth Regina. It stands for the Queen."

CHAPTER
SIX

"Are you sure about all this crossword stuff?"

They were sitting in General Petre's office under the map of Europe. Edgar had telephoned the general on Saturday night after his conversation with Max. The general's answer was to summon them both to a meeting in London. Edgar had demurred. They were busy at the station and he thought that his boss, Frank Hodges, wouldn't take kindly to another London jaunt. "I'll talk to Hodges," Petre had said and he must have done because, on Monday morning, Edgar had found a note from the superintendent on his desk. "Understand you need to be in London today. Make it quick." And it had been quick thanks to the wonders of modern travel. An hour on the train, ten minutes on the underground and Edgar was explaining the mysteries of crossword-solving to a sceptical Petre.

"Edgar is good at cracking codes," said Max. "I remember that from our army days."

It was something he had in common with the late Peter Cartwright, thought Edgar, remembering the unfinished crossword under the bed.

"I can't be sure that's what Hitchcock meant," he said, "but it seems possible. Max said he gave the words a lot of emphasis."

Petre looked at Max who said, "He definitely seemed to be giving a clue of some kind."

"And he knew about the newspaper cutting?"

"He definitely knew about that."

The general surveyed them in silence for a few seconds under his alarming eyebrows. Then he said, "There's nothing else for it. You'll have to go and see him."

Max and Edgar looked at each other. "But he's in America," said Edgar.

"I know *that*." The general rolled his eyes towards the ceiling. "You'll have to go to America."

"But the crossing will take weeks," said Edgar.

"Who's talking about going by sea? These days you can fly to New York in fifteen hours."

Edgar was conscious of feeling slightly dizzy. He had never been in a plane though he had, once, contemplated joining the RAF. Was the general really telling him to fly to America?

Max said, "I can't, I'm afraid. I need to be on stage every day."

"Surely this is more important?"

"Of course it's more important. It's just that it's my job to appear on stage at the Theatre Royal every night."

Petre grunted as if he didn't think much of that as a job but he seemed to accept the point. He turned his cold gooseberry eyes on Edgar.

"Stephens, you'll have to go. I'll sort out the paperwork. Be ready to leave tomorrow."

"Tomorrow?"

"Yes. The coronation is in two weeks. If this man is plotting something to spoil it, then we've got to stop him, haven't we?"

Such was the force of his personality that both men agreed that they had to stop him. It was only afterwards that they wondered why — of all the police and secret-service men in England — the job had been left to them.

Edgar was back in Brighton by lunchtime. As he walked down from the station, the sea at the bottom of the hill seeming impossibly high and blue, he thought about the amazing fact that he might be in America by the day after tomorrow.

"But I haven't even got a passport," he had said.

"We can sort that out for you," said Petre, with the air of one brushing aside trivialities. "I'll have one of the secretaries take a photograph. The documents can be waiting for you at London Airport."

The cavernous outer room was today filled with women hunched industriously over typewriters. Petre selected one of them — apparently at random — and she fetched a box brownie and took a photograph of Edgar standing wide-eyed in front of a white wall. Then Edgar and Max found themselves outside in the bright May sunshine.

"You lucky bastard," said Max. "I'd kill to go to New York."

48

"I don't feel lucky," said Edgar.

"No," said Max, "you never do."

Edgar was still smarting from this as he pushed his way through the aimless midday crowds around the Clock Tower. Was he really being ungrateful about this unexpected opportunity to see the world? Maybe this was the chance to recapture the surge of excitement he had experienced when driving through Whitehall at night. The feeling you used to get in the war when you were not sure what was going to happen tomorrow, or even if there would be a tomorrow. Now his life sometimes felt dull and unadventurous: working in his underground office all day, walking back to a solitary evening in his flat enlivened only by the possibility of ringing Ruby. Marrying Ruby would shake up this dull routine, like agitating the snow globe his mother used to keep on the mantelpiece, the glittery flakes enveloping and transforming the dull woodland scene within. But, when he'd seen her yesterday, Ruby had been in one of her infuriatingly vague moods. "Oh, don't let's talk about that, Ed," she'd said when he broached the subject of their wedding.

By the time he had reached Bartholomew Square he had almost convinced himself that he should go to America, do something that would make Ruby proud of him (or, at the very least, curious about him). Bob Willis and Emma Holmes were in the incident room arguing about something. His two sergeants had a fractious, competitive relationship which sometimes worked well when they battled to outdo each other on investigations but was often rather trying to witness.

Edgar couldn't work out whether they actually disliked each other or were secretly in love. Either way, their bickering sometimes made him feel uncomfortable.

"They didn't ask for you, they asked for the DI," Emma was saying.

"They asked for the DI." Bob mimicked her voice. "You're such a teacher's pet."

"I'm not even going to answer that," said Emma in her loftiest voice.

"Who asked for me?" Edgar pushed open the door. Bob, who had been leaning over Emma's desk, stood up straight. Sometimes he treated Edgar like a senile uncle, sometimes like his commanding officer.

"The Barton family," said Emma. Her neck was pink, always the sign that Bob had got under her defences.

For the moment Edgar's mind was blank. He was in America with Wild Bill Hitchcock, Al Capone and any other cinema cliche he could think of. Then he remembered. Doreen Barton. Aka Madame Zabini.

"I thought we'd released the body to the family?"

"Yes, we have. The funeral's tomorrow. I've warned the traffic police. No, it was the son who rang. He wanted to talk to you urgently, he said. He asked for you by name."

Edgar considered. He could send Bob or Emma but they *had* asked for him and the thought of a brisk walk somewhere was better than an afternoon in the underground office worrying about transatlantic air travel.

"OK," he said. "I'll go and see them. One of you had better come with me. I'm going away for a few days and the family might need a contact."

Emma looked like she wanted to ask but Bob did. "Where are you going? Sir," he added as an afterthought.

"To America," said Edgar. Both sergeants stared at him. "Now, who spoke to the son on the phone?"

"Emma," said Bob sulkily.

"You come with me then, Emma."

The Barton family lived at number 87 Marine Parade, a Regency terrace facing onto the sea. The houses were once grand family dwellings, with servants in the attics and gracious first-floor drawing rooms with wrought-iron balconies. But now they were mostly divided into flats, the cream façades fading and the balconies displaying either wind-blown plants or broken deckchairs. But number eighty-seven showed no signs of multiple occupancy, no bicycles chained to the railings or names sellotaped to flat numbers. Instead there was a discreet brass plate bearing the legend "Zabini". Clearly this was still a family house.

The door was opened by a tall man wearing a dark suit. Apart from hair that was slightly longer than average, he didn't look particularly gypsyish. In fact, he had the abrupt, abstracted manner of a businessman interrupted in the middle of a meeting.

"Tol Barton." The handshake was businesslike too and this man clearly had no truck with Zabini. But what sort of a name was Tol?

Edgar introduced himself and Emma. "I believe you spoke to my sergeant on the telephone?"

"Yes." Tol gave Emma a hard stare. His eyes were an extraordinary colour, somewhere between blue and grey and green. Like the sea, Edgar thought.

"What does Tol stand for?" asked Emma.

"Ptolemy." The man gave them another look, perhaps daring them to laugh, but Edgar was thinking of Inverness and the fake battleship they had constructed from an old pleasure cruiser. The ship had been Max's greatest triumph and their greatest disaster. It had been called *The Ptolemy*. He couldn't decide if this was a good omen or a bad one.

"Please come up." They followed Tol through a dark hall, darker because the doors to all the rooms were firmly shut, and up a rather grand staircase. The room they entered was impressive too, with a grand piano in the corner and red velvet curtains at the French windows. On closer examination, though, the curtains looked threadbare and the once-lush pink sofas had holes where the straw showed through. Clearly there may once have been money in the fortune-telling business but times were harsher now. But nothing could change the splendour of the view: the sea, the promenade and the pier, like an advertisement for Brighton.

There were two other people in the room, both dressed in deepest black. One was an elderly woman and the other a slight, blonde girl. Despite the advanced age of one and the ethereal beauty of the other, the two women looked oddly alike and both also resembled Tol. Perhaps it was the eyes, the grey-blue-green sea-changing eyes.

Tol offered brusque introductions. "My grandmother Isobel Zabini, my daughter Astarte Zabini."

Several thoughts presented themselves to Edgar. Did Doreen, who was sixty when she died, really have a mother who was still alive? It was possible, he supposed, and the woman on the sofa looked at least eighty. Why were these women being introduced to him, of all the numerous Zabini clan? He noticed, as well, that the name Zabini seemed reserved for the women of the family.

Tol didn't waste much more time on pleasantries. "I've asked you to come today because we've had a letter. Delivered by hand today." He reached behind him to a desk, the old-fashioned bureau type with a leather-bound lid that lowered down onto wooden rests. There was an envelope lying on the green leather. Tol opened it to reveal a short letter, almost a note, handwritten on thick, expensive paper.

Edgar read the bold, black words, conscious that all eyes were on him and that Emma was trying to look over his shoulder.

If you wonder why Madame Zabini was killed, ask Detective Inspector Edgar Stephens. Ask him what the Magic Men knew. Or ask the spirits, if they will speak to you.

There was no signature. Edgar passed the letter to Emma. For a moment he felt almost queasy from the accumulated shocks of the past few days. Colonel Cartwright, the blood card, Wild Bill Hitchcock, "Stephens, you'll have to go". And now, the Magic Men.

"Do you know what this means?" Tol asked. "Who are the Magic Men?"

Edgar took a deep breath. "The Magic Men were a group I was seconded to during the war. It was an espionage group."

"What can that have to do with my mother's death?"

"I don't know," said Edgar.

"Because this fellow —" Tol pointed at the letter, now lying on the coffee table in front of Emma — "this fellow seems to think that the two are connected."

"How do you know it was written by a man?" asked Emma.

Tol glared at her but it was Astarte who answered. "Oh, we know it was a man. A tall man, sad and angry in his heart."

"Astarte has the sight," said Tol, as if announcing that she had measles. "I don't have it. She inherited it from my mum."

"Who inherited it from me," said the older woman with a disconcerting cackle. "The sight has always run in the female line. There's never been a male seer."

Was Astarte the next Madame Zabini? Edgar looked at her with new interest. The girl couldn't be more than eighteen, as blonde as Emma but wispier, less healthy-looking. Was it usual for a Romany gypsy to be so blonde? There was something strange, almost albino,

54

about her colouring. Astarte saw him looking and stared coolly back at him with those astonishing eyes.

"Did your mother ever mention the Magic Men?" Edgar asked Tol. "Could she have come across us in the war? We were based in Inverness."

"We stayed in Brighton during the war," said Isobel, the old woman. "They were dark time for us gypsies. Hundreds of Roma killed in the concentration camps. We had so many refugees staying with us. Doreen didn't have time to go gallivanting up to Inverness."

Edgar tried a different tack. "Did Doreen ever mention Max Mephisto?" All eyes turned to him again.

"Max Mephisto?" Tol repeated. "The magician?"

"He was one of the Magic Men," said Edgar. He knew that Emma, too, was listening intently. He'd never told anyone at work about his war years.

"Grandma saw him at the Theatre Royal once," said Astarte. "She thought he was very good. For a *gadjo*."

"A non-Romany," Isobel explained. "Mephisto has no real magic powers but he's a good showman."

"Did she mention Stan Parks?" Edgar asked. "Also known as The Great Diablo? Tony Mulholland?"

There was a movement in the room, a reverberation, as if the last word were a stone thrown into a deep pool.

"Tony Mulholland," said Edgar again. "Did she ever mention a magician, a mind reader, called Tony Mulholland?"

Tol looked at his mother and daughter. Then he turned to the desk again and pulled out a sheet of paper, emblazoned with red and blue print.

"This was in her caravan. Astarte found it when she collected Mum's crystal ball and tarot cards."

It was a flyer for the Liverpool Empire, the one featuring Tony "The Mind" Mulholland. The same flyer that had been found in Colonel Cartwright's bedside cabinet.

CHAPTER
SEVEN

Edgar and Emma walked back along the seafront. It was a lovely afternoon, the sea limpid and flat, the sky a clear, pale blue. Two promettes — young women employed to patrol Brighton, exuding glamour and answering tourist questions — were wandering along the promenade, offering to pose for photographs with visitors. The police directing traffic by the pier were wearing white helmets, a sure sign that summer had come.

Emma broke the silence. "Well, that was interesting."

Because the visit hadn't ended with the production of the flyer. As they descended the dark staircase, Isobel Zabini had said, "I expect you'll want to see Doreen."

For a moment Edgar thought that the old lady was offering to set up a seance but then Tol had opened one of the ground-floor doors to reveal a room lit only by candles. It was a few moments before Edgar realised that there was a coffin in the middle of the room.

He tried to back out, only to find Isobel and Astarte close behind him.

"You won't want strangers in here."

"You'll want to pay your respects," said Isobel, in a tone that did not brook the possibility of refusal.

57

Edgar and Emma made their way slowly into the shadowy room. It smelt of lilies and something else that Edgar did not care to identify. The open coffin was lying on what was obviously the dining room table. Edgar, who knew that there had been an autopsy, was relieved to see that Doreen's hair was covered by a black lace scarf, tied securely under the chin. Her face looked waxy and serene, quite unlike the cheerful woman who stared out from the photograph on the incident board. A rosary was clasped in her unreal-looking hands, and tucked into the crook of her arm was . . .

"Is that a playing card?" Edgar asked.

"Yes," said Astarte, who was lighting another candle behind him. "The ace of hearts. In Romany culture it symbolises the mother being the heart of the home."

But to a magician the ace of hearts was the blood card. Could there really be a link between this dead gypsy fortune-teller and the high-ranking government official murdered in his Kensington flat? Edgar stared down at the coffin, sumptuously lined with crimson silk, until Emma's slight cough recalled him to the present. At least Isobel seemed to feel that they had spent a respectable amount of time paying their respects. At the door she shook Edgar's hand and told him that he had a good heart. Then she turned to Emma. "You've got a lovely face, my dear. Don't worry, you'll be lucky in love one day." Emma had blushed deep red. Coffin-lining red.

Now Emma said, "Do you think her death might have been suspicious?"

"I don't know," said Edgar. "The note itself isn't evidence of foul play, of course, but there's always the possibility in cases like this. She fell from the pier in the dark. She could have been pushed but with no witnesses it's going to be hard to prove." He'd told Tol that he would take the note "so that our experts can look at it" but, unless they had genuine Romany magic powers, it was hard to tell what these so-called experts could make of the few words. *If you wonder why Madame Zabini was killed, ask Detective Inspector Edgar Stephens. Ask him what the Magic Men knew. Or ask the spirits, if they will speak to you.*

Someone in the Brighton area thought that he, Edgar, knew why Doreen Barton, aka Madame Zabini, had died. But there were mad people all over Brighton; he'd lived in the area long enough to know that.

"Why would someone think your espionage group was linked to her death?" said Emma.

"I've no idea," said Edgar, trying to close down the conversation. Emma could be tenacious in pursuit of a clue, worse even than Bob.

"They didn't refer to you by your military rank," said Emma. "So they must know that you've joined the police. They must be following your career."

This was an uncomfortable thought and one that had already occurred to Edgar.

"Go to the funeral tomorrow," he said. "Keep your eyes open, get talking to the family. There are some similarities between this case and the one I'm working on in London. I can't say more."

They were waiting to cross the road by the aquarium. Emma looked at him, her eyes round.

"Is the London case why you're going to America?"

Edgar laughed. "I said I couldn't say more."

"I heard you," Emma said cheerfully. "Won't stop me asking though."

Max stared at himself in the mirror. He usually enjoyed this time before the first show of the evening: the orchestra tuning up, the chorus girls running past in curlers, the stagehands moving scenery behind the drawn curtains, the theatre manager checking his running list and warning the acts not to overstay their welcome on stage. But today something was making him feel unsettled, even discontented. He had come straight from a meeting with Joe Passolini where he had signed a contract to appear on *Those Were the Days* and a longer contract promising Passolini ten per cent of his earnings. Was that what was worrying him? He had managed without an agent for so long, would it be a bore having someone organising him and protesting if he took a month off in the south of France? He'd liked Passolini, liked his cheerful pushiness and lack of the sort of deference that made people grovel to his father just because he signed his name surname only. But how charming would the agent seem after a year of touring Number Two playhouses or appearing in gormless TV shows?

Or was it this ridiculous case that was getting to him? He still couldn't quite believe that Ed would be off to America tomorrow while he was left behind making a shaggy dog appear and disappear. Was this it? Was he jealous of him? Of *Ed*. Surely not, it was just the whole weird set-up: the playing card, the playbill, Wild Bill Hitchcock's voice on the telephone, Tony Mulholland rising from the dead. Something was up, there was no doubt about that, but would they ever find the answers to the multiplying riddles? Or would Ed find them, emerging both guns blazing from some Wild West shoot-out, while he remained behind, a tiny figure on the television screen dressed in top hat and tails (apparently the director insisted on this).

Max rubbed greasepaint into his face. The fashion now was for the natural look, comics going on stage looking dishevelled and pale, their ill-fitting suits apparently eliciting sympathy from the audience. Well, Max would never go on stage looking anything less than *soigné*. He always wore a dinner jacket and his only concession to nonchalance was occasionally leaving his bow tie undone. Nevertheless, he had no desire to look like some over-painted pantomime dame (memories of *Aladdin* two years ago and the Dame drinking brandy in his dressing room after the show, blood-red lips and five o'clock shadow). So just a thin layer of five and nine and some definition to his already dark eyebrows.

"Overture and beginners, Mr Mephisto."

He could hear the orchestra playing "Happy Days Are Here Again". He wasn't on until the last slot before the interval but suddenly Max had a desire to see the start of the show from the wings. It was a good bill and the opening act, a family of contortionists from

61

Bulgaria, well worth seeing from any angle. He left the number one dressing room and started to climb the narrow stairs. The Theatre Royal was built on the site of an older theatre which burnt down in 1663 and on the lowest levels you could still see charred beams and blackened walls. As he climbed the stairs there was a sense of returning to civilisation, the walls were painted and there was overhead lighting, even carpet in places. Max stood in the wings watching the Bulgarian contortionists rubbing resin into their feet. The air smelt of greasepaint and machinery and lavender oil. For some reason this last scent made Max feel even more uneasy. The orchestra had segued into the Bulgarians' tab music and he watched as the heavy curtains parted and the two men and three women leapt onto the stage, their twisting bodies very black against the blazing lights.

Max looked round. He was alone in the wings but the sense of foreboding remained. Perhaps he should return to his dressing room, play a game of patience and get ready for his entrance. As he turned to go, he saw a flash of white just behind him. He swung round. There shouldn't be anyone in the wings now except the next act, Eloise Hanley, the Croydon Nightingale. But the place was empty except for the scent of lavender oil, now strong enough to make him feel slightly sick.

CHAPTER
EIGHT

Edgar felt surprisingly calm as he reached London Airport the next morning. This was because right up to the last minute — the train to Victoria, the underground to Hammersmith and the green-line bus to Heathrow — he never really thought that it was going to happen. He could see the planes on the runway, giant unwieldy things with propellers bigger than a man, and thought that he would never sit inside one of these monsters and look down on the world from above the clouds. It just wasn't going to happen.

But when he entered the modern glass and concrete building, there was a woman standing under the clock as arranged. Edgar thought he recognised her as one of the girls from Petre's office but he couldn't be sure. She had a symmetrical face and smooth brown hair, pretty but forgettable. In silence she handed him an envelope. Inside was a passport, another sealed envelope and a wad of cash, dollars Edgar assumed.

"Your plane's in an hour," said the woman, shutting her handbag. Edgar suddenly felt a ridiculous desire to ask her to stay. He asked her name instead.

"Conchita," said the woman unexpectedly. She gave him a quick smile, showing slightly uneven teeth. "Good luck." And Conchita was gone.

Edgar put the passport and dollars in his inside pocket. Then he looked at the envelope which was marked "To whom it may concern". Well, whatever it was, it concerned him. He opened it carefully.

To whom it may concern,
    The bearer, Detective Inspector Edgar Stephens, is under the protection of Her Majesty's Government. Please offer him every assistance.

It was signed General D.N. Petre DSO. Despite its official letter heading the note seemed a poor sort of defence. And how strange it was to read "Her Majesty" instead of "His Majesty". Emma would disagree, of course, but it felt odd to be under the protection of a woman, rather feeble in fact. Edgar put the letter in his pocket and walked towards the sign for "Transatlantic Flights".

Half an hour later he was queuing to get onto one of the monstrous planes. The other passengers seemed to be either military personnel or businessmen, all of them appearing completely blasé about flying over five thousand miles in a metal box. There was only one woman in the line, a beautiful creature in a tightly fitted black suit and feathery hat, carrying a tiny vanity case. In her glamour and stylishness, she reminded him of an older Ruby. Where was the rest of her luggage? Edgar had been told to put his suitcase on a trolley, they had labelled it "Idlewild" and it had been whisked away. Would he ever see it again? All he had for the journey was the newspaper and a book (Sherlock Holmes, it had seemed appropriate). As he stood in the queue a woman in a smart navy blue uniform gave him two colour postcards of the plane.

"What are these for?"

"Some people like to write postcards on the flight. It helps while away the time."

She gave him a professional smile and carried on along the line. Edgar wondered who would like to receive a mid-air postcard from him. Ruby? His mother? Max? He hadn't told his mother about the trip. Rose viewed even train travel as beset with danger. What would she think about a fifteen-hour flight to America? Even if he survived the journey she would be sure that he would be murdered by a machine-gun-toting gangster within minutes of arrival in New York (his mother was surprisingly fond of this sort of film).

He had told Ruby, though, and she had been gratifyingly impressed. "America! You must be working on a really important case then. In a way, you're a sort of spy." Edgar had demurred but he hadn't minded Ruby thinking that he was a sort of spy. He had also neglected to tell her that Max, her father, was also involved in the case.

He climbed the steps and found his seat on the upper deck. It seemed impossible that all the passengers would fit onto the plane but, before long, more uniformed girls (they were called "air hostesses", he found out later) had directed everyone to their allotted place. The beautiful woman was sitting across the aisle from Edgar and, for this reason alone, he was determined not to show any unease when the plane took off. It was difficult to feel nervous anyway when seated in a comfortable chair being offered a drink by another charming air hostess. Edgar asked for a gin and tonic and his next-door neighbour, a grim-faced man with an American drawl, ordered "Scotch on the rocks" and lit up the first of many cigarettes. By the time that the disembodied voice of the captain welcomed them aboard the Boeing 377 Stratocruiser and informed them that there was a bar and dining area on the lower deck, Edgar felt as if he had been flying his entire life.

The gypsy funeral was in full swing. Madeira Drive had been closed to traffic and the hearse, drawn by two plumed black horses, made its way past the crazy golf and the amusement arcade, pausing for a moment in front of the Palace Pier so that Madame Zabini could bid farewell to the place where, for the last thirty years, she had plied her spiritual trade. Behind the hearse came a small band, playing their violins as they walked. Tol and Astarte walked behind the musicians, followed by five men in deepest black.

Emma, watching from the promenade above, saw Astarte's white-blonde hair gleaming against her black coat and thought that Doreen's granddaughter was making some sort of a statement by not wearing a hat. Was it that she was the old woman's spiritual heir? Astarte carried herself regally too, head up, not needing the comfort of her father's arm. Who were the men walking behind her? Emma knew that Doreen had three sons, were the other two following her coffin alongside their brother? Two of the men looked about the right age, one with greying hair and another with a piratical-looking beard. The other men looked younger, all of them black-haired and black-suited. Astarte carried a wreath of red roses. Was the ace of hearts buried amongst the foliage? For the tenth time that morning, Emma wondered what the DI was doing. He had said that his plane took off at midday. Emma looked up at the sky, bright blue with a scattering of feathery clouds. Please God, she prayed to the deity she only half believed in, keep him safe. She was profoundly grateful that she was not within the psychic reach of anyone with "the sight". Her feelings for Edgar were as intense as they were secret. It was hopeless, she knew that. Everyone at the station knew about Ruby, the beautiful showgirl whose photograph (head turned over bare shoulder, black curls tumbling) adorned the DI's desk. The best Emma could hope for was that the DI never knew of her devotion. At least that way she retained a bit of dignity.

As the cortège wound its way around the Aquarium roundabout and back up the coast road, Emma took a shortcut through the backstreets of Kemp Town to St John the Baptist Catholic Church. "Oh yes, we're devout Catholics," old Isobel had told them yesterday, not seeming to see any contradiction between the rosary in the dead woman's hands and the crystal ball and tarot cards in her caravan. Despite her expensive education, Emma knew very little about religion. Her parents would both declare themselves C of E, partly because any other faith would seem rather déclassé. Catholicism was for Irish navvies and Italian prisoners-of-war. They'd once had a cook who was a Methodist but they'd had to let her go when the hymn singing became too much for Emma's mother. Emma's school, too, had been nominally Christian; chapel and morning prayer and a muttered Latin grace before meals. If she thought about it, though, maybe there was a link between Romany and Roman Catholic. She'd have to do some research.

St John the Baptist was certainly a church for the devout. Looking it up later, Emma learnt that it had been built by George IV for Maria Fitzherbert and, whilst the outside was stolid and plain, inside the decorators hadn't left a single Catholic cliché unexplored. Candles? Tick. Gruesome old paintings of the Resurrection and St John's head on a platter? Tick. Confessional boxes? High altar? Sense of gloom and incense and mystery? All present and correct. There was a bas-relief of Maria Fitzherbert on the wall too, her three wedding rings picked out in gold, as if to emphasise that she really was married to George.

Emma sat herself near the back of the church. It was hard to find a seat because the place was absolutely packed. Where had they come from, all these people? Emma had been expecting some jewelled scarves and bright colours but all she could see was a sea of black, mourners solid and respectable enough to be her parents' friends (perhaps some of them were?). But, just as she was feeling rather disappointed with the whole affair, the congregation rose to their feet and the musicians entered the church, still playing as they walked up the aisle. Outside, the music had sounded discordant and strange but now the tortured strings formed themselves into a tune so wild and sad and passionate that Emma found herself wanting to laugh or cry, or both. To the sound of this gypsy lament Madame Zabini's coffin was borne into the church by the six men who had been following the hearse. Astarte walked alone behind them, carrying the wreath of red roses.

"Ah," said a large woman in front of Emma, "she's a true Romany, that one."

It was obviously a compliment of the highest order.

An hour later the service was drawing to a close; the priest sprinkling holy water on the coffin and his acolytes wafting incense around with such abandon that the high altar was lost in a cloud of blue smoke. Emma sat back in her pew, trying not to breathe in. The combination of gypsy violins, incense and Latin chanting had left her feeling rather dazed. She had no way of knowing how much of the service was traditional Catholic requiem and how much was Romany tradition, but, one thing was certain, Doreen Barton, aka Madame Zabini, had been given a thorough send-off. Her three sons (Emma was right about Tol's brothers) had all spoken at length about "Ma", her kindness, her practicality and her extraordinary psychic powers. What had happened to their father? Emma wondered. Apart from a passing mention of "when Pa died", Mr Barton had been conspicuous by his absence.

Then Astarte had made her way to the pulpit. Emma had expected more reminiscences, perhaps some charming anecdotes about Grandma Doreen. Instead Astarte had simply opened her mouth and sung. Her unaccompanied voice, sweet and clear, rose to the painted ceiling of the church, almost causing the plaster angels to take flight. "Sleep well, my love," sang Astarte, "sleep while the night sky weaves its spell." The woman in front of Emma was sobbing openly and, all around the church, handkerchiefs were emerging. For Emma, though, the song was not so much sad as strangely disturbing. She could feel her nerve endings jangling as Astarte sang on, staring straight in front of her, a tiny figure in the huge church. "Earth to earth," she sang, "Grow like the willow tree." Was this magic, was Astarte actually weaving a spell? At all events, Emma was glad when the girl stopped singing and stepped back to stand beside her father. Tol put a hand on her shoulder but Emma was unable to see his face. What was he feeling? Paternal pride or something altogether more complicated?

At last the Mass ended and the coffin made its way back down the aisle, borne by the Zabini men. As Tol passed Emma he nodded to her slightly, encumbered as he was by the heavy coffin. Emma was annoyed to find herself blushing.

As she stood outside the church, wondering whether to gatecrash the wake (the DI had told her to watch the family, after all), a young man approached her. He was dark with beetle-brows and had a definite Zabini family look to him.

"Miss Holmes?"

"Yes."

"I'm Adam Barton. Uncle Tol told me to give you a lift to the wake."

Emma thanked him but, as she accompanied Adam to his car, she was conscious of a slight feeling of unease. She wished that she hadn't insisted on attending the funeral alone. At that moment she would have been happy to be accompanied by any one of her police colleagues. Even Bob.

CHAPTER
NINE

The wake was held at Marine Parade but Emma would not have recognised the shabby house she had visited yesterday. Double doors had been opened on the first floor, creating a long room full of flowers and glittering with cut-glass and white china. The sofa had been covered with a blue cloth decorated with gold stars and, somewhere amongst the throng of people, the gypsy band was still playing. Adam told Emma that only the immediate family had gone to the cemetery. "Just Great-Grandma, Uncle Tol, Uncle Merlin and Dad. And Astarte, of course." Why Astarte when the other cousins — Adam, his brother Joseph and Merlin's son David — had stayed behind? But Adam seemed to find nothing strange in the arrangement. He found Emma a glass of champagne and offered her a sandwich. "They're really good, turkey and ham. My mum made them." Emma had not worked out which of the women, most of them wearing old-fashioned black lace veils, was Adam's mother. At any rate she was not considered worthy to attend the burial. She thought to ask Adam his father's name. "Peter," said Adam. Merlin, Ptolemy and Peter. Had Doreen lost faith in Romany traditions by the time that her last child was born?

Emma took the champagne and politely refused a sandwich. Adam hovered for a few minutes but then was called away to move a table. Emma was left in the company of an elderly man in a black velvet smoking jacket.

"Are you a family member?" she asked.

The old man laughed. He had a brown leathery face and white hair, like a troll. But he seemed friendly enough. "I should say I am. I'm Doreen's uncle. Isobel's brother."

They were a long-lived family, the Zabinis. Except Doreen, of course. Emma wondered why the uncle — who'd introduced himself as Lucian Zabini — hadn't accompanied his sister to the cemetery. She ventured that it had been a lovely service.

"It was all right," said Lucian, taking a silver flask from his pocket and adding a generous splash of its contents to his champagne, "but in my day we had real Romany funerals. They would last all day, music and singing and story-telling. Then, in the evening, we'd burn the dead person's caravan."

"Why would you do that?"

"Romany tradition. Some Roma believe that the dead will need their possessions in the afterlife. But the most important reason is that there's no *marimé*."

"What's *marimé*?"

"Contamination. It's dangerous to touch the body or the possessions of the dead. If there's *marimé* there's a danger that the dead one will become a *mulŏ*, an undead spirit looking for revenge."

He sounded quite cheerful about it so Emma felt able to say, "That doesn't sound very friendly."

"The dead aren't friendly," said Uncle Lucian. "In the old days, the bereaved families didn't eat at all until the dead one was buried. They were only allowed to drink water. And brandy." He gestured with the silver flask.

"Do all . . . all Romanies believe this?"

"The young don't believe," said Lucian. "Why do you think Doreen's sons buried her away from all us old ones? So that we can't see if there's any *marimé*."

But Isobel was there, thought Emma. Surely she counted as one of the old ones?

"Does Tol believe?" she asked.

Lucian shot her a look from tortoise-like eyes. "Take my advice, my dear young lady, and don't get involved with Ptolemy. He's been trouble from the day he was born. He treated his poor wife terribly, almost blinded her once. Why do you think the girl died only two years after their wedding? Because he's trouble."

"I'm not involved with Tol." In the effort to make herself clear, Emma heard her voice rising. "I hardly know him."

"We can remedy that," said a voice behind her. It was Tol, back from the cemetery, sombre and dangerous in his black suit. "Hallo, Emma Holmes. Has Uncle Lucian been amusing you?"

Emma could feel herself blushing again but she answered coolly enough. "We've been having a very interesting conversation."

74

Lucian, quite unabashed, said, "I've been explaining Roma burial customs to this delightful young policewoman."

Policewoman? Did the whole family know who she was? Had they been discussing her?

"Thank you, Uncle," said Tol, gravely. "Now, do you think you could look after Grandma for me? She was quite upset by the burial."

It was definitely an order. Lucian took a quick swig from his flask and headed off across the room. There was a rise in noise levels as people greeted the newcomers. Emma could see Astarte's bright hair in a group by the doorway.

Emma, left alone with Tol, took a nervous sip of her drink and was surprised to find her glass empty.

"Can I get you another?" asked Tol.

"No, thank you. I'm meant to be on duty." After all, they all knew she was a policewoman. Might as well be open about it. She tried to give Tol a straight look but he was so tall that she ended up having to back away slightly.

Tol smiled. "And have you seen anything suspicious today?"

Not suspicious exactly, thought Emma. Unsettling, certainly. Weird, perhaps. She thought of Astarte singing in the church. Uncle Lucian talking about *marimé*.

"I don't know," she said. "Have you?"

"Maybe," said Tol unexpectedly. "I'm not sure exactly."

Emma watched Astarte moving through the crowds. They parted to let her through, the Gypsy Queen, head held aloft.

"Your daughter sang beautifully," she said.

"Yes." Tol gave a short laugh. "Father O'Brien didn't want her to sing. He's not keen on women in the pulpit but Astarte wanted to. And what Astarte wants, she gets."

That was quite something to say about your daughter, thought Emma, a girl who was probably not yet twenty. Still, her own father probably said the same thing about her when she refused to go to finishing school.

"Astarte was very fond of Mum," said Tol. "She was brought up by her really. Sally, Astarte's mother, died when she was little."

Did Tol guess that Lucian was talking about his dead wife? wondered Emma. He *treated his poor wife terribly, almost blinded her once.*

"It must have been difficult for you," she said.

"It was hard," said Tol, "but I had my mother and grandmother. Romany families are very matriarchal."

That might be true, thought Emma, but Tol was definitely in charge of this family. She thought of the way Adam had escorted her to the wake, the way even Lucian hastened to obey Tol's orders.

"You said you might have seen something suspicious," she said. "What was it?"

Tol fixed her with his strange blue-green gaze. "I'm not sure yet."

76

This was irritating, to say the least. Emma decided to go for the direct approach.

"Do you have any idea who sent that note?"

Ask him what the Magic Men knew. Or ask the spirits, if they will speak to you.

"No," said Tol. "I thought you were getting it checked by your experts." He put a faint, slightly malicious emphasis on the last word.

"We are," said Emma, although the experts were only her and Bob, peering at the handwriting and concluding that it was "someone artistic".

"Well then," said Tol, scanning the room from his superior height. "We have nothing to fear."

Emma did not dignify this with an answer.

By the time that the captain told them to prepare for landing, Edgar felt as if he had been on the plane for ever. He had eaten in the dining area, slept in his chair (there were sleeping compartments available but he hadn't felt like climbing into the tiny overhead bunks) and enjoyed breakfast while the plane was still over the ocean. They had refuelled in Canada and now they were approaching New York City (the pilot gave the words a jokey American twang). He had chatted to his next-door neighbour, a shoe salesman called Hank, and was on first-name terms with two of the hostesses, Sylvia and Nancy. He had not managed to speak to the beautiful woman passenger but she had passed him the marmalade at breakfast with a slightly suggestive smile. Max, he was sure, would have made something of this.

He had written two postcards.

Dearest Ruby, I'm writing this five miles in the air! Should be in New York by afternoon tomorrow. Love always Ed.

Dear Mum, Guess where I'm writing this? In a plane flying to New York! Nothing to worry about. Will be home next week. Love Edgar.

Nancy collected the cards and assured him that BOAC would post them. "Though you might be home again by the time they arrive." The thought of being home again was both comforting and unreal.

Now they were flying low over Idlewild Airport. The captain told them to look out for the Empire State Building but Edgar couldn't locate it in the mass of tall buildings. Who knew that there were so many skyscrapers in the world? How tiny and insubstantial they looked from the air. The landing seemed frighteningly abrupt, a shocking return to earth. Sylvia and Nancy were helping people collect their belongings and saying goodbye with professional warmth. Edgar felt a ridiculous pang at the thought of never seeing them again.

"Goodbye," said Nancy. "Have a nice day. That's what they say in America."

"Have a nice day," echoed Edgar with a weak smile. He had no idea what to do next.

What he did in the end, after endless queues at customs and a long, anxious wait for his suitcase, was to hire a car using some of the dollars given to him by General Petre. He had an address for Bill Hitchcock but no idea how to get there by public transport. Having a car would give him the illusion of being in control. He also bought a map of New York State which, comfortingly, showed Albany on the cover.

The car was a black Buick, not as opulent as Max's pre-war Bentley but still light years ahead of the police issue Wolseley which was the car Edgar drove most often. This car had gears on the steering wheel and a radio which gave him a shock when it came on with a shout of: "Mrs Filbert's margarine — buy some today!" Drive on the right, he told himself, drive on the right. But, coming out of the airport, he went straight into oncoming traffic, horns blaring, lights flashing. He switched to the other side of the road, wondering if he was going to die before he reached Albany. Negotiating the maze of signposts he seemed to be constantly in the wrong lane, having taxi drivers mouth obscenities from within their incongruously cheerful yellow cabs. Suddenly, almost without knowing it, he was on a bridge, terrifyingly high, with cars on both sides of him. The airport was on a narrow spit of land, he remembered that, but the emergence of water below was a shock. Coming off the bridge, he was once more in a queue of traffic. He needed to come off the road and look at the map. What if he never stopped? What if he continued to circle New York for the rest of his life?

Eventually he found a garage (or Gas Station, according to the sign), pulled up and opened out the map. He then made the unwelcome discovery that Albany, which looked so close on the cover picture, was actually more than a hundred and sixty miles away. On the map it looked as if it was almost in Canada. The journey would probably take him four hours and it was six o'clock now. At least it looked like a fairly straight highway, number 87, leading all the way. Edgar bought a sandwich and a bottle of drink which the garage attendant called a soda. It tasted like cherry medicine but wasn't entirely unpleasant. He also asked for directions to Highway 87, feeling as if he was speaking in code, and received a complicated set of words in return. He had to head for the Bronx, that was the main thing. He thanked the attendant profusely.

"You're welcome. You British?"

"Yes."

"We ain't helping you folks enough, that's what I think. You still got rationing?"

"For some things, yes."

"It ain't right." The young man shook his head sorrowfully.

After a hellish tangle with the Bronx, Edgar found himself enjoying the drive. The highway was blissfully straight and easy to negotiate and the Buick a joy to drive. He even mastered the radio, singing along to advertisements for Colgate toothpaste and deodorant ("No, no, to underarm O"). It was only when it started to get dark that the charm palled and tiredness overcame him. He had only slept for a few hours since he had boarded the plane at midday yesterday. He couldn't really turn up at Hitchcock's door at ten in the evening. Maybe he'd better look for a place to spend the night.

As he neared Albany, he started to see signs for Canada as well as illuminated posters for bars and grills. One place, in particular, seemed very insistent.

"Shangri-La Motor Court, twenty-five panelled units of Spanish Design. Five miles." Then four miles, three miles, two and finally one. "Vacancy", shouted the neon sign. Was the Shangri-La some sort of hotel? At any rate, it seemed to want his patronage. At the next sign — "Stop here for the Shangri-La Motor Court" — he obeyed and pulled up outside a row of little huts.

At reception he was told that the Shangri-La was a motel, a hotel where people parked in front of their bedroom and drove off again in the morning. He was given the keys to number three and told that breakfast was in reception from seven a.m. "You British? Thought as much."

By now, Edgar was practically sleepwalking. He let himself into number three, which was a large clean room with two double beds. There was also an armchair and a television set. Edgar turned on the television and was rewarded by a black and white picture of Buckingham Palace. "Great Britain prepares for the coronation of young Queen Elizabeth."

Edgar turned off the television and found a door that led to a small but well-equipped bathroom. He washed his face and cleaned his teeth ("Brush your teeth with Colgate. It cleans your breath — what a toothpaste! — while it cleans your teeth"). Then he threw himself onto the bed and, at once, fell into a deep sleep.

CHAPTER
TEN

Max should have felt at home. He was in a theatre that he knew and loved, the Empire, Shepherd's Bush, a grand old Number One in its day. But now it seemed like a foreign land. He remembered appearing here in 1935, the first year that he'd topped the bill. "A star is born," the papers had said and, appearing under the lights at the Empire, he had certainly felt — perhaps for the first time in his life — that he was where he belonged. The exquisite pause when the girl first vanished and the audience had been too shocked to applaud. The ovation, minutes later, when she appeared in the Royal Circle balcony. That was Ethel, Max's best ever assistant, but now she was dead and the Empire was . . .

"It's a television theatre," Joe Passolini had explained. "The BBC bought it this year. Paid £120,000 for it, I'm told. They're going to film all the live TV shows there. *Those Were the Days* will be one of the first."

The director, Derek Conroy, had called all the acts together for a first run-through. The show was due to be aired in thirteen days' time, on the evening after the coronation. Max wondered what the run-through would entail. He hadn't really thought much about his act and, anyway, he didn't like to rehearse in front of the others. Surprise was essential in magic and pros were such awful gossips. He supposed he'd have to think of something.

Walking through the auditorium, Max told himself that he should be glad that the old theatre was still standing. He had heard about other theatres being knocked down and turned into flats or offices. At least this was still show business, albeit a new and strange branch of it.

Joe, wearing a pinstriped suit with shoulders so wide that his head looked tiny, came down the aisle to meet him.

"Maxie boy, you made it. Come and meet Derek."

Max followed his agent into the orchestra pit which was full of men pushing giant cameras on wheels. Were there no orchestras in this brave new television world? And why, in the name of God, was Joe calling him "Maxie boy"?

"Max, this is Derek Conroy, the director. Derek, this is Max Mephisto." Joe said the name with an aural flourish. Max winced but Derek shook his hand with genuine enthusiasm. He was a tall man, probably in his fifties, with greying hair and a still-boyish grin.

"Max Mephisto. Gosh, this is an honour. I've been a fan of yours for years. I'm delighted that you've agreed to be on *Days*. You're just the headline act we need."

Max smiled politely. He wondered whether Joe had suggested him to the director or the other way round.

"Let me show you round." Derek Conroy led Max up onto the stage where several carpenters were hard at work.

"We're extending the stage over the orchestra pit to give more depth," he explained. "We can put the camera dolly on a tracking platform in front. The other cameras will be on tripods around the auditorium."

Max only understood two or three words in this statement so he fixed on one of them. "Where will the orchestra go?"

"They'll be in the front rows of the stalls. We'll have a lighting rig over the top. Eventually, we'll build a band room to the right of the stage."

Max looked at the workmen and the electricians and the men pushing cameras. "Do you think you'll be ready by the second of June?" he asked. What was the date today? Twentieth of May, he thought. Edgar would be in New York by now.

"It'll be all right on the night," said Derek. "That's what you professionals say, isn't it?"

We say it, thought Max, but we don't really mean it. Mind you, he had seen theatres in worse states than the Empire scrub up pretty well for the opening night.

"Let's go to the Green Room," said Derek. "Meet the other acts."

Joe had been rather tight-lipped about the other performers. This meant they were either has-beens or famous enough to make Max feel insecure. He didn't know which scenario he would prefer.

Derek led the way through the wings which were a tangle of cables and wood shavings. "We were so lucky to acquire this place," he told Max. "We're going to film all sorts of shows here. In the future, when people think about variety they'll think about the BBC Television Theatre."

Max wasn't sure how he felt about this. On the one hand, it looked as if variety was going to have some sort of future. On the other, the real experience of variety was not about sitting in front of a television, it was going out in the night to a brightly lit and exotic building called a theatre. The Empire had been one of the best and its transformation made Max feel rather sad.

Derek seemed to sense this. "It looks a bit of a mess now," he said, "but wait until you see it all lit up on the second. It'll be just like the Theatre Royal, Drury Lane, except that you'll be playing to an audience of millions. They say that there are two million television sets in Britain. Just think of three or four people to a set."

There was that, of course.

"The other pros are an exciting bunch," said Derek, leading the way up some stone stairs. Backstage was, comfortingly, as shabby as backstage anywhere. "There's a ventriloquist. His dummy's bloody scary but he does an amazing trick where they sing a duet. Then there are some Russian dancers, an impressionist, a fabulous singer, two comedians and some incredible acrobats, the Fantinis. Oh, and there's another magic act."

Max stopped dead. It was usually in his contract that he had to be the only magician on the bill. Had he neglected to mention this to Joe Passolini or had the agent just ignored him?

Derek saw his face. "Don't worry. You'll be top billing. This is a very new act. I asked Joe and he said he was sure you wouldn't mind."

Did he indeed? Max was still finding words to disabuse the director of this idea when the Green Room door opened and Derek was saying, "This, boys and girls, is the famous Max Mephisto. And this, Max, is the other magician. We're really excited about her."

And Max found himself looking into the smiling face of his daughter, Ruby.

Emma and Bob peered at jaunty blue and red letters.

Roman and Renée: Husband and Wife Songbirds
Tommy Lang: Not Quite Himself
Val and Monty: Australia's Ace Ventriloquist
Tony "The Mind" Mulholland: He Knows What
    You're Thinking Before You Do
Raydini: The Gay Deceiver
Charlie Haystack: Man of a Thousand Voices
Lou Lenny and her Unrideable Mule.

"Blimey," said Bob, "I wonder if it was a real mule."

"I don't see how it could have been," said Emma. "Maybe it was like a pantomime horse."

"Well, that would be unrideable all right."

Emma stared at the words Tony "The Mind" Mulholland. It was a name she knew well. Although she hadn't been at the station when they were hunting the Conjuror Killer, everyone knew the names of the victims. Why had Madame Zabini kept this flyer, fourteen years old now, in her caravan? Tony Mulholland had been one of the Magic Men, as had the DI and his mysterious friend, Max Mephisto. What did the letter writer mean by, *Ask him what the Magic Men knew?* The DI didn't talk about his war years but, once, in a mellow moment, he had mentioned being involved in "a doomed attempt to stop Hitler by magic powers." Was this what the Magic Men were all about and, if so, how could a wartime espionage group be linked to the death of an obscure Brighton fortune-teller? And what was the link with the DI's hush-hush American case? She looked at the calendar tacked up on the wall which showed the Royal Pavilion in spring sunshine. He must be over there by now.

Not that she and Bob had had much time to spend on the Zabini case. With the boss away their time was mostly taken up with the burglaries and petty thefts that always coincided with the summer season. They were both keen to keep their heads down and avoid the super, who might think that they should be reporting directly to him in the DI's absence. Anyway, as far as the super was concerned, the Zabini case was over. The coroner had recorded death by accidental causes and Madame Zabini had been laid to rest. "Madeira Drive shut all morning," the DI reported Superintendent Hodges as saying. "Gypsy violinists wandering up and down the promenade. Let that be an end to it."

Except that Emma didn't really think that it was the end. The letter writer obviously thought that there was something suspicious about Doreen Barton's death. Tol clearly had his suspicions too. Emma was not going to let the case rest just yet. Which was why she had asked Bob to look at the flyer. Bob was annoying but he wasn't stupid and he often spotted things that other people missed.

Now, though, he seemed stubbornly fixated on the wrong things.

"Raydini sounds a bit dicey. Wonder who he was deceiving?"

"But why did Doreen keep the flyer all those years? That's the point."

The door flew open and a young uniformed policeman burst into the room. "Fire on the Palace Pier!" he panted.

"What the . . ." Bob started up.

"Are the fire brigade there?" asked Emma.

"Yes, but I thought you should know."

"Why?"

"It's the old gypsy caravan. Someone's set it alight."

"Hallo, Max," said Ruby.

At least she wasn't going to call him Dad and force him to explain the whole thing in front of Derek Conroy and Joe Passolini.

"Ah, that's right," said the director. "Joe said he thought you knew each other."

"Ruby was Max's assistant once," said Joe, obviously pleased to have this inside knowledge.

88

"For a short time," said Max. "Before she went up in the world." He turned to Ruby. "I thought you were appearing in Bournemouth, at the Pavilion."

"The show's over," said Ruby. "It ended on Saturday. So, when Joe told me about this . . ."

An unwelcome thought struck Max. "Is Joe your agent then?"

Ruby dimpled at Passolini, who actually blushed. "Yes, he's been my agent for a while now."

Trust Ruby to find one of the hottest agents around. But the knowledge made Max feel wrong-footed, something he seldom experienced. Did Ruby already know that he would be in the show? Had Joe only asked him because of the connection with Ruby? He didn't get a chance to ask because Derek Conroy was continuing the introductions.

"This is Jim Jones, the ventriloquist. And Reggie, of course." Max found himself looking into the terrifying face of a large dummy. Was it his imagination or did Reggie wink at him?

"Olga and Natasha, our lovely dancers. Stew Stewart, a very funny new comedian. Leonora Lorenzo, a wonderful singer. Tommy Lang, the impressionist. Marco Fantini and his sons Pietro and Lucca."

Max had worked with the Fantinis before and they exchanged a few words in Italian. Marco expressed the opinion that the ventriloquist's dummy was possessed by the devil and warned Max to steer clear of him. Max glanced at Joe Passolini to see if he'd understood but the agent was still looking at Ruby.

Introductions over, Derek Conroy announced the running order. Max was the last act on the programme, befitting his headline status, and the Fantinis had second billing, appearing just before the interval, which would also give the stagehands time to move their apparatus. What would the television viewers see during the interval? someone asked. "Oh, we'll just play them some music or something," said Derek. Ruby was midway through the first half, not a great spot, but obviously Derek hadn't wanted two magicians in the same half. The Russian dancers would be the first act, followed by Jim Jones and Reggie. Max could see the ventriloquist looking doubtful about this.

"It's a big honour," said Derek. "Got to open the show with a bang."

Stew Stewart was now looking rather disconsolate.

Derek clapped his hands. "I think I speak for all of us when I say that this is an exciting, a *thrilling* moment. *Those Were the Days* is not just a show, it's an *event* . . . people will remember where they were the first time they saw it . . . audiences dressed up in Victorian clothes . . . all the glamour of the music hall . . . costumes . . . music . . . yesteryear . . . old time . . ." Max sat back in his chair and let the words wash over him. Jim Jones was still looking put out. Next to him, Reggie slumped in his chair, mouth open in a silent scream. The Fantinis looked cynical, Stew Stewart depressed and Tommy Lang worried. Olga and Natasha listened politely, their long limbs arranged in mirror symmetry. Only Ruby, leaning forward, eyes

90

sparkling, was displaying the right kind of awe and excitement.

Derek then introduced a young woman called Pearl who was to be the stage manager. Pearl, who was armed with a clipboard, asked the performers about their music and effects. Max requested the "Danse Macabre", his signature tune, but was rather vague about his act. He didn't want to do the trick with the stage manager's dog again. There was no doubt that Alfie would be as big a hit with the BBC Television Theatre audience as he was at the Theatre Royal. It was just that he didn't want his first television appearance to be upstaged by a dog. If he wasn't careful, he'd find himself in a double act, just like Jim Jones and Reggie. But he'd have to do something impressive. The trouble was, if he wanted to perform a cabinet trick, he would have to get something made in the next few days and the best theatrical cabinetmaker was Declan Fitzgerald in Hove. "I'll do some tricks with the audience first," he told Pearl. "Find doves in women's handbags, that sort of thing. Then I'll do my set-piece illusion. It'll be good, I promise." Pearl looked doubtful but made a note.

Then, it seemed, they were free to leave. "We'll meet next week for the technical rehearsal. The stage should be finished by then."

Max and Ruby found themselves walking back through the auditorium together.

"Isn't it exciting?" said Ruby. "To think we'll be on television."

Max looked at Ruby's glowing face. He didn't find it exciting, he found it rather depressing. The Empire had become a giant television set and he was reduced to fifteen minutes of prancing around the specially extended stage in a top hat and tails. But Ruby was different. This was her generation. She had no nostalgia for the draughty digs and faded glamour of music hall. She was made for the bright lights of television. Max was sure that she would be a big success.

"What does Em — your mother make of it?" he asked. He was usually careful not to mention Emerald, a former snake-charmer with whom he'd had a brief relationship twenty-three years ago, but he was curious. He knew that Ruby's mother and stepfather disapproved of her stage career.

"Oh, she thinks television is more respectable than variety," said Ruby. "She says I'll meet a nicer sort of chap."

Well, Emerald should know, thought Max. But he didn't like the idea that Emerald was still matchmaking for her daughter. He might be ambivalent about Edgar marrying Ruby but Emerald should realise that he was worth a million of the sort of "chap" Ruby would meet in television.

"Doesn't she approve of you marrying Ed?" he asked.

"Oh, she likes Ed," said Ruby, stopping in the foyer to adjust her hat. "She just thinks I'm too young to get married, that's all."

Max had nothing to say to that because he agreed. Emerald got pregnant with Ruby at twenty and made the decision not to involve him, the father. Max could never decide if he found this unforgivable or amazingly noble. In any case, he was sure that Emerald's situation had been an unenviable one. He looked at Ruby's reflection in one of the foyer's many mirrors. She was as pretty and smiling as ever — Joe hadn't been able to take his eyes off her in the Green Room — but there was something slightly brittle about her today all the same. He wondered if he could take her to lunch without Joe Passolini tagging along. It was a long time since he'd been alone with his daughter. He was just about to suggest an Italian restaurant nearby when Ruby said, "Did you know that Ed was in America?"

"Yes. Yes, I did."

"He's gone all the way to New York. *In an aeroplane.* And he won't even tell me what he's doing there."

So that's what she was sulking about.

By the time that Emma and Bob reached the Palace Pier, the fire was out. A red fire engine stood at the entrance to the pier and hoses snaked their way along its length until they reached the gypsy caravan, now just a pile of charred and sodden wood. On one blackened plank the word "Tarot" was still visible. The pier had been cleared of customers but a few employees stood in a huddle under a nearby awning. Emma recognised one of them, Lou Abrahams, from a previous investigation.

"Hi, Lou. What happened?"

"I don't know." Lou had a mobile face, like a cheerful clown, but now all the lines pointed downwards. "Cherry, who runs the candyfloss stall, just shouted out that Doreen's caravan was on fire. I called the fire brigade and we got everyone off sharpish. It's a crying shame. Doreen's granddaughter was going to carry on the business. Have you met her? She's a lovely girl."

"I have met her, yes."

Emma spoke to Cherry who had nothing much to add. She hadn't seen anyone approaching the caravan but then she'd been quite busy. They'd had a lot of customers for May. Must be the good weather and the coronation coming up. People were taking their holidays early.

Emma joined Bob, who was talking to the leading fireman.

"It was deliberate, all right," the fireman was saying. "There was petrol in that fire. We can tell by the flames. Someone must have poured petrol onto the caravan and thrown a match on top. Went up like a firework."

"Why would anyone want to set the old lady's caravan on fire?" asked Bob as they made their way back along the seafront, past the carousel and the big wheel and the crowds enjoying an early holiday.

Emma said nothing. She was thinking of the funeral and Uncle Lucian. *In the evening, we'd burn the dead person's caravan ... It's dangerous to touch the possessions of the dead.*

CHAPTER
ELEVEN

Max took Ruby to an Italian restaurant that he knew. It was a dark, backstreet place but the food was good and he was confident that they wouldn't run into any other members of the cast. But, no sooner had they sat at their table and the waiters exclaimed over Ruby's beauty, than he heard a familiar, half cockney, half American voice. Only this time it was speaking Sicilian.

"Well blow me down if it isn't my two favourite clients." The voice switched back into a version of English.

There was nothing for it but to acknowledge him. Besides, Ruby was twinkling and sparkling for all she was worth. Max turned, trying to make sure that his body language did not spell out "please join us".

"Hallo, Joe. Fancy seeing you here."

"Oh, the owner is a friend of Pa's. *Grazie*, Daniele." Giving his coat to the waiter Joe somehow managed to ease himself into the chair between Max and Ruby.

"You're a dark horse, Maxie boy. Fancy sneaking off here with the most beautiful girl in London. Shall we have a bottle of something? Maurizio's got some good stuff locked away for his regulars."

Where to start? Max contented himself with saying, "Ruby's my daughter and I've already ordered a bottle. You're welcome to join us, of course. Oh, and please stop calling me Maxie boy."

At least he had the pleasure of seeing Joe's mouth drop open in surprise.

"Your daughter? I had no idea. Why didn't you tell me, Ruby?"

Ruby gave Joe her frankest look, lashes fluttering. "I wanted to make it on my own, not because I had a famous father."

"You're a diamond," said Joe. He turned to Max, and possibly the whole restaurant. "Isn't she a diamond?" Max agreed that she was and Joe continued to extol Ruby's virtues as the waiter brought and poured the wine. There was no way of knowing if it was one of Maurizio's special bottles, thought Max, but it was pretty good none the less.

"All the same," said Joe, having exhausted the subject of Ruby's beauty, brains and general star quality, "you should have told me. There are all sorts of things we can do. Publicity, special features in the papers. 'My daughter the magician.' 'The hidden daughter: Max Mephisto's greatest conjuring trick.' Maybe even a TV show. *Magician and Daughter*. This could be big. This could be sensational." He lapsed into his American accent again.

Max was still reeling from "The hidden daughter". "I don't think we're quite ready for it to be generally known yet. Are we, Ruby?"

"No," said Ruby. But she sounded rather regretful.

96

"You see," said Max, "Ruby was brought up by her mother and stepfather and they might feel . . ."

"Say no more," said Joe. "I understand. I'm a sensitive soul. Hey, Daniele!" He shouted across the room to the waiter. "Bring us some pasta here. We're starving."

Max might deplore the agent's manners but there was no denying that Daniele took their orders very quickly and that the pasta, when it came, was delicious.

"Maurizio was interned with my dad on the Isle of Man," said Joe. " 'Collar the lot', that's what Churchill said, and they interned all of them, all the London Italians. Maurizio's family had owned this restaurant for years. My dad was a baker in Clerkenwell. Neither of them were Mussolini supporters. My dad was the other way, to tell you the truth. A bit of a communist. But they were locked away for the duration. The only good thing to come out of it, Pa said, were the friendships. They all became really close. And the music. They had all these Jewish musicians, you see. Pa used to say that there was this string quartet, the best in Europe, that used to play to them on Sunday evenings. It was almost worth being interned to listen to them, Pa said."

"I've got a friend, a violinist and conductor, who was interned on the Isle of Man," said Max. "He's German Jewish and it always seemed very unjust that he was locked up as a potential Nazi sympathiser."

"But you fought, didn't you, Max?" said Joe, tucking his napkin into his collar. "You fought for the British." Something in the way he said "the British" made Max

97

think that Joe, for all his Londoner's charm, still considered himself Italian.

"I signed up," he said. "I wouldn't say that it was out of patriotism though. I think I mostly did it to annoy my father. Now he *was* a bit of a Nazi-sympathiser. Like a lot of the British aristocracy."

"I don't believe it," said Ruby. "Grandpa wouldn't have supported Hitler."

Ruby didn't know the first thing about the man she called Grandpa, thought Max, but she often stuck up for him in conversations with her father. Max had initially been reluctant to introduce Ruby to Lord Massingham but he needn't have worried. The old boy had been absolutely charmed by his granddaughter, despite the (to him) massive drawback of her being the daughter of a snake-charmer and the stepdaughter of a plasterer. Well, Ruby had certainly charmed her snake of an ancestor. Max lived in hope that his father would cut him out of his will in Ruby's favour. There was nothing he wanted less than to be Lord Massingham one day.

"He may not have supported Hitler," he conceded. "But he was definitely all for appeasement before the war. And he wasn't happy when I joined up in the ranks either."

"Hard to think of you as an aristo, Max," said Joe. "Ever use it on bills? The Lord of Levitation? The Prince of Performers?"

"No," said Max, with a shudder.

"You've got to think about the publicity," said Joe. "Especially these days. Doesn't matter how good you are, if the public don't know about you, what's the point of going on? That's the great thing about this show, *Those Were the Days*. It'll put you on the map. It'll make people sit up and notice you."

"It's really exciting," said Ruby. "To think that all those people will be watching us. On coronation day too."

"They might be watching us," said Max, "but suppose they don't like what they see?"

Joe made an impatient gesture that almost knocked his empty plate to the floor. "That doesn't matter, don't you see, Max? People will automatically like performers that they see on the TV. Doesn't matter if they're not very good. If you're on TV, you're in their home, you're one of the family. In a few years' time, they'll probably have TV shows that just show people living their ordinary lives, eating, drinking, talking, even having a bath. And those people, those ordinary people, they'll be stars. That'll be their entertainment."

"Christ, I hope I don't live to see it," said Max. He was rather surprised that Joe hadn't leapt in to say that of course people would like him because he was brilliant, he was the best. He didn't like all this "it doesn't matter how good you are" stuff. It did matter, for a magician. If you were good, you could do magic; if you weren't, you couldn't. It was as simple as that.

"Don't be defeatist, Max," said Joe. "This is the future. What did you think of your fellow TV stars today?"

"Well, the dummy was bloody frightening," said Max.

"I've heard Leonora Lorenzo on the wireless," said Ruby. "Mum really likes her."

"Derek's put a good bill together," said Joe. "Tommy Lang's a bit past it but Stew Stewart's a new face. That's important in a show like this."

"I've worked with the Fantinis before," said Max. "They're a first-class act."

"Ah, Italians always stick together," said Joe with a wink, accepting a glass of grappa from Daniele. "But, the real star of the show is sitting at this table."

Max looked modest and took a sip of grappa.

"Yes, the star of the night will be Ruby here. She'll be famous after June the second or I'm a Dutchman."

"And we all know you're Italian," said Max.

Max walked Ruby back to the tube station. He had offered to pay for a taxi but Ruby was in one of her independent moods and said that it would be "fun" to take the tube to Victoria. Fun wasn't exactly how Max would have described trying to cross the Uxbridge Road as the traffic descended from all directions. There were more cars every day — something he approved of, in principle — but it made being a pedestrian a little trying sometimes. He thought of Edgar on the American highways. Would he have hired a car? Would he even now be sailing along Route Whatsit in a giant Cadillac?

Once the road had been safely navigated, he moved to be on the traffic side of Ruby.

"You're making me nervous," she complained.

"Sorry," he said, "just saving you from possible runaway horses. You know there weren't any cars around when I was growing up."

She laughed, although it wasn't far from the truth. As they neared the tube station entrance, he said what he had been planning to say: "Edgar was talking about your wedding the other day."

"Was he?" Ruby was searching for something in her bag and didn't meet his eyes.

"Yes. He seemed to think it was imminent. Before the end of the year anyway."

"That's ages away."

"It isn't really," said Max.

Ruby looked up at him, her chin tilted. "What's it got to do with you?"

"Well, I am your father." He knew it was wrong as soon as he said it. The words "Are you?" hovered, unsaid, in the air.

"It's just —" he tried for a gentler tone — "if you're not sure, don't you think you should tell Ed?"

"I am sure," said Ruby. "And Grandpa said that he'd come to the wedding. He said he'd give me away if you didn't want to."

What with him, Lord Massingham and Ruby's stepfather there would be quite a queue at the altar, thought Max as he kissed Ruby goodbye and set off towards Kensington. It had been an unsatisfactory lunch, one way or another. First Joe Passolini turning up and ruining their tête-à-tête, rabbiting on about the war and predicting that Ruby would be the star of the TV show. Then the slight argument with Ruby at

101

the tube station. Why hadn't he just kept his mouth shut? As Ruby had said, her love life really wasn't any of his business.

What would it be like if he was Ruby's real father, if he'd brought her up from birth? But he couldn't imagine it, any more than he could imagine what Edgar was doing in America. He'd better concentrate on what he knew best: magic tricks. He walked along Holland Park Avenue, thinking of the best way to make a woman disappear.

CHAPTER
TWELVE

Edgar woke up feeling curiously relaxed. He was lying in an exceptionally comfortable bed and the smell of damp that normally assailed his nostrils on waking was entirely absent. He rolled over and saw another bed next to him, rather sinister in its pristine whiteness. Where the hell was he? If it was heaven, it was a rather utilitarian version of it. He sat up. Pine-clad walls, his suitcase lying in the middle of the floor, a television set. He got up and opened the curtains. Grass, trees and, closer than he would have thought possible, a city with smoke, and large buildings. Were they skyscrapers? That must be Albany. He was nearly there. As he watched, a squirrel scampered over the grass and climbed a tree. It seemed odd to see such a familiar creature in such an unfamiliar place. You'd expect American squirrels to be different somehow, in the way that American soldiers had been different, even to the cut of their uniforms.

Edgar went into the bathroom and had a shower in the little glass cubicle. Then he shaved and dressed in clean clothes. It was only seven a.m. He'd have breakfast and then he'd set out to find Wild Bill Hitchcock.

Breakfast was served on the wide porch in front of the reception area and it was delicious. Crispy bacon, eggs, gallons of coffee. Edgar ate and ate, enjoying the sensation of eating good food in the open air. The owner, a rather depressed-looking woman called Irma, seemed charmed by Edgar's appetite and hovered at his elbow to offer more bacon and flat cakes which she inexplicably called biscuits.

"Don't you have bacon in Britain?" she asked.

"We have it," said Edgar, "but meat's still rationed. Cheese too."

"Still rationed?" said Irma. "But the war's been over eight years."

Except that somehow it's not over in England, thought Edgar. Everything — clothes, furniture, food — still seemed to be shrouded in the greyness of war. Well, maybe the coronation would change all that. The new Elizabethan age, that's what they were calling it in the papers.

He showed Irma Hitchcock's address and was gratified that she seemed to recognise it. "Just a few blocks from downtown," she told him, speaking that foreign language again. But she did draw him a map and even wrapped up some "biscuits" for him to eat later. Edgar booked another night at the Shangri-La. He wasn't sure what his meeting with Hitchcock would bring but his flight home wasn't until Saturday and, besides, he was starting to feel rather fond of the motel.

Hitchcock lived at number 59 Meadow Lane, on the outskirts of Albany. It was a nice area, Edgar decided, large houses set back from the road, lots of grass and trees. He passed a yellow school bus and older children walking to school, the girls in white knee socks and the boys in colourful jackets with numbers on the back. Number fifty-nine was an attractive house, built of slatted wooden boards with a wide porch like the one at the Shangri-La. There must be money in the mesmerism business, thought Edgar, as he parked the Buick and made his way up the path.

The door was opened by a middle-aged woman in a black dress.

"Good morning." Edgar raised his hat and attempted a charming British smile. "I wonder if I could speak to William Hitchcock, Bill Hitchcock. I understand he lives here?"

The woman's face crumpled in distress.

"Bill's dead," she said. "He died yesterday."

The room seemed to be full of people but, after a few moments, Edgar had sorted them into: Helen, Bill's widow, who'd opened the door; Gardiner, his son; Eunice, his daughter; and Gardiner's wife, Alice. There was also the sleeping presence of Gardiner and Alice's baby, William Junior ("He was so proud to have his grandson named for him," Helen told Edgar tearfully). Edgar hadn't really wanted to come in and intrude on the family in mourning but Helen had insisted and he knew that he should be investigating Hitchcock's death. Because it had to be suspicious, surely? A few days ago Bill Hitchcock had spoken to Max on the telephone, teasing him with wordplay and crossword clues. And now he was dead. His body was lying in the mortuary in Albany and his family had gathered in his house.

"How did it happen?" he asked, as tactfully as he could, sitting on the leather sofa with a glass of iced tea in his hand.

"He was run over," said Helen. "He was leaving work yesterday when a car just knocked him down and carried on driving. Didn't even stop." She held a handkerchief to her eyes.

"Out-of-town plates," said Gardiner darkly.

"Travelling too fast to catch," said Alice.

"I'm so sorry," said Edgar. "It must be a terrible shock."

"For you too," said Helen, "after coming all this way. Bill would have been so pleased . . . How did you say you knew him again?"

"We've got a mutual friend, Tony Mulholland," said Edgar. This was the story he had prepared with Max. "I met Bill when he was doing a show with Tony a few years ago."

If Helen recognised the name she was hiding it well.

"Bill loved doing shows," she said. "He was so sad when he had to give it up."

This was news. "He'd given up mesmerism?" he asked.

The Hitchcocks exchanged glances. Eventually Gardiner said, "There was this case last year when a woman fainted after one of his shows. It was nothing really but the woman's family got nasty and so Dad gave up the act."

106

"He was really unhappy about it," said Eunice. "His father and grandfather had both been famous hypnotists. It's a family tradition."

Something in the way she said it made Edgar wonder if Eunice felt that she should be the one to carry on the tradition. He thought of Astarte Zabini, the slight young girl who was supposedly the inheritor of her grandmother's gift. He must telephone Emma and ask about Madame Zabini's funeral.

"He was wonderful at it, as I remember," Edgar lied. "He definitely had a gift."

It was the right thing to say. Helen's face lightened. "Oh, he *was* wonderful. You could draw something on a piece of paper in another room and he'd know what you'd drawn. He could guess your favourite colour or astrological sign. He could do card tricks like you wouldn't believe."

Tony Mulholland had done the drawing trick too. Edgar couldn't remember the details but it was something about planting an idea in the other person's head before they even set pencil to paper. He decided to take a chance.

"Bill was good at crosswords too, wasn't he?"

"Oh, wonderful at them," said Helen. "He could do the crossword in the *Albany Times Union* in under a minute. He timed himself with my egg timer. He used to get the *Evening Standard* crossword sent all the way over from England. It was the special British sort. What do you call them? Cryptic crosswords."

"With hesitation" was definitely a cryptic type of clue. It seemed more unlikely than ever that Bill

107

Hitchcock said these words by accident. Edgar asked what job Bill had done after he abandoned show business.

"He worked in a television repair shop," said Helen. "He was fascinated by televisions and radios."

It was only then that Edgar realised that the room boasted no fewer than three television sets, monstrous objects encased in mahogany cabinets. It was these, combined with the three-piece suite and the baby carriage, that made the room seem so crowded.

Helen saw him looking.

"He used to bring televisions home and tinker with them," she said, her eyes filling with tears. "It used to bother me but now I'd give anything to have him back here, all the nuts and bolts spread out on my good carpet."

And she began to cry in earnest.

After Edgar had escaped from number fifty-nine, promising to keep in touch and never to let Bill's memory die, he sat in his car for a few minutes, unsure what to do next. He had been all set to interview Hitchcock, to find out how he knew Colonel Cartwright and Tony Mulholland, to discover whether the shadowy anarchist cell actually existed or whether it was a figment of General Petre's imagination. But now Hitchcock was dead and his secrets would die with him. Get a grip, he told himself. You're a detective, you need to do some detecting. The least he could do was talk to the local police. He could always show them Petre's letter and claim Her Majesty's protection.

Central, or downtown, Albany was a revelation. "It's a small town really," Irma had told him, "not like New York City." But there was nothing small-town about the solid government buildings, all with their fluttering American flags, or the shops on Main Street. The Albany Police headquarters, in particular, seemed designed to make you feel about an inch high. The police station at Bartholomew Square had been an impressive building once but now it was squalid in the extreme and the CID offices had actually been condemned in the 1930s. This place looked like a wedding cake, complete with marble steps and soaring columns. Edgar climbed the steps, holding the letter from General Petre in front of him like a shield.

It took some time to convince the desk sergeant that he wasn't a lunatic but the letter helped and, in a fairly short time, Edgar was sitting in a windowless interview room opposite Detective Brendan O'Grady and Detective Patrick O'Flynn. He wondered if it was the law that all policemen in America had to be Irish.

"So why are you interested in this Hitchcock guy?" asked O'Grady, shifting the gum to the other side of his mouth.

Edgar explained again. "Colonel Cartwright had a newspaper cutting about Bill Hitchcock on his bedside table and we thought that it was worth investigating. Especially as he'd jotted down Hitchcock's telephone number."

"Nobody from Scotland Yard has contacted us," said O'Grady, sounding disappointed.

"It's a rather hush-hush inquiry," said Edgar, "but it's very high level." He pointed to Petre's letter.

The two officers looked at each other. Edgar felt a twinge of excitement. There *was* something going on after all.

After another pause, O'Grady said, "What do you know about William Hitchcock the third?"

The number startled Edgar for a moment but then he remembered that Americans often did this with family names. Presumably the baby he met earlier was William Hitchcock the fourth.

"Not much," he said. "I know that he was a mesmerist, a mind reader, who appeared on stage and at state fairs. That's all."

"Oh that." O'Grady waved this aside. "Fellow was a charlatan, that's all, pretending to be able to read minds, hypnotising fool women at fairs. No, what I meant was, did you know that he was a commie?"

"A communist," interjected O'Flynn helpfully.

"I didn't know that," said Edgar.

"Hitchcock was an open member of the communist party during the war," said O'Grady. "Since then he's been lying low but we know he's been mixing with other commies. He knew the Rosenbergs, for example. We also know that he's part of a communist cell that meets in the old picture house in town."

"How do you know?" asked Edgar.

"We infiltrate the meetings," said O'Grady. "We have to keep a watch on these red bastards. For all we know, they could be planning to murder us in our beds."

O'Flynn looked uncomfortable. "Aw, come on, Brendan. They're just a bunch of deadbeats who meet and talk about Karl Marx and Mao Zedong. You've listened to the transcripts."

"Do you know if Hitchcock was in touch with any British communists or anarchists?" asked Edgar.

O'Grady gave him a sharp look. "So that's what's going on, is it? Do you think the commies killed your colonel?"

Edgar remembered Petre talking about anarchist groups wanting to disrupt the coronation. He hadn't given this much credence at the time and it still didn't seem very likely, no matter how much Hitchcock had talked about Karl Marx. He couldn't quite get used to the way O'Grady talked about communists, as if they were a dangerous and potentially treacherous subsection of society. Back home, people like Superintendent Hodges might talk about "commies" but, to lots of people Edgar knew, communism represented a charming but unattainable ideal, like universal love. He remembered many conversations of this sort from his university days. The death of Stalin, a couple of months ago, and rumours of his atrocities, may have changed people's minds, he supposed. Somehow he doubted it though.

"We don't know who killed Colonel Cartwright," he said. "We just know that he'd jotted Bill Hitchcock's name down on a piece of paper. Then there was the newspaper cutting, about a woman fainting at one of his displays. I think you mentioned it just now."

111

O'Flynn laughed. "Velma Edwards. It doesn't take much to make her faint. She's a friend of my mom's, one of those highly strung types. Apparently Hitchcock hypnotised her and made her sing and dance. When she came to she was embarrassed as hell so she fainted to make Hitchcock feel bad."

"His son said something about Mrs Edwards' family being angry."

"Oh, the Edwards are big shots round here," said O'Grady. "He owns the sawmill down by the river. They threatened to sue but nothing came of it. Like Pat said, I think Velma just felt foolish."

"But it made Hitchcock give up mesmerism."

"Good thing too," said O'Grady. "It made him get a proper job. He worked at Mike Moretti's TV repair shop. Hitchcock was pretty good with televisions, by all accounts."

"And he was run over as he left work yesterday?"

"Yeah." O'Grady spat his gum neatly into the wastepaper basket. "Bastard just drove off without stopping. We're getting a lot of these now. Hit-and-run, they call it. If you ask me it's another sign that the world's going to hell."

He sounded quite cheerful about the prospect. Edgar thanked the two detectives and said goodbye. O'Flynn asked him to pass on their best wishes to Queen Elizabeth and Edgar promised to do so.

He walked down the marble steps, deep in thought. O'Grady and O'Flynn might not think that there was anything suspicious in Bill Hitchcock's death but Edgar wasn't so sure. What if someone, somewhere, had got wind of Edgar's visit and was willing to kill to prevent the two men meeting? He stepped into the road.

It all happened so quickly. A black car racing towards him, a woman's scream, tyres squealing and then a strong hand pulling Edgar back onto the pavement. The shock made him stagger and sit heavily on the kerb. The black car screeched off around the corner.

Edgar was willing to bet that it had out-of-town plates.

CHAPTER
THIRTEEN

Max was surprised to receive an invitation that evening, addressed to the Theatre Royal, to have supper with Derek Conroy. He'd liked the director — not least because he'd seemed to be a genuine fan — but nothing in the man's demeanour had led him to think that they were set to be bosom pals. Some directors were like that, they wanted to be friends with their star, to have a relationship that extended beyond the theatre, but Conroy had seemed professional in the extreme.

The letter, though, was rather different.

Dear Max,

Irene (lady wife) and I were wondering if you'd like to come for supper after the show tonight. Nothing formal but we would be honoured if you'd join us. Say 10 o'clock? We live just round the corner, in Covent Garden. Address below. Just telephone if you can't make it, otherwise we'll look forward to seeing you.

Warmest,
Derek

Warmest? Warmest what? And how warm did Max want to feel towards his director, to say nothing of his "lady wife"? But, on the other hand, it wouldn't hurt to be on good terms with the man and there was something enticing about having a home-cooked meal after the show instead of drinking with the other pros or dining in solitary splendour at the Strand Palace (they always served him late, as a special favour, but it was a bit grim sometimes). So Max didn't telephone with an excuse. He put the letter in his pocket and went to check on his props for the show.

He still felt a bit unsettled by the morning at the television theatre and his lunch with Ruby. Was the future, as Joe had predicted, a place where a performer didn't count unless they had appeared on television? Or was the future going to be a place where his daughter was married to his best friend? This somehow was the hardest thing of all to picture.

The props room was empty. Max checked the box that would hold Alfie, the white fluffy dog. On stage, he held the box up and opened it to show that it was empty but, of course, Alfie would already have escaped through the false back and scampered off to the wings where his owner, the stage manager, was waiting with tempting dog treats. Max put the box down, looking round at the little room with the chairs lined up for the chorus girls' act and the swing in which Eloise Hanley would sit to sing "In an English Country Garden". He couldn't escape the feeling that someone was watching him. Of course, you were always being watched

115

backstage in a theatre; walls turned out to be made of cardboard and there were spyholes everywhere to allow the stagehands to see what was going on out front. But this was different, there was a palpable sense of menace. He remembered the other day, when he'd felt so spooked waiting in the wings. And then he realised that his unease was actually being triggered by a smell. The scent of lavender.

Edgar got to his feet, feeling rather foolish. Two women who had been on the other side of the street now crossed over, exclaiming as they came.

"Are you OK, honey? Seems like they came straight at you."

"Didn't even slow down. Must be one of those run-and-hit drivers we've been reading about."

Edgar turned to face his rescuer, a stocky young man with shirtsleeves held up by metal bands.

"Thank you. I think you saved my life."

His accent seemed to enchant the women.

"Oh my! You're British."

"To think that a Britisher could be run over in our streets."

"Are you all right?" the young man asked.

"Yes, fine. Just a bit shaken."

"You need to lie down," one of the women suggested.

"I'm fine," said Edgar again. He turned to the man. "Thank you so much for pulling me out of the way."

The man smiled. "No problem." He held out his hand. "Mike Moretti."

116

"Edgar Stephens." They shook hands and Edgar said, "You own the TV repair shop, don't you?"

"Yes." Mike Moretti looked surprised, an expression that didn't fit easily on his square, swarthy face. "How do you know?"

"I was wanting to talk to you."

The women were looking back and forth between the two of them as if they were watching a tennis match. Mike shrugged and said, "I was just going to get some lunch. Want to join me?"

"I'd like that, thanks," said Edgar.

Mike led him to something called a diner, a type of restaurant that was completely new to Edgar. It seemed to be a cross between a cafe and a dance hall, brightly lit and chrome-plated with a juke box playing in the background. They sat in a booth by the window and a cheerful waitress ("My name is Wanda" according to her badge) brought them iced water and coffee as soon as they sat down. Mike ordered a steak and fries and Edgar — temporarily unable to think for himself — asked for the same.

"So," said Mike, taking a long drink of water. "Why did you want to talk to me?"

"It's about Bill Hitchcock," said Edgar. "I understand he worked for you."

Mike put his hand to his neck and Edgar saw that he was wearing a black tie. "Poor old Bill. Did you hear what happened to him?"

"Yes," said Edgar levelly. "He was hit by a car."

They looked at each other for a long moment and then Mike said, "You'd better tell me who you are."

117

Edgar told him some of it, that he was a policeman investigating the death of an English colonel who may have had some link with Bill Hitchcock of Albany. Mike listened in silence, his face giving nothing away. Their food came and Mike turned his attention to his plate, cutting up his steak and then transferring his fork into his right hand and eating with that. Edgar ate too, hungry again despite his enormous breakfast. Whatever else you might say about America, he thought, cutting into the tender meat, it was a cornucopia of food, overflowing with milk and honey.

When he had finished eating, Mike said, "How do you think Bill knew this colonel of yours?"

"I don't know," said Edgar, "but I think it may have had to do with mesmerism. I know that Bill knew an acquaintance of mine called Tony Mulholland, who also had a mind-reading act. Did you ever see Bill perform?"

Mike laughed. "I knew he had some sort of act but we never talked about it. We only talked about televisions. Bill was really interested in them."

"How long had he worked for you?"

"About six months but I knew him before then. He used to come in and talk about radios and televisions. He read up on all the new makes and everything."

"What sort of a man was he?" Edgar asked. "I didn't like to ask his wife too many questions."

Mike paused before replying, wiping his hands on his napkin. "He was a nice guy," he said at last. "He could be a bit . . . a bit intense, but he was a good guy deep down."

"What was he intense about?"

118

Mike looked at him shrewdly. "I can guess what you were talking to the goons at the police station about. Did they tell you that Bill was a dangerous communist?"

"Something like that," Edgar said.

"Man, those guys. Typical Irish. Get an idea in their heads and you can't shift it. Bill may have been a communist once but he wasn't any more. He used to say that Stalin was as bad as Hitler."

"I heard that he still went to meetings."

"I guess he did. Those meetings at the picture house are full of guys like Bill, people who've read a lot of books and think they have all the answers."

"Did Bill think he had the answers?"

"No," said Mike, "but he sure had a lot of questions. He used to say that was what his mind-reading act was really about, asking the right questions."

Tony Mulholland had said the same, Edgar remembered.

"I hear he got into trouble with a hypnotism act," he said, "and a woman fainted."

"Velma Edwards," said Mike, in the same tone the policemen had used. "She's the kind that would faint, if you know what I mean. Just because Bill hypnotised her and made her sing some fool song."

"Do you remember the song?"

"Something about a Christmas tree, I think."

"And after that Bill gave up hypnotism?"

"Yeah. Said it was more trouble than it was worth. Said that he'd rather work on a television set, said that was the way to get your message across."

"What did he mean by that, do you think?"

"He'd read somewhere that you could send messages by television. They'd flash up on screen real quick and people watching wouldn't know they'd seen them but, after a while, they'd start to become brainwashed. Sub-something advertising, he called it."

"Do you know where Bill got that idea?"

"No. Like I said, he'd read a lot of books. He had a ton of crazy ideas."

But what if he had an idea that wasn't crazy? thought Edgar. And what if someone killed Bill Hitchcock to stop him having any more ideas?

The show went well. The slight unease Max had felt backstage didn't make its way into his act. Alfie disappeared and appeared again with the ease of a pro (though Max felt he was milking his applause a bit) and the audience whooped and cheered at the end. The show had been a hit, Dan Napier told Max backstage. "Shows there's still life in variety yet. Pity Saturday's the last night."

"What are you showing next?" Max asked.

"*Private Lives*. You can't go wrong with Noël Coward."

"And you haven't seen the ghost of Grimaldi yet?"

"No," said Dan. "I suppose he wouldn't appear just for a two-week run."

"You mean you believe that story?"

Dan looked shocked. "Of course I believe it. I haven't seen him but I know plenty who have. You mean to tell me that you haven't had the feeling of being watched, that you've never seen something out of the corner of your eye, never heard or seen something you couldn't explain?"

Max said nothing. Dan laughed. "I knew it. All theatres have ghosts, that's why we light the spirit lamps at night, so they can see the show."

Max thought about this as he changed and took off his make-up. It wasn't that he believed in ghosts exactly, more that he found himself increasingly haunted by his past, his theatrical past, that is. Backstage or in his dressing room, they trooped through his thoughts like a phantom army: Ethel, his best ever assistant, Tony Mulholland, The Great Diablo, the Diller Twins, Emerald and her python, Sonia and Tanya the exotic dancers (he'd had an affair with one of them, which one was it?). It was as if he knew that all these acts were either dead or dying. The Empire was being turned into a TV studio, the Theatre Royal was showing *Private Lives*. Soon variety would have no home at all, unless it was on the television screen and — whatever Joe Passolini said — he couldn't really see that happening. Who on earth would watch an entertainment show on the television?

All in all, he wasn't in a very cheerful mood when he knocked on Derek Conroy's door. The director lived in a narrow townhouse in Floral Street. It could have been Max's perfect address, close to restaurants, theatres and bars, almost near enough to hear the music from the Opera House. Inside, the house was full of slightly scruffy charm: framed posters from variety shows, red brocade sofas, books lining the walls and piled up on.

the stairs, a parrot in a cage. Irene ("Call me Reenie") gave him a martini as soon as he got through the door.

"I make a mean martini, though I say so myself."

Max took a grateful sip. She did too. Reenie was an attractive woman in her fifties, with reddish hair (possibly dyed) and a beautiful, slightly sad, smile. She had an interesting personality, thought Max, like her house. He felt himself relaxing for the first time in a week.

Derek Conroy, wearing a velvet smoking jacket, was sitting on the red sofa, drinking a martini. Something told Max that it wasn't his first. On the chair opposite sat a thin, dark young man. "My son, Lazlo," said Reenie. "He's just on his way out to work. He plays the saxophone in a jazz band."

"Lots of late nights," said Max. And Lazlo did have a rather haunted look, the skin around his eyes shadowed and delicate-looking.

Lazlo laughed. "Well, let's say the milkman is a very good friend."

Derek sang a few bars of the song. "'My very good friend the milkman says I'm losing too much sleep.' I love Fats Waller."

Max wasn't much of a jazz fan but he remembered feeling sad when he heard of Waller's death. It didn't seem right that someone so life-affirming should die young. But, then again, the nickname hardly hinted at a lack of excess.

"I'd better be going," said Lazlo, standing up. "It was good to meet you, Mr Mephisto, I'm a big fan."

122

"Thank you very much," said Max. He hoped no one was going to ask him to do a magic trick. Many a dinner party had been ruined because the hostess wanted him to make the plates disappear or conjure a rabbit from the soup tureen. But Lazlo just smiled and picked up his saxophone case.

"Bye, darling," said Reenie.

"Bye, Mum, bye, Dad. Goodbye, Mr Mephisto."

"Nice boy," said Max as the door slammed and Lazlo's footsteps echoed in the street.

"Lazlo's a dear," said Derek. "He's my stepson really but I think of him as my own." Max felt a slight pang, imagining Ruby's stepfather saying the same thing.

"Shall we eat?" said Reenie. "It's all ready."

"We'd better," said Derek. "I need to soak up some alcohol."

They descended the stairs, Reenie carrying a tureen and Derek two bottles of red wine. The dining room was in the basement but the Conroys hadn't tried to disguise this fact. Instead the room was shadowy and mysterious, with fringed lamps and red velvet curtains.

"It's goulash," said Reenie. "I hope that's all right."

"Delicious," said Max. And it was, helped by the extremely good red wine. Max found his opinion of Derek Conroy rising as the level of the bottle went down.

"I'm so glad you're in the show, Max," said Derek, cleaning his plate with bread. "I wanted you from the first but I wasn't sure if you'd be prepared to do television. Passolini promised me that he could persuade you." Derek seemed less drunk now, even

123

though he had certainly had his fair share of the wine. Maybe it was the sobering effects of the goulash.

"Joe is very persuasive," said Max. He thought back to his first meeting with the agent, sitting in the deserted theatre stalls: *If you do this show, millions of people will watch it. Millions. Think about that, Max.* No, he hadn't really needed persuading. He'd been seduced, like everyone else, by the thought of an audience of millions. So why was he regretting it now?

"He certainly is," said Derek. "He insisted that we employ that young girl magician, Ruby French. I was doubtful at first but when I saw her today . . . even if she can't do a single magic trick, she'll be a hit."

"Oh, she can do magic," said Max. As succinctly as possible, he told the Conroys that Ruby was his daughter.

"Well, I'm jiggered," said Derek. "I had no idea."

"I've seen her picture," said Reenie. "She does look a bit like you."

"Maybe we could make something of this on the advertising," said Derek. Max thought of Joe Passolini. *The hidden daughter: Max Mephisto's greatest conjuring trick.*

"No," he said, too quickly. Derek and Reenie looked at each other.

"Of course not," said Derek, "not if you don't want it known."

"It's not a secret," said Max, "but I'd be uncomfortable shouting about it. I'm sure Ruby would too. She's very keen to make it on her own merits."

"I'm sorry," said Derek, with a rueful glance at his wife. "I do get carried away sometimes. It's television, it turns you into a monster."

"It certainly does," said Reenie. But she said it fondly with a glance that, just for a second, made Max wish he had a wife. "I'm going upstairs to make coffee," she went on. "No —" as both men made half-hearted attempts to rise — "you stay here and chat."

This, of course, temporarily robbed them both of the power of speech. Eventually Max asked, "How did you get into television?"

Derek emptied the last of the wine into Max's glass. "I was an actor before the war, then I was in ENSA. The BBC started recording some of our concerts and I got interested. Later on I directed a couple of broadcasts and realised I was a better director than I was an actor."

Derek seemed slightly embarrassed about his past, twice mentioning that childhood TB had made him unfit for service, but Max never felt resentment towards actors who had spent their war years entertaining the troops. The Entertainments National Service Association (otherwise known as Every Night Something Awful) had travelled to most theatres of war, offering cut-price Shakespeare and hastily put-together variety shows, Max had never been tempted to take the ENSA shilling. As he had told Joe, he had joined up as soon as he could, partly to annoy his father who couldn't bear the thought of his son serving as a private.

"My friend Stan was in ENSA," he said. "Stan Parks. The Great Diablo. Did you ever come across him?"

"The Great Diablo! Yes, I directed him in a show in Egypt. He was a good magician but he drank like a fish. Is he still around?"

"Alive and kicking and living in Hastings. I did a panto with him a few years ago."

"You and Stan were involved with that camouflage group, weren't you?" said Derek. "There was a lot of talk about it in North Africa."

"Yes," said Max, not wanting to get onto the subject of the Magic Men. It was in Egypt that he had come across Stan, whom he'd known slightly before the war, and enlisted his help with the camouflage unit. Stan had travelled to Inverness with him to set up the Magic Men. In Scotland they had met Edgar, recently invalided home from Norway. Edgar had been the respectable face of the Magic Men, a regular soldier with a decent record who had been recruited by MI5. By Colonel Cartwright, who had been found dead with a playbill beside him.

"What about Tony Mulholland?" he asked. "Did you know him at all? Had a mind-reading act. Quite big before the war."

"I don't think so," said Derek.

"I remember the name," said Reenie, coming in with a tray of coffee and liqueurs. "I think I saw him up north somewhere. He used to guess the colour of girls' underwear."

That sounded like Tony. Max asked how Reenie and Derek had met.

"The usual story," said Reenie. "I was a singer, not a very good one. I was in a couple of shows with Derek before the war. My first husband was a Jewish refugee, interned as an enemy alien. He died soon after the war. I met Derek again and, well, the rest is history."

"I'd never forgotten her," said Derek gallantly.

Max wondered how old the couple were. Derek looked at least fifty but there was an almost childlike charm about the pair stemming, Max now realised, from their pleasure in each other's company. The only woman he had ever felt that comfortable with was Joyce Markham, the Brighton landlady with whom he had a sporadic relationship. But he couldn't see himself married to Joyce.

Max sat back in his chair, drinking brandy. Reenie had put a record on, something orchestral and moody. The red-lit room felt dreamlike and soporific, the curtains drawn against the world outside. It must have been after midnight. Max knew that he really ought to leave before he fell asleep but he couldn't bring himself to move. Then he realised that Reenie was speaking again. "Was it Tony Mulholland who did the Russian roulette thing with the gun?"

"No, that was an American," said Derek and his voice too sounded sleepy and slurred. "What was his name? Something like a cowboy. Hickok. Hitchcock. That's right. Wild Bill Hitchcock."

CHAPTER
FOURTEEN

Edgar wasn't quite sure what to do next. He could go back to the police station and tell O'Flynn and O'Grady that a car had tried to run him down but he had a feeling that the two officers wouldn't take him seriously. "Welcome to America," they'd say. "Cars travel fast here. You're not in sleepy old Brighton now." He felt oddly reluctant to say goodbye to Mike Moretti who suddenly felt like his only friend in a strange land. But Mike was obviously keen to get back to work. He gave Edgar his card and said to call him if he needed anything. Edgar said thank you and stood, irresolute, on the pavement (it was called the sidewalk in America, he had learnt).

"Do you have an address for Velma Edwards?" he said at last. He might as well continue with his investigations and the newspaper cutting was one of the only leads he had.

"You can't miss the Edwards' place," said Mike but Edgar assured him that he could so Mike drew him a map on the back of the card. Edgar said goodbye and thank you and watched as Mike unlocked the TV repair shop and turned the sign to "Open". Then he went back to his car.

Mike was right. The Edwards' place was hard to miss. It was a large house on the outskirts of town, painted pale blue with a turret at each corner. What had the policemen said about the family? That they owned a sawmill or something? Clearly there was money in wood.

The door was opened by a maid, a middle-aged black woman in uniform, complete with white apron. Edgar began to feel that he had strayed into *Gone with the Wind* (a film that he had watched, on sufferance, with his mother). He knew that some parts of America were more equal than others but this was the north. Almost Canada, for God's sake. Surely they didn't still have coloured servants? He asked for Mrs Velma Edwards and was told that "Miss Velma" was resting. "I'll see if she can come down."

Edgar waited in the hall, watched by sundry stuffed animal heads and a large painting of a ballet dancer. He wondered if Velma Edwards was an invalid. Why else would she be resting at three o'clock in the afternoon? Maybe that was why she had fainted at the mind-reading show.

But a few minutes later he was shaking hands with a divine blonde creature, as coquettish and charming as Scarlett O'Hara herself.

"Have you really come all the way from England to see me?"

In his head she said "little old me" but she wasn't really southern, just the sort of woman who flirted with all men on principle. And, once he'd got over the gauzy dress and the floral scent, she was older than he first thought, at least fifty, and her hair was more ash than blonde. But she was still powerfully attractive, propelling him into a sitting room glittering with chandeliers and mirrors and asking the maid (Charlene) to fetch him a bourbon.

"I don't . . . just water is fine."

"Nonsense, all men like bourbon."

By now, Edgar was feeling rather dazed, especially when he'd drunk some of the strongest liquor he had ever tasted. Was he really here, in America, drinking bourbon with a woman who seemed to belong to the silent film era? Surely he should be in Brighton, tracking down petty criminals or sitting at his underground desk dreaming of Ruby? The disorientated feeling was not helped by Velma chattering on about the beauties of the state as if he were just another weekend visitor.

"And the Hudson's so pretty. You can take a boat out. Or you can go to Saratoga to see the races —"

"Mrs Edwards —" Edgar cut in as politely as he could — "as I explained, I'm a British police officer. I came to Albany to talk to Bill Hitchcock but . . ."

Velma leant forward, her blue eyes round. "Is it because he was a communist?" she breathed.

"No. I mean that's not relevant." Edgar shook his head to clear it. "Did you know about Mr Hitchcock's fatal accident?"

"The whole town knows," said Velma, taking out a tiny lace handkerchief. "My nerves were so upset when I heard that I had to lie down with vinegar on my eyelids."

130

Edgar couldn't quite work out the significance of the vinegar. He ploughed on, "I don't want to upset you, Mrs Edwards, but I understand that you were present at a mind-reading demonstration given by Mr Hitchcock about six months ago."

"That's right. I fainted." This was said with a certain degree of pride.

"I wonder if you'd mind telling me what happened. As far as you can remember."

For almost the first time since they'd met, Velma Edwards fell silent. Her face was still serene but she was pleating and repleating the lace handkerchief in her hands.

"Did he hypnotise you?" asked Edgar.

"Yes," said Velma at last. "I knew Bill Hitchcock, of course. Everyone in town knew him. His father had a circus act years ago, rather tacky to my mind but still. Benson, my husband, remembers going to see him when he was a little boy. Well, Bill followed the family tradition. I think he appeared on stage in New York a few times. I don't know, I don't go to those sort of shows. Anyway, this was at the Albany state show, so it was a different matter, of course. I went along just to show willing. It was a silly act, Bill guessing what people were thinking, that sort of thing. Then he asked for a volunteer to be hypnotised."

"And you volunteered?"

"Hardly. It was like he picked on me. He practically hauled me out of the audience. Then he stared at me. His eyes. They were . . ." She held the handkerchief up to her own eyes.

"His eyes?" Edgar prompted.

"They were positively *demonic*. Staring and awful. He told me to look into his eyes and the next thing I knew I was lying on the floor in a dead faint."

"Do you remember doing anything when you were hypnotised?"

"No." Said very firmly. "I looked into his eyes and then I fainted."

Sergeant O'Flynn and Mike Moretti had both mentioned a dance, thought Edgar.

But either Velma didn't remember or she wanted to forget.

"Did you complain to Mr Hitchcock afterwards?"

"That was Benson. He's very protective of me, Inspector Stephens. I'm sure you're the same about your wife."

"I'm not married."

"What are British girls thinking of? Why, if you lived here I could fix you up with a nice girl in a second."

"That's very kind of you but I'm going back to England on Saturday."

"Where are you staying?"

"The Shangri-La motel."

Velma made a moue of distaste. "I wish I could offer for you to stay here but Benson —"

"Thank you but really, there's no need. The Shangri-La is very nice. You know, we don't have motels in England."

"You don't?" The blue eyes opened wider still. "You poor darlings."

132

It was four o'clock when Edgar left the Edwards' place. Once again, he felt rather at a loss. Beyond discovering that Bill Hitchcock had a passion for televisions and had once been a communist, he didn't seem to have learnt anything from his visit to Albany. Or rather he had learnt one important thing: Bill Hitchcock, who had been in good health a few days ago, was now dead. He had been run down by a hit-and-run driver and it was possible that the same driver had tried to kill Edgar. But why? What was there about the small-town mesmerist that made him a possible target for murder? Could the unseen Benson have done it to preserve his wife's honour? It seemed unlikely, although Velma Edwards was the kind of woman who inspired protective feelings in men. Edgar still thought that it was likely that Hitchcock's death was in some way related to his act, to Tony Mulholland and the mysterious playbill beside Colonel Cartwright's bed. Perhaps he should telephone General Petre and tell him about the latest developments. Or maybe he should ring Max, who had at least spoken to Hitchcock once. This idea cheered him up. He could go back downtown, find a telephone and speak to Max. Then he remembered. It was four o'clock in New York State so it would be nine o'clock in England. Max would be on stage. There was no point trying to talk to him until tomorrow.

He drove back towards Albany, the Hudson River on one side, keeping a wary eye out for the car that had nearly run him over outside the police station (he

133

wasn't even sure of the make, boxier than the Buick, not as flashy as a Cadillac). Suddenly, popping up from behind a pine tree, he saw one of the Shangri-La's famous posters. *Shangri-La Motor Court, twenty-five panelled units of Spanish Design.* That was what he'd do. He'd go back to the motel, rest, maybe have a cup of tea (the Englishman in him longed for a cup of tea), decide what to do next.

The Shangri-La was quiet in the afternoon sun. The blinds were drawn in the main house but he could see Irma sweeping the porch. He waved as he drove past to his own unit. It was a really wonderful invention, a hotel where you had your own front door, free to come and go as you pleased. He stopped the car and stared. He had his own front door, certainly, but it was wide open. He was certain that he had shut it that morning, locked it too and put the keys in his pocket. His hand closed around them now. He approached slowly. If someone was in the room, he wanted to catch them in the act of . . . what? Maybe what he would find was a man with a gun trained on the door.

The room was empty. Edgar's suitcase was upside down and his belongings strewn around the room. His Sherlock Holmes novel was open on the bed, the breeze riffling gently through the pages.

CHAPTER
FIFTEEN

Irma was very upset. "Nothing like this has ever happened in the Shangri-La before." She seemed inclined to blame Edgar for the whole thing, especially when he insisted on calling the police. "I've never had the police here. What will people think?" O'Grady and O'Flynn arrived very promptly in a black and white car with a red light on top and "State Police" written on the bonnet. There was no way that this was going to be an anonymous visit.

"You certainly seem to be having an eventful holiday, Inspector Stephens," was O'Grady's opening remark, gum working furiously in his back teeth.

"I'm not on holiday," said Edgar.

"Well, someone is certainly putting out the welcome mat," said O'Flynn, examining the door of Edgar's room. "They shot right through the lock. Didn't you hear anything, Irma?"

"No." Irma shook her head. "I've been inside all day with the wireless on. I only came out to sweep the porch a few minutes ago."

Edgar couldn't stop himself pointing out the obvious. "They had a gun?"

"Oh, most folk round here have a gun," said O'Flynn. "It's hunting country."

Edgar thought of the hunting trophies in the Edwards' place. He had told Velma that he was staying at the Shangri-La but surely she wouldn't have had time to organise some anonymous heavies (and who would these people be anyway?) to break into Edgar's room. Besides, you'd need a handgun, not a hunting rifle, to shoot out a lock. O'Grady was asking him who knew where he was staying.

"I think I mentioned it to Bill Hitchcock's family and to Mike Moretti and Velma Edwards."

The two officers looked at each other.

"Mike Moretti?" said O'Flynn.

"Yes. I had lunch with him, I wanted to talk to him about Bill Hitchcock. Why?" Catching the expression on O'Grady's face. "What's wrong with him? I liked him."

"Italian," said O'Grady succinctly.

"Probably got links to the mob," said O'Flynn.

Edgar thought of the way that Moretti had talked about "the Irish". Clearly there were undercurrents here that he didn't understand. But it was hard to believe that the TV repair man had links with the Mafia, if that was what O'Flynn was implying.

"Mike Moretti's a good man," said Irma. "He fixed my television for nothing last year. I've got his televisions in all my rooms," she added rather proudly.

"He may have saved my life earlier," said Edgar. He told the policemen about the car that had nearly run him down. This led to more gum-chewing from O'Grady.

"I don't like this," he said.

"Nor do I," Edgar couldn't help adding.

"Of course it could have been an accident," said O'Flynn.

"Pretty big coincidence though," said O'Grady. "Someone tries to kill Stephens and then someone else breaks into his motel room. What were they trying to find?"

"I don't know," said Edgar. His suitcase had only contained clean shirts and underwear. Oh, and a photograph of Ruby.

"There's something you're not telling us," said O'Grady.

"I've told you everything I know," said Edgar, not wanting to go through the story with Irma listening. Besides, he had told them almost everything.

"It's the reds," said O'Grady. "The reds are after you." It was hard to know whether he was being ironical. Irma, at any rate, didn't seem to think so. "No!"

Edgar tried to reassure her. "That's not true. This has nothing to do with the communists."

"You think not?" said O'Grady.

"I'm sure," said Edgar, wondering if he was sure of anything any more. "I think that it has more to do with Hitchcock's vaudeville past than his political past."

"Vaudeville?" O'Flynn looked incredulous.

"I know it sounds incredible but —"

"Too damn right it sounds incredible," said O'Grady, walking back towards his police car. "Take my advice, Mr Stephens, leave town as quickly as you can."

Edgar looked at Irma and knew he would have to find somewhere else to spend the night.

He didn't know quite how he ended up sleeping on Mike Moretti's sofa. It was six o'clock by the time the police left the motel and he just knew that he didn't want to drive back to New York, arriving there in the middle of the night with nowhere to stay, and Mike's was the only number he had. It was his work number so Edgar didn't know if he'd still be there but Mike answered on the second ring.

"Come and stay here," he said after listening to Edgar's garbled explanation. "We live over the shop."

Edgar drove back into town and was surprised to find a grocery store still open on Main Street. He went in and bought flowers and chocolates for Mike's wife. He was pretty sure that Mike had said "we" on the telephone.

He was glad that he had brought presents because the door was opened by a pretty dark-haired woman who introduced herself as Genevieve, Mike's wife. Genevieve was heavily pregnant and holding a small child in her arms. Edgar felt extremely guilty about turning up on her doorstep but Genevieve just smiled and said it was no trouble. "I always cook for an army anyhow."

Mike took the child from her. "This is Sal. Our son and heir."

"Sal?"

"Salvatore, after my dad."

"It could have been worse," said Genevieve, "my dad's called Baldassare."

Edgar thought about the way the policemen had talked about Mike being Italian. Mike and Genevieve seemed to take their heritage very seriously — it was present in the religious paintings on the walls, in the lullaby Mike sang to his son and in the delicious pasta fagioli cooked by Genevieve — but they also thought of themselves as Americans. Mike had served in the navy during the war, he learnt, and Genevieve belonged to a woman's group called Daughters of America ("we mostly chat and make cookies"). There were lots of British Italians, of course, but, remembering the war when Italians young and old had been rounded up and put into camps, Edgar suspected that most people still thought of them as "foreigners". He was fascinated by the way the Morettis managed to be both foreign and American at the same time.

He hadn't wanted to say much about the day's experiences for fear of upsetting Genevieve (he always felt nervous around pregnant women) but as they sat eating cheese and fruit, Mike came right out with it.

"So why do you think someone ransacked your place? What were they trying to find?"

"I wish I knew," said Edgar. "I just think it has to do with Bill Hitchcock."

"Bill Hitchcock who worked for you?" said Genevieve. "But he was a nice old boy. I was so sad about him being killed like that." She stopped and looked at Edgar, a quarter of pear halfway to her mouth. "Or do you think he was killed on purpose? Was he *murdered?*"

"I don't know," said Edgar. "There are just too many unanswered questions."

"How did you get on with Velma?" asked Mike.

"She claimed not to remember anything about being hypnotised."

Mike laughed. "She's probably embarrassed. Velma puts a lot of store on being the perfect lady."

"But she wasn't always a lady," said Genevieve. "She was a burlesque dancer once."

Both men stared at her. Genevieve grinned, reminding Edgar suddenly and painfully of Ruby. "I was a dancer when Mike met me. Not anything big but I did a few variety shows. My mom was in the business too and she remembered Velma. She'd been a really big Broadway star before the war. But Mom mentioned it to her once, just being friendly, and Velma denied it. As soon as Velma married Benson Edwards, she wanted to forget all about her past. She used to pretend that she'd been a ballet dancer. At the Royal Ballay." She attempted to sound like a British person sounding French.

So maybe that explains why Velma didn't want to remember being hypnotised, thought Edgar. Maybe why she fainted in the first place. Because she didn't want to remember the young girl who had danced on the stage and captured the heart of a sawmill owner. Had Bill Hitchcock known about her past, was that why he had singled her out from the crowd? Edgar wouldn't rule it out. It was very much the sort of thing Tony would have done, he often used mind reading as a cover for small cruelties. Edgar remembered the painting of the ballet dancer in the hall of the Edwards' house. Velma must have been determined to paint her own picture of the past. How far would she go to preserve it?

"Tell us about your life, Edgar," said Genevieve. "Where do you live? I visited England once, when I was younger."

"Brighton. Do you know it?"

"Yes. I stayed there in digs once. It's a fun place. Are you married, Ed?"

"No. I'm engaged though." He told them about Ruby. Genevieve was intrigued. "So she's a lady magician. That's so cool. Will she keep the act going when you're married?"

"I'm not sure," said Ed. This was something he had never dared broach with Ruby.

"It's tough," said Genevieve. "One minute you're on stage wearing a sequinned dress, crowd yelling for you, next minute you're at home doing the cooking and cleaning. Looking like this." She gestured towards her stomach.

Mike, who had appeared to be dozing over his coffee, said, "I think you look great, Genny."

Genevieve gave him a look that was half exasperation, half affection. "Yeah, you do, Mike. But sometimes I want to wear the sequinned dress again, you know?"

Edgar didn't know but he had the uneasy feeling that Ruby would understand all too well. He wanted to say more, to ask Genevieve's advice about marrying a beautiful showgirl and keeping her happy, but Mike was still yawning and Genevieve started clearing the table. Edgar got up to help her.

In the morning he awoke with a start to find himself lying on the sofa with Sal staring solemnly down at him. He felt like Gulliver waking up on the beach surrounded by the Lilliputians.

CHAPTER
SIXTEEN

Max was about to go out to lunch when the bellboy stopped him by the revolving doors.

"Mr Mephisto? Telephone call for you."

Max went back to the reception desk where an awed-looking clerk handed him the telephone receiver. "Long distance call," she breathed.

"Hallo, Max. It's Ed."

"Ed! I've been wondering how you've been doing."

A hollow laugh, echoing across the miles. "I've been having a whale of a time. For a start, Bill Hitchcock is dead."

"What?"

"I turned up at his house yesterday morning to find that he'd been killed the day before, knocked down by a car that didn't stop."

"Jesus. Do you think it was deliberate?"

"Well, I started to think so after someone tried to run me over yesterday."

"What?" Max saw the receptionist looking at him and tried to lower his voice. "Are you serious?"

"Afraid so." Max thought that Edgar sounded rather satisfied with the impression he was creating. "I went to see the local police to find out more and I was almost

143

knocked down in the road outside. Then, when I went back to my motel . . . hotel last night it had been ransacked."

"My God, you are having fun, aren't you?"

"Holiday of a lifetime. I spent the night with some people I met yesterday. Lovely couple. Italian-American. I've just left their apartment."

"What did the local police say about Hitchcock bring killed?"

"Oh they think it's all because he's a dangerous communist."

"Was he? A communist, I mean?"

"I think he was once but Mike, his employer, thought that he'd become disillusioned. Hitchcock seemed a respectable citizen to me. He had a wife and grown-up children. Oh, and a job mending televisions."

"Televisions?" Max thought of the Empire theatre and the seats being ripped out for the cameras. The spectre of TV was everywhere.

"He was fascinated by them apparently."

"Someone told me that he used to do an act with a gun. Russian roulette, she called it."

"I'm sure he did a lot of weird things in his time but he'd given up the act. After that woman fainted at his show he got a hard time from her family and gave up show business. Everyone in town seemed to agree on that."

"What are you going to do now?"

"Drive to New York and find somewhere to stay tonight. My plane leaves at midday tomorrow. With any

144

luck I'll be back in England on Sunday evening. I'd better go. My money's running out."

"Come to London on Sunday night. I'll book you a room here. I'll pay."

"Thanks, Max. I'll see you then. Bye."

"Bye, Ed. Be careful." But he was talking to the dialling tone.

Max brooded on this conversation as he walked to Bertorelli's in Charlotte Street. He was worried about Edgar (could someone really have tried to run him over?) but, much as he hated to admit it, his dominant emotion was still envy. Edgar might be dodging homicidal cars in a strange city but he was still talking casually about driving to New York, about this "lovely" Italian American couple he had stayed with (in their *apartment*, he was already speaking a different language), about people and places that seemed as exotic as the dark side of the moon. Well, strictly speaking, they seemed familiar as well as exotic; a strange combination. Max knew about apartments and sidewalks and American cops from films, it was just odd, and slightly unsettling, to think of steady old Edgar actually getting a starring role in one of those films. Max never liked anyone else to have top billing.

Bertorelli's soothed him slightly. The waiters made a fuss of him, calling him "Maestro Mephisto" and conjuring up a bottle of his favourite Montepulciano. At least here — in any Italian restaurant anywhere in the world — he felt at home. And, thankfully, Joe Passolini hadn't showed up yet. Drinking the wine and watching the waiters scurrying past with plates, Max wondered if he should contact General Petre and tell him about Bill Hitchcock. But it was Edgar's news really and he'd be back on Sunday. Did Hitchcock's death mean that there really was a conspiracy linked to Cartwright's murder? Were Cartwright and Hitchcock actually on the same side? He remembered the, odd, teasing telephone conversation. *I come from a long line of seers and mystics. I do a mind-reading act that blows people's minds. Why, I could tell you what you're thinking now, Mr Mephisto.* Hitchcock's act had certainly blown one woman's mind and now he was dead. *These are dark times*, that's what he'd said. Could the woman (he'd forgotten her name) have taken out a contract on Hitchcock or was he thinking in films again? Come to think of it, though, didn't Hitchcock say that he wasn't in good health? Maybe he had simply suffered a heart attack after some car came too close? But Ed had said that he was run down. What's more, Edgar had said that the same car had tried to run *him* down. Was this likely? Could it be that Ed too was imagining himself in a gangster film complete with Jimmy Cagney and Pat O'Brien as a good-hearted priest?

Max embarked on his spaghetti carbonara with slightly less than his usual relish. Either Edgar was in danger or he was having the adventure of a lifetime. Max hated to admit it but both possibilities made him feel extremely depressed.

Emma was not quite sure what she was doing back at Marine Parade. The police inquiry into the suspected

146

arson of the gypsy caravan had been opened but Superintendent Hodges had told them, in no uncertain terms, not to spend too much time on it. "It'll be a couple of gyppos having an argument, that's all. Just go through the motions — talk to pier staff and the like — but don't get too involved with the family. They'll only make trouble. I know the sort." So why was Emma making an unscheduled trip to Marine Parade on her way home?

Partly it was because of the conversation with Uncle Lucian, partly it was just a desire to do the job properly and not just "go through the motions", and partly it was because it was Friday and the thought of a weekend with her parents (a tennis party on Saturday, friends for lunch on Sunday) made her feel like becoming a Romany gypsy herself. Emma was a Brighton girl but her life sometimes seemed a million miles away from the lives around her. Her parents lived in a grand art deco house in Roedean with a swimming pool and tennis court. Emma went to Roedean School and, if her parents had had their way, she would have continued on the same treadmill as her school mates: finishing school in Switzerland, being presented at court, marriage to a dull man with enough money to make it unnecessary for her ever to have to work. But, when she had finally finished school, all Emma had wanted to do was *live*, to do something useful in the world. Her parents had tried to stop her joining the police. Anything — even university or teaching — was better than that, but Emma was adamant. She wanted to do a job where she could use her brain and make a difference and, by and large, the police force had given her that opportunity. She knew that this had a lot to do with the DI and his enlightened attitude towards women police officers. Most of her female friends from training school were trapped in a nightmare of making tea and filing traffic reports. Ros, who had a languages degree from Cambridge, even had to collect her DI's dry cleaning for him. So Emma thanked God for Edgar.

That was the other thing. She was also going mad with not knowing what was happening to the DI. He had flown to America on Tuesday and was due back in the office on Monday. "What do you think he's doing?" she asked Bob. "Oh, going to a speakeasy or something," said Bob, whose knowledge of America dated from pre-war films. "They don't have prohibition any more," said Emma but the image remained: darkened rooms, jazz, girls dancing on the tables. At least it was better than imagining his weekends with Ruby.

So, at five-thirty on Friday evening Emma was knocking on the door of number eighty-seven. A few minutes later the door was opened not by Tol (as Emma had secretly hoped) but by Astarte in remarkably un-Romany costume of slacks and a check shirt knotted at the waist.

"Oh, it's you," said Astarte.

Surely your sixth sense told you that already, thought Emma. Aloud she said, "Can I come in? I just wanted a quick word about your grandmother's caravan. Is your father home?"

148

"He's not back from work," said Astarte, still holding the door half-closed.

Emma hadn't thought of Tol having a job beyond being a member of the Zabini family. The two women looked at each other and both jumped when a voice from upstairs called, "Let her in, Star." It was the grandmother, Isobel. Did she know who was at the door or was her hearing abnormally good for an elderly woman?

Emma followed Astarte up the stairs. The sitting room had reverted to its previous shabby state but the flowers from the funeral remained on every surface and banked up around the walls. A wreath bearing the legend "Mum" was propped up against the fireplace. Isobel was sitting on the sofa, an embroidery frame in her lap.

"Come in," she said. "I was wondering when you'd turn up."

"Were you?" said Emma, taking a seat opposite. Astarte sat next to her grandmother, her expression still more sulky teen than mystic fortune-teller.

"Yes," said Isobel. "You'll have worked out by now that Doreen's caravan was set on fire deliberately. The fire brigade can tell things like that."

"Do you think it was deliberate?" said Emma.

"Of course," said Isobel, taking up her needle. "It's traditional. You need to burn the dead person's caravan otherwise there's *marimé*."

"Do you know who did it?" asked Emma.

"No," said Isobel, "that's men's work."

149

Emma had had enough. "It's also a criminal offence," she said. "And so is withholding information."

The old woman laughed. "So arrest me."

"If it's men's work I'll need to talk to your three sons," said Emma. "And your brother Lucian."

"It wasn't Dad," Astarte burst out. "He was in London that day."

"Be quiet, Astarte." Isobel's voice was low but none the less frightening for that.

"Which day was that?" asked Emma.

"Everyone knows it happened on Wednesday," said Astarte. "It was in the paper. Well, Dad was in London on Wednesday. Anyway, Dad said . . ."

"Astarte." Isobel turned with her needle raised. Emma thought of the bad fairy, the abandoned castle, Sleeping Beauty pricking her finger and sleeping for a hundred years. Come to think of it, Astarte did rather resemble a fairytale princess.

"What did he say?" asked Emma, unable to believe that Astarte, the heiress apparent, was speaking out like this.

Astarte looked at her grandmother but obviously decided to speak anyway. "He said that nobody should touch the caravan. He said it was mine now."

Now she sounded less like a princess and more like a spoilt child.

Edgar felt quite sad when he said goodbye to Mike Moretti. Last night had felt like a refuge in this strange, bewildering land. He couldn't remember the last time that he'd stayed in an actual home. His mother's house

150

no longer felt like home and he wondered if it ever had. He liked staying with his sister Lucy, her husband and their three boys but he realised guiltily that it was two years since he'd done so. Being with Mike and Genevieve had made him imagine what it might be like to have a home with Ruby, perhaps even to have children. All this made the parting rather emotional, on Edgar's side at least.

"Thanks for everything, Mike. You've been really kind."

"No problem." Mike stood by his shop door, obviously itching to turn the sign to "Open".

"Good luck with . . . with the baby and everything. You've got my address. Let me know if it's a little Mario or Maria." They had discussed names last night.

Mike grinned. "Genny will have changed her mind again tomorrow."

"Well, goodbye then." Edgar held out his hand.

"Goodbye." They shook hands. Then, as Mike turned towards the door, he said, "Say, Edgar. I found a couple of Bill's old magazines yesterday. I don't think the family would want them but seeing as you were interested in his ideas . . ."

"I'd like to have them. Thank you."

A few minutes later Edgar was heading off to find his car, armed with several closely written journals with titles like, "How Psychiatric Measures can be Applied to Market Research."

He reached New York by midday. He knew that the sensible thing would be to find a hotel — or a motel — close to Idlewild airport but it seemed rather feeble to come all this way and not to see Manhattan. Besides, he reasoned, if he was being followed it would be easier to throw off his pursuers in a big city. So he followed the signs to Manhattan and found himself driving along streets Where the skyscrapers cast deep shadows and where the Empire State Building popped up like an illustration in a children's book. After driving around aimlessly, being hooted at by aggressive yellow taxis he eventually found a small hotel on Times Square West. It was in what he later learnt was the "Garment District" and seemed reassuringly unsmart, surrounded by tailors' shops where men with tape measures around their necks worked on cutting tables and where racks of clothes clattered along the street, pushed by unseen hands.

Edgar spent the last of General Petre's money on a room for the night. He would have to find somewhere to cash a cheque if he wanted to eat that evening. But, despite everything that had happened to him on this trip, he felt strangely optimistic as he parked the Buick in an underground garage and caught the lift (elevator) up to his room. The sight of New York had revived his spirits to an extraordinary degree. The city seemed to be seething with life, crowds of all shapes and sizes surging across the roads and along the sidewalks, lights flashing, car horns blaring, the world turning. Surely no one could fail to be energised by this place.

His bedroom was small but comfortable, a grey cube with the obligatory en-suite bathroom (though this one contained a shower only). He dumped his suitcase, washed his face and set out to explore New York.

CHAPTER
SEVENTEEN

The last night was a success. Of course, last nights are always claimed as successes as relief and euphoria create a party atmosphere even if audiences have been sparse and reviews scathing. But the last night at the Theatre Royal, Drury Lane, really was a success, with several curtain calls and cheers for Max and the Bulgarian contortionists. Backstage Max hugged Eloise Hanley, the Croydon Nightingale, and even patted Alfie on the head.

"Why don't we celebrate later." Eloise pressed her body against his.

"Sounds lovely," said Max, disengaging himself. "I think we're all going for drinks at the Lemon Tree."

"Well done, Max." Dan Napier pumped his hand. "Great show. I told you variety isn't dead yet."

"What are you doing next?" asked Eloise, linking her arm with his.

"A television show at the Empire."

"Oh." Eloise looked at him, her previous interest now becoming something more calculated. "How wonderful."

"Television will never beat this," said Dan, gesturing at the flats leaning up against the wings, the stagehands taking down the backcloth. "This is the real thing."

They all congregated in Max's dressing room, which was the biggest. Max tried to take his greasepaint off but it was difficult with Eloise sitting on his lap and Paddy O'Leary ("Ireland's tap-dancing sensation") constantly leaning across the mirror to help himself to Max's best brandy.

"Max is going to be a TV star," Eloise announced to the room. A murmur of interest and congratulation spiced — Max was sure — with a dash of envy.

"Are you going to do the act with Alfie?" asked the stage manager. "Alfie would love to be on television."

"The lights would be too hot for him," said Max. "I've got another trick planned." It was still in the embryo stages, an idea combining a television set with the famous, and ill-fated, Zig Zag Girl illusion.

"You'll miss the Royal though," said Fred Daniels, a sharp-faced Londoner who was one of the new comedians. "The ghost of Grimaldi, the scent of lavender . . ."

"What?" Max turned so sharply that he almost unseated Eloise.

"Haven't you heard that one?" said Fred. "One of the usherettes told me. The theatre's haunted by the ghost of Dan Leno — you know, the famous pantomime dame. He appeared here loads of times, Mother Goose was his most famous part. Anyway, sometimes you can hear him practising his clog-dancing routine or you just smell his lavender scent in the wings."

"I'd heard that Leno was an alcoholic by then," said Dan, "and the lavender was to mask the smell of drink, or worse. He ended up in a mad house, you know."

"Don't we all," said Paddy O'Leary, helping himself to more brandy.

"Is it good or bad luck if he appears to you?" asked Eloise, getting off Max's lap to refill her glass.

"Oh, bad I should think," said Fred. "Shows you're on your way out."

Max looked at himself in the mirror. His make-up was streaked with sweat and he thought he looked every day of his forty-three years. He didn't really feel like celebrating any more.

Edgar arrived back in London at six o'clock on Sunday evening. The plane had been slightly delayed by heavy winds (Edgar didn't like to think of the great airliner being affected by something as frivolous as wind) and, by the time that they landed at London Airport, the passengers were tired and inclined to be bad-tempered. Edgar had been unable to sleep; his head was still too full of America. Last night he had wandered through New York, looking up at the Empire State Building, like a rocket about to take off into the night sky, watching the lights on Broadway, the flashing advertisements for shows he couldn't afford to see. *Dancing! Girls! Entertainment! Tonite only!* Did Velma Edwards dream of the bright lights from the safety of her pale-blue mansion built with sawmill money? And what about Ruby? Was this what she dreamt of, her name ten feet high in multicoloured lights? If she did, he was unable to give it to her.

He'd walked for hours until, after a thorough inspection of his pockets, he found enough money to

155

buy a beer in a dingy bar off Madison Square, where boxing gloves hung from the wall and the patrons gathered around a tiny television screen watching a fight. He thought of Bill Hitchcock, the man who had been fascinated by televisions. A funny thing to be fascinated by, in Edgar's opinion, but, according to an article he had read on the plane, more than twenty per cent of British families had purchased a set to watch the coronation. Was this the future? People gathered in bars watching a screen, not needing to speak? Well it was rather restful, if so. No one even commented on his British accent. Perhaps he was losing it already.

When he finally found himself back at his hotel he had been unable to sleep. The traffic seemed to roar past all night, a never-ending stream of cars going . . . who knew where? Perhaps they just drove round and round all night, like modern-day *Flying Dutchmans*. But Edgar found it exhilarating rather than otherwise. Perhaps he could bring Ruby here on their honeymoon. Eventually he opened "How Psychiatric Measures can be Applied to Market Research" in the hope that it would get him to sleep. But the strange words and phrases started to chase each other round his head. *The circular test of bias. Subliminal advertising. The operational potential of subliminal suggestion. Must be one of those run-and-hit drivers we've been reading about. Someone is certainly putting out the welcome mat. He told me to look into his eyes . . .*

Now, back in London, the lack of sleep was catching up with him. He wandered out of the airport in a daze and caught a bus back towards the centre of town. At

156

Hammersmith he gave up and hailed a taxi (at least he had some British money on him). London, so exciting a few days ago, seemed a pale imitation of New York, the cabbie astonishingly friendly and polite, the cars boxy and staid, stopping to let each other go first at the lights. The cabbie dropped Edgar outside the Strand Palace with an exhortation not to go spending all his money at once. Edgar tipped him generously for this advice.

The bellboy took his bag and offered to show him to his room. Edgar longed for a hotel room, cool sheets and soft pillows, but he wanted to see Max first.

"Is Mr Mephisto in, do you know?"

"Yes, sir. He's in the bar."

Of course he was.

"Ed! How are you?"

"Exhausted."

"I'll get you a whisky." Max gestured towards the barman. To Edgar, creased and travel-stained, Max seemed the epitome of ease and sophistication, dressed in a well-cut grey suit with a cravat at his throat. A pack of cards lay fanned out on the table beside him. The bar was elegant too: leather sofas, chrome tables, cool jazz playing in the background.

"It seems incredible that I was in New York yesterday," said Edgar, gratefully accepting a large whisky.

Max threw him a rather sardonic glance. "I'm sure London seems like a village to you now."

"No," said Edgar, though he had been thinking something of the kind. "It's just all so strange."

157

"It must be." Max seemed to relent slightly. "Do you really think Bill Hitchcock was murdered?"

"Yes, I do. He was run down in the street and the driver didn't stop. That sounds like murder to me."

"And someone also tried to run you down?"

"Yes. It was just after I'd come out of the police station in Albany."

"What are the American police like?"

"The ones I spoke to were pleasant enough, two big chaps, both Irish. But they seemed obsessed with Hitchcock being a communist."

"Do you think that had anything to do with it?"

"I can't imagine that it did but you never know. Hitchcock's communism seemed to boil down to meeting up with a group of fellow dreamers in an old cinema. The police had infiltrated the meetings and they had to admit that all they ever did was chat about politics. I checked up and none of them had a criminal record of any kind. Besides, Bill's boss, Mike Moretti, said that Bill had become disillusioned with communism."

"Was this the man at the television repair place?"

"Yes. He was a nice chap. I stayed with him and his wife on Thursday night, after my room was ransacked."

"Who could have done that? What were they trying to find?"

"I've no idea. Word must have got round that I was in town. It's an odd place, Albany. I mean it's the state capital but it's like a village in some ways. The policemen that I met, they knew everything about everyone."

158

"What did they say?"

"Oh, that it was all down to the commies again. I just don't buy that. All the links were to Hitchcock's mind-reading act, not to his politics."

"I bet you Petre will think the reds have got something to do with it, all the same."

"Did you tell General Petre? About Hitchcock being killed?"

"No. I thought you might want to do that."

"Yes. I'll go round to Whitehall tomorrow morning."

"In the meantime," said Max, signalling for more drinks, "there's nothing else you can do."

Edgar leant back against the leather sofa. It was a truly wonderful thought.

CHAPTER
EIGHTEEN

At first Edgar couldn't remember where he was. Was he still in America? There was a faint hum of traffic from outside but the first object he saw when he focused his eyes was a hulking mahogany wardrobe that could only be English. Ditto the net curtains covering the sash window, the floral counterpane on the bed, the glass bottles on the dressing table (the dressing table itself). He was home. He was in England.

He reached out for his watch. Two o'clock. How could that be? Had he slept right through the morning? No, it was still on American time. Two a.m. That must make it seven a.m. in England. Last night he and Max had eaten in the hotel and Edgar had almost fallen asleep in his steak (so far removed from American steaks that it seemed to come from a different animal altogether). He had been in bed by ten, English time, and must have slept for a solid nine hours. He felt like a new man. He was meeting Max at nine and they were going to walk down to Whitehall to confront General Petre. Time for a leisurely bath and breakfast first. Edgar got up and switched on the wireless — another massive piece of mahogany. The reassuring BBC tones of the announcer filled the room. They were talking about the coronation. "In just over a week's time this young woman will ascend the throne and rule over a country and a Commonwealth united in peace and goodwill . . ." It was as if Edgar had never been away.

Was it too early to ring Ruby? Her Bournemouth show was over so she would be back in her digs in Brighton. There was a communal telephone in the hall. If he rang, would anyone answer it? The house seemed to be occupied by a transient population of young women: typists, teachers', usherettes and clippies. Would one of them be passing on their way to an early shift? He decided to risk it but the phone rang on, unanswered.

Edgar knew that Max wouldn't join him at breakfast so he ploughed through his fried eggs alone. But, at nine o'clock, Max was waiting on the steps outside, wearing his trilby and smoking a cigarette. They set off along the Strand, Edgar enjoying the feeling of not being at work on a Monday morning. London was looking its best, all red buses and cheerful flower sellers, like a propaganda film, but as they turned down Whitehall, past the statue of Charles I ("Poor bastard," said Max) and the tall, blank-faced buildings, everything suddenly seemed greyer and more sombre. How would General Petre react to the news of Hitchcock's death? wondered Edgar. Would he think that Edgar had squandered government money on a trip that had gained them nothing? Would he, as Max suggested, blame the red menace? It was hard to know. At any rate, Edgar couldn't waste too much time debriefing the general. He needed to be back at work by midday.

"I'll come down to Brighton with you," said Max. "I need to see my cabinetmaker in Hove."

"Is this for the TV show?" Max had told him about *Those Were the Days* last night. Including the slightly unwelcome news that Ruby was also on the bill.

"Yes, I'm planning to do a version of the Zig Zag Girl with three televisions, one on top of the other."

Edgar still couldn't hear the name of that illusion without an inward shudder. He thought of the boxes that had contained a woman's severed body, the connection that had led him to the Zig Zag Girl and to Max. He was amazed to hear that Max was performing the trick again, however modified.

"That's not very Victorian," he said. "I thought this show was meant to be all music hall and the good old days."

"It's ironic," said Max. "I'm going to call it the Magic Cabinet." He sounded quite pleased with himself.

Edgar rapped on the door of number twelve. He had wondered whether Petre himself would come to the door again but he was greeted by a supercilious-looking man in pinstripes.

"Good morning," said Edgar. "We'd like to speak to General Petre."

Pinstripes stared at him as if he'd never heard something so preposterous in his life.

"It's rather urgent," said Edgar. He had to stop himself adding "a matter of life and death".

162

Pinstripes spoke at last.

"There's no one called General Petre here."

"What do you mean?" said Edgar. "We met him here last week." He scrabbled in his pocket for Petre's card, now impossibly crumpled and dirty. Pinstripes took it with obvious reluctance.

"There's no General D.N. Petre here," he repeated. "And, as far as I know, no one of that name on the staff. Good day to you." And, taking advantage of their stunned silence, he shut the door very firmly indeed.

Max and Edgar stared at each other. Pinstripes' door slam still reverberated in the air. Edgar found himself stupidly looking down at the card that had been handed back to him.

"But . . . he was here . . . he told me to go to America . . . gave me a passport and money . . ."

"We never had anyone else's word for it that he really was General Petre," said Max.

"What do you mean? We saw him here, at Whitehall. He was in the office. The room was full of secretaries."

"Misdirection," said Max. "If you tell the audience enough times that the cabinet is empty, eventually they'll believe you. Petre had all the props — the uniform, the office, the manner. We swallowed the whole thing."

"But how could he have got me the passport?" said Edgar. "And he gave me a letter on headed notepaper."

"He was good, I grant you," said Max, lighting a cigarette.

A girl approached the door, looking at them curiously as she passed. Something about her, the smooth hair and the coolly competent manner, sparked a memory in Edgar.

"Conchita?"

She turned in surprise; she was holding a paper bag which contained a cake of some kind. Grease was oozing out unpleasantly, turning the paper transparent.

"We met at the airport," said Edgar. "You gave me the passport."

"Oh yes," said Conchita. "Did you have a good trip?"

"Conchita." Edgar stepped closer, causing the woman to back away slightly. "The man who gave you the passport and told you to meet me, did you know who he was?"

"No," said Conchita. "I never know anyone's name. I'm just a secretary. No one knows my name either. This general just came out of the back office and asked me to take a photo of you. The next day there was a parcel and a note on my desk telling me to meet you at London Airport. You don't ask questions in this job. To be honest, I was just glad to get out of the office."

"How did you know he was a general?" asked Edgar.

Conchita looked at him as if he was insane. "He had a general's uniform on."

Max let out a bark of laughter. "Brilliant. If it looks like a general it must be a general."

Conchita coloured slightly. "Like I say, I don't ask questions. We're told never to address senior staff directly."

164

"Conchita —" Edgar tried his most honest, persuasive look, the one that sometimes worked with the WPCs at the station — "this is really important. Do you know anything about the man who told you to take the photograph? Anything at all."

Conchita considered. "I've got a photograph," she said at last.

"You have? That's wonderful."

"Yes, when I took the picture of you for the passport, he was in the background. I got two copies developed in case he needed a spare."

"Could you, would you lend it to me?"

"I don't see why not." Conchita shrugged. "I can't see anyone else wanting it. Wait here a sec and I'll go and get it. Got to give my boss his morning doughnut first." She held up the paper bag which was now bleeding jam profusely. "Well worth passing that civil service exam for, I must say."

"It's a pity it's not a bigger picture." In the first-class compartment of the Brighton train, Edgar squinted at the black and white photograph.

"We should have seen it all along," said Max. "That hair, those eyebrows, the way he talked. It was a disguise."

"But what about the passport?" said Edgar, for what felt like the tenth time. "And the headed paper? And how did he know about Colonel Cartwright's death in the first place? He had a key to his flat."

"And we were taken there in an official car," said Max. "Mind you, those fellows would probably drive the devil if he was wearing a general's uniform."

165

"Maybe he was a general, maybe he just didn't work in that department. When I get back to the station, I'll have someone check the army records." Emma would do that, he thought. He wondered how she and Bob were getting on in his absence. Up until that moment he hadn't realised how he was looking forward to seeing them.

"No," said Max. "I'll bet my life he was an imposter. We believed he was a general because he told us he was."

Edgar looked at the picture again. There he was in the foreground looking, as he thought he always did in photographs, completely gormless and, in the background, a tall, grey-haired figure, ramrod straight, the perfect caricature of an army man. Petre probably hadn't realised that he was in the picture. He was frowning slightly and Edgar wondered what had been in the man's mind. Was he pleased that his trick was going so well? But what was the trick and why had it been performed? Edgar looked out of the window as the suburbs of London gave way to the South Downs. They were alone in the compartment (one reason why Max had insisted on first class) and the train wheels provided a relentless counterpoint to his thoughts. They were missing something. What was it? He thought of Colonel Cartwright's bedroom, the newspaper cutting, the playbill and the playing card. The ace of hearts. The blood card. The train rumbled on, Max had his eyes closed. Edgar remembered turning off the lamp by the colonel's bed and seeing something half-hidden by the counterpane. The unfinished cryptic crossword. Carthorse is an anagram for orchestra.

"Of course," he said.

"What?" Max opened his eyes.

"We should have known. D.N. Petre is an anagram for Pretend."

Max and Edgar parted at the Clock Tower; Max to walk into Hove, Edgar to make his way to the station. Max didn't suggest meeting up that evening and Edgar wondered if he was planning to see Mrs M. He knew better than to ask about his friend's plans though. Besides, he was hoping to see Ruby.

It was nearly one o'clock so he hadn't expected anyone to be in the CID offices but Emma was in the incident room going through some papers. She coloured when she saw him as if she'd been caught doing something disreputable.

"Hallo, sir," she said. "How was America?"

"It was interesting," said Edgar. Emma was looking at him expectantly and he knew he should make a better story of it or at least offer some pungent observation on the differences between America and England. But where to start really? Should he have brought something back for Emma and Bob? Some American chocolate or a snow globe showing the Statue of Liberty? He hadn't even got any nylons for Ruby. What sort of a boyfriend was he?

"We've had some developments on the Zabini case," said Emma after waiting a few moments for him to say some more. She started to tell him about Madame

Zabini's caravan being set alight and how she suspected a family member because of some old gypsy superstition. Edgar found it hard to concentrate, he kept thinking about the fact that he had apparently been sent on a transatlantic trip by a man who didn't exist. General Pretend himself. Eventually he said, "Good. You've done well. Sorry. It's just I'm a bit distracted." Emma looked expectant again and he ended up telling her the whole story. She listened with a rapt attention that he found rather soothing.

"So I was going to ask you if you could check the army records, see if there ever was a General Petre. I mean it's possible that he was just from a different department. I could be making too much of the thing with the name."

Emma had her notebook out. "Do you know anything else about him? His first name? Where he lived?"

"No." Edgar shook his head, feeling stupid. General Petre hadn't been the sort of person for idle chit-chat about your home town. But had that Petre, the brusque army man, been a complete construction?

"I do have a photograph," he said. He held out the picture. "There's Petre, in the background. Ignore the idiot in the foreground."

Emma smiled and took the photograph. Then she leant forward with a small exclamation.

"What is it?"

"That man." She went to stand under the naked light bulb that was the only illumination in the basement room. "That man . . ."

"What about him?"

Emma turned, her face glowing with excitement. "I'm almost sure that man was at Madame Zabini's funeral."

CHAPTER
NINETEEN

Edgar stared at her.

"Are you sure?"

"I can't be completely sure but I think so. When I was talking to Lucian, Doreen's brother, I think he was sitting close to us. He's quite striking with that white hair and those eyebrows."

Edgar's mind was racing. Could this possibly be true? Could this be the link between Madame Zabini and Colonel Cartwright that had bothered him ever since he saw the ace of hearts on the old lady's coffin? His instinct was to go round to the Zabini house immediately but he forced himself to be sensible. Superintendent Hodges would certainly expect him to report in to him and not to rush off again on what he would definitely class as a wild goose chase. He also needed to see Bob and catch up on paperwork.

"We'll go round to the Zabinis at the end of the day," he said. "Is that all right with you? More chance of somebody being in at that time too."

"Of course," said Emma. "Tol, the son, works as a chef at the Grand. He normally comes home at five-thirty for a rest before starting the evening shift. Astarte told me that the other day."

170

"Then we'll go round at five-thirty."

Edgar knocked on Hodges' door to be told that the superintendent was at lunch, which meant he'd be away for at least another hour (the super's lunches were notorious). When he got back to the incident room Bob was there, full of questions about New York and police chases — he'd obviously been watching gangster films too. Edgar quite enjoyed telling his sergeants about Times Square and Fifth Avenue, about motels and diners and hit-and-run drivers. But he didn't tell Bob about General Petre. He wasn't sure why unless it was because he wanted to preserve the role of the seasoned traveller and not to reveal himself as a gullible dupe.

Back in his office Edgar put a call in to Alan Deacon, a London policeman whom he knew from a previous case. He asked Deacon if he'd check his records for a General Petre and also asked him what he knew about Colonel Cartwright's death.

"He was that top brass killed in Kensington, wasn't he? Not my beat but I'll check up if you like. How come you're involved?"

"He was my old commanding officer."

Deacon didn't ask any more. He was the same age as Edgar and had served in the war. He knew about the mysterious ties that bound you to your old unit and comrades, however much you had disliked them at the time.

"Deacon, have you ever heard anything about a plot to disrupt the coronation?"

Deacon laughed. "We get a dozen calls a day. Crackpots mostly. People who don't think a woman

171

should be on the throne or who think it should be some Scottish chap because of a rebellion hundreds of years ago."

Edgar didn't think it was worth going into intricacies of the Jacobite cause with Deacon. Instead he said, "But nothing serious. No anarchist or communist groups?"

"Plenty of those too," said Deacon but his voice was more serious. "What's going on?"

"It's just a lead I'm following," said Edgar. "I'll let you know if there's anything in it."

"You do that," said Deacon. "And I'll let you know about your general."

By mid-afternoon Edgar was feeling as if he'd never been away. Superintendent Hodges returned from his golf club lunch in a belligerent mood. He informed Edgar that, whilst he had been enjoying himself "with the Yanks", Hodges and his team had been rushed off their feet dealing with a tidal wave of crime in Brighton. When Edgar asked for further details of the tidal wave, Hodges was strangely unforthcoming but he muttered something about gangs and pickpockets. "Even got the gyppos burning down their own caravans," he said. "Your girl Holmes got herself quite worked up about that one." Edgar didn't say that Emma wasn't "his girl", she was a qualified and decorated police sergeant, but he did ask about the telephone call from General Petre, the one that had convinced Hodges to let Edgar have the time off in the first place. "Of course I spoke to him," said Hodges, sounding affronted. "He said the inquiry was pretty high level. I'd never have given my permission otherwise." But it seemed that Petre had offered no proof beyond his own, obviously convincing, assurance.

Deacon rang at three o'clock to say that there was no General D.N. Petre in the British army. Emma had already given him this information but Edgar was grateful for the double confirmation.

"And your colonel," said Deacon. "Scotland Yard are treating his death as a break-in gone wrong."

"Was anything taken from his flat?" said Edgar, thinking of the sitting room with its upturned tables.

"I can't tell you," said Deacon. "I've called in enough favours as it is."

"I know. I'm very grateful. Scotland Yard didn't mention anything found at the crime scene, any newspaper cuttings or playbills, for example?"

"Playbills? What are you talking about, Stephens? Has that sea air finally sent you doolally?"

So Edgar didn't mention the playing card. He spent the rest of the afternoon reading reports and trying to remember every detail about the man who had called himself General Petre. There wasn't much, to be honest. The so-called general had been tall and white-haired, he claimed to have seen Max perform at the Chiswick Empire, he knew Colonel Cartwright's first name and had a key to his flat. Why had he performed the elaborate charade for Max and Edgar? How had he managed to get a passport at such short notice? What was the real reason behind the American trip? Edgar felt as if he were getting further and further away from the truth. He was relieved when Emma knocked on his office door at five twenty-five. He had also failed to get in touch with Ruby.

"What was the funeral like?" he asked Emma, as they walked along the promenade towards Marine Parade. "Did you find out anything about the Zabini family?"

"It was quite a spectacle," said Emma. "They closed off Madeira Drive and there was a horse-drawn hearse. Black horses, plumes, the lot. Oh, and a gypsy band."

"A gypsy band with the hearse?"

"Yes, walking in front. Tol and his brothers walked behind with their children."

"Was the girl there, Astarte?"

"Yes. She was carrying red roses."

"Well, she is Madame Zabini's spiritual heir."

He'd meant it as a joke but Emma said seriously, "She certainly is. She sang a Romany song in the church and it was the weirdest thing ever. Made my blood run cold."

Edgar glanced at Emma who was, if anything, looking less cold-blooded than usual. She had taken her hair out of its plait and she seemed to be enjoying her walk in the sunshine. It was a beautiful late afternoon, all yellow and blue, the sea smooth as glass. From the pier they could hear the distant carousel music, somehow sad and joyful at the same time. "Coconuts," someone was shouting. "Lovely coconuts."

"Did you get a chance to talk to Tol?" Edgar said. "He looked as if he could be an ugly customer, I thought."

174

"I talked to him a bit," said Emma. "He said that he'd noticed a few suspicious things but wouldn't elaborate about what they were. I thought he might be making it up. But I did talk to his uncle Lucian, Madame Zabini's brother. He said that Tol was dangerous, something about him almost blinding his wife."

"Almost blinding her?"

"Yes but I checked and he hasn't got a criminal record." Edgar suppressed a smile; you could always trust Emma to check the records. "His wife died of cancer when Astarte was still a baby."

"Sounds as if Uncle Lucian has a grudge against Tol."

"Yes, and when I went round to ask about the caravan Astarte was very anxious to say that her father couldn't have started the fire. She said he was in London that day. Isobel, the grandmother, got quite angry about it."

Edgar noted that Emma had been continuing with her own investigations while he was away. This was one of the things that made her a good officer, of course, but she had to be careful. Edgar didn't like to think of her being in close contact with the dangerous Tol Barton.

The door of number eighty-seven was opened by Astarte who told them that her father wasn't back yet. "But he won't be long. Sometimes he stops for a drink at the Fortune of War." The Fortune of War was a rather disreputable pub under the arches between the piers. If Tol was drinking there at five-thirty p.m., the pub was open at least half an hour before it should be. Edgar wondered whether Tol drank there alone. Astarte seemed to have no objection to them coming in to wait so Edgar and Emma followed her up the stairs to the sitting room.

Astarte had obviously been sitting alone at the table by the balcony. On the table was the crystal ball with tarot cards laid out in front of it. She had been practising her trade. Edgar was suddenly reminded of Max in the bar at the Strand Palace with a pack of cards beside him.

Emma was looking at the table too. Astarte intercepted her look and said, in a parody of a gypsy crone, but sounding not unlike her great-grandmother Isobel, "Want your fortune told, dearie? Well, cross my palm with silver and I'll do it for you."

"No, thank you," said Emma.

Astarte turned to Edgar and he was struck again by her extraordinary silvery-blue eyes. They were eyes that made you believe in sirens and mermaids, creatures that lured men to their deaths. "Is this about the fire?" she said. "I told you Dad had nothing to do with it."

"It's not about the fire," said Edgar, "though that is an ongoing investigation."

"What's it about then?" Astarte sat down at the table and stared into the crystal ball as if expecting to find the answer there. Edgar was rather fascinated by the object. It wasn't crystal at all, rather it seemed to be made of opaque glass and was a shimmering blue colour, or perhaps it was just reflecting the sky. It looked as if it would be icy cold to touch.

176

Edgar took the photograph out of his inside pocket and put it on the table next to the tarot cards. "Do you recognise this man?"

Astarte gave the photograph a quick glance. "Oh yes," she said, "that's Uncle Charlie."

Edgar and Emma looked at each other. "Is he your uncle?" asked Edgar.

"He's not really my uncle but he's a family friend. He's been down to visit a few times."

"And his name's Charlie? Charlie what?"

"Who are you talking about?" Tol Barton had made a noiseless entrance, crossing the room to stand by his daughter. Although Edgar had been speaking, Tol seemed to address his question to Emma.

"I was asking your daughter about this man." Edgar passed the photograph to Tol, stepping between him and Emma. Edgar was tall but Tol was taller still which gave him a slight advantage. Edgar gave him his straightest look but Tol's shifting turquoise gaze didn't quite meet his. Edgar wondered if the man was slightly drunk.

"Astarte says you know the man in this photograph," said Edgar.

"You're the man in the photograph."

"I mean the man in the background."

"Yes," said Tol and Edgar got the impression that he was weighing his words carefully. "I think that's Charlie Halász."

"And who is Charlie Halász?" The name had a strange sibilant quality that made Edgar distrust it. Or was this simple Hodges-like xenophobia?

177

"He was a Hungarian refugee who stayed with my mother before the war. Lots of Roma were killed in Hungary. I think Charlie must have got out just in time."

So General Petre was actually a Romany gypsy from Hungary? It seemed too fantastic to be true.

"He had a music hall act," Tol was saying. "Quite big at one time. He did all these different voices, accents, stuff like that."

"Charlie Haystack," said Emma. "Man of a thousand voices."

They all turned to stare at her. Edgar couldn't have been more surprised if the crystal ball itself had spoken.

"His name was on the playbill," said Emma, colouring slightly. "The playbill that was found in Madame Zabini's caravan."

In the street outside, Edgar said, "That was brilliant. You remembering the name like that."

"It just came to me," said Emma, "when Tol said that thing about the voices." But she sounded rather pleased with herself all the same.

According to Tol, Charlie Halász had stayed in touch with his mother after the war. "She'd been kind to him and he didn't forget that." Charlie had been down to Brighton a few times over the years. Astarte remembered him because he'd once given her a beautiful doll called Queen Mab. Tol didn't know who had told Charlie about Doreen's funeral but it wouldn't have been difficult to find out. "The Romany world is

178

quite small," he said. "And a gypsy funeral is a big event. Charlie would have wanted to pay his respects."

"So General Petre was a music hall impressionist." Edgar looked at the picture again. It was still hard to believe but, as Max had said, the military persona was so perfect that perhaps it could only have been an act. Thinking of Max gave him an idea.

"Come on," he said to Emma. "We're going to pay a visit."

He started to walk quickly along Marine Parade. Emma kept pace with him, not saying anything, seeming quite happy with this new plan. It was only when they reached the bottom of Upper Rock Gardens that she said, "Who are we visiting?"

"Mrs M," said Edgar. "She's a theatrical landlady. If anyone knows Charlie Haystack, it'll be Mrs M."

Edgar had thought that Max might be there but he was unprepared for the sight of his friend sitting in Mrs M's front parlour mending a clock.

"Max is very good with his hands," said Mrs M. It sounded filthy but then so did most things the landlady said. She was very attractive, Edgar thought, but in a rather overripe way. She was also wearing a silk housecoat that left very little — or perhaps too much — to the imagination.

"Sorry to burst in like this," said Edgar, "but I wanted to ask your advice about something, Mrs . . ." He paused because he couldn't remember what the M stood for.

"Joyce, please," said the landlady. "I'm always happy to help the police with their enquiries."

Max laughed. "Be careful what you promise, Joyce." Sitting in the armchair with his sleeves rolled up Max looked almost — Edgar couldn't believe he was even thinking this word in relation to Max — domesticated. The clock innards were spread out on a small table and Edgar could see that Max was giving them the concentrated attention he had given to his decoy tanks back in the Magic Men days.

Emma was still standing in the doorway looking rather wide-eyed.

"Max, you remember my sergeant Emma, don't you? Mrs . . . er, Joyce, this is Sergeant Emma Holmes."

"Hallo, Emma." Joyce gave her a friendly smile. "I must say you're the prettiest policeman I've ever seen. I thought Edgar was pretty until I met you."

Edgar felt himself blushing — Joyce was good at making people blush — but Emma laughed, not seeming to mind this description.

"Take a seat, Emma," said Joyce. "Can I offer you something hot? Or a beer?"

"No, thank you very much," said Emma, taking the armchair opposite Max. Edgar suddenly felt desperate for a cold beer but didn't want to look like a sad alcoholic in front of Emma.

"Let's all have a beer," said Max, seeing Edgar's face. "It's Monday night, after all. We need cheering up."

Edgar wasn't sure that Max did need cheering up, in fact he looked happier than he'd seen him for a long time. While Joyce was out of the room, Max chatted

180

easily to Emma about growing up in Brighton. Edgar was surprised how relaxed Emma seemed with him, he even heard her admit to being a Roedean girl, something which she often went to considerable lengths to conceal. Joyce came back with the beers and Edgar got up to help her. As he took the tray, he smelt her perfume, something floral, gardenia or rose. He wondered whether she was wearing anything under the housecoat and felt horrified with himself for even having the thought. It was just something about Joyce, he told himself. She was the sort of woman you couldn't stop yourself from undressing mentally.

As Joyce poured the beers, Edgar got the photograph out again. Max gave him a sharp look but said nothing.

"Joyce," he said, "do you recognise this man?"

"Of course," said Joyce, handing Emma a glass. "That's Charlie Haystack."

"Good God," said Max. "Do you really know him?"

"Oh yes," said Joyce, settling herself in a chair. "He's a pro. He stayed here a few times. He's a foreigner but he can do all sorts of accents. When he first came here he put on an Irish accent all the time he was here, talked about County Clare and the Fenians and the cows in the long grass. I even got him Guinness in specially. Then I found out he wasn't Irish at all."

Edgar looked at Max. Clearly Charlie Haystack was a man who liked to immerse himself in a part.

"Do you know anything else about him?" he asked.

"Like I say, he was foreign. I think he was a prisoner of war for a time. He was a nice enough man though. I felt a bit sore after the whole Irish thing but, next time he came, he bought me this beautiful vase made from Irish crystal to say sorry. Then he talked like a Frenchman for the whole of that run. Made everyone call him Monsieur Botte de something. Apparently that's haystack in French."

"*Botte de foin*," said Max, who often knew surprising words in different languages. "When was the last time you saw Charlie?"

"A good five or six years ago. I heard he'd gone straight. Left show business," she added, for Emma's benefit. "What's he done? Why are you after him?"

"He fooled us," said Max, "and we're wondering why."

"Ah," said Joyce, getting out a cigarette lighter. "That's what he did, you see. That was his act."

"Man of a thousand voices," said Emma.

"That's right, dear," said Joyce. "I don't think there was an accent he couldn't do."

"Do you know anyone who might still be in touch with him?" asked Edgar. When he'd asked Tol where Charlie lived he had pleaded ignorance — "Gypsies don't have address books," he'd said — but Edgar hadn't been entirely convinced.

"I don't know," said Joyce, breathing smoke through her nostrils. "Like I say, I haven't seen him for a good few years."

"Have you heard of Tony Mulholland?" asked Edgar. "He had a mind-reading act before the war. Do you know if he was a friend of Haystack's?"

"I know of him," said Joyce. "Poor boy got himself killed, didn't he? He never stayed here though. I counted myself lucky at the time. Apparently, he wasn't above doing a moonlight flit if money was tight."

That figured. Tony was one of the meanest men Edgar had ever met, as well as completely lacking in moral scruples.

"Do you remember any of the other names on the playbill?" Edgar asked Emma.

"Roman and Renée were top of the bill," she said. "And there was Lou Lenny and her unrideable mule. I'll never forget that one."

"Roman and Renée were a nice act," said Joyce. "They were singers, classically trained, I think. Lou was all right too until the drink got to her."

"Was it a real mule?" asked Emma.

"Of course it was," said Joyce, sounding surprised. "Dear little animal. When Lou stayed here we kept Bubbles — that was the mule — in the garden shed."

"Anyone else?" asked Edgar. He knew that Emma had a phenomenal memory, something that she often used against Bob.

"Raydini the gay deceiver was one."

"Raydini's dead," said Max. "I heard it a few years ago."

"Some Australian ventriloquists," said Emma. "I can't remember their names. Val and someone, I think. Oh, and Tommy something. His line was something about being not quite himself."

"Tommy Lang," said Max. "He's in the show I'm doing at the Empire."

"Could you ask him about Haystack?" asked Edgar.

183

"I certainly could," said Max. "Even if he's left the business, someone is bound to know where he is. It's a small world, variety."

Tol had said the same thing about the Romany community, thought Edgar. The two worlds probably had a lot in common.

"Was Charlie Haystack married?" asked Emma.

"Not as far as I know," said Joyce. "I never heard any gossip about him and the girls either. He was a bit of a loner. I mean, very nice to talk to and all that, but he kept himself to himself."

It was funny, thought Edgar, but, if he'd considered it at all, he would have imagined that General Petre was married with children and perhaps grandchildren. But General Petre didn't exist and in his place was a much less substantial figure, one who changed accents by the minute and could slide in and out of a Whitehall office without being noticed.

"I'm going back to London tomorrow," said Max. "I'll find Tommy Lang's address and go and talk to him."

"I'll ask the Bartons again," said Edgar. "One of them must know where dear old Uncle Charlie lives. I'll do the heavy policeman act if I have to." He felt happier now that they had this definite lead. He was almost forgetting the real fear that he'd felt in Albany, the nightmarish sensation outside the Whitehall offices. *No one of that name works here.* It was really very cosy in Mrs M's front room, drinking beer and listening to one of the resident pros play the piano in the other room. *If you were the only girl in the world . . .*

"Are you seeing Ruby tonight?" asked Max. "I know she's back in Brighton for a few days."

Ruby. Edgar felt as if he'd been shaken awake. He hadn't thought about her for a whole two hours.

CHAPTER
TWENTY

Tracking down Tommy Lang turned out to be fairly easy. Max telephoned Derek Conroy and was given an address in Hammersmith.

"Good to know you're all getting to know each other," said the director. "How's the act coming on?"

"Very well. I went to see my cabinetmaker yesterday. I think I'll have something really good."

"That's great. Technical rehearsal on Saturday, remember."

"I'll be there," said Max, thinking again how little time they had to put on the television show. The coronation was in a week's time, and *Those Were the Days* would be shown at seven-thirty that evening. There would be a dress rehearsal the day before and, on the night, they would have to muddle through as best they could. Just like the real thing, in fact.

Tommy Lang lived in a terraced house behind the Hammersmith Palais. Max remembered going dancing at the Palais before the war, the names of the various girls merged into one though he could still recall the exact tones of the trumpets in Harry Roy's jazz band. During the war the theatre had been used to store trams and he'd heard someone say that the rails were still there, under the dance floor.

Lang himself opened the door — shirtsleeves, cigarette in hand — and gaped to see Max on his doorstep.

"Bloody hell. Max Mephisto."

"Good morning. I hope I'm not intruding?"

"No. Not at all. I was just listening to the wireless."

The wireless set dominated the small front room, which also contained a rather threadbare three-piece suite. Max sat on the sofa and Tommy on an armchair but they were so close that their knees were almost touching.

"The missus wants to buy a television for the coronation," said Tommy. "But where would we put it?"

"She could watch the show on it though," said Max. "Or will she be in the audience?"

"She'll be in the audience," said Tommy. "She wouldn't miss a TV show. It's the chance of a lifetime."

Max was surprised to hear Tommy sounding so enthusiastic. He'd looked rather bored that day at the Empire. But he supposed that a live TV show was a lifeline to an ageing variety artiste and, in the daylight, Tommy was older than he had first appeared; his hair was suspiciously black but his face was lined and his hands slightly shaky. Life on the circuit was no fun after fifty. Less fun at sixty, torture at seventy. Diablo had still been performing in his seventies, eking out a living at seedy strip clubs and bingo halls. Max would be fifty in seven years' time.

"I'm calling because I'm trying to trace someone," said Max. "I think you may have been on the bill with him at the Liverpool Empire before the war. His name's Charlie Haystack."

"Charlie?" said Tommy. "Why are you trying to trace him?"

"I've got a friend who's in the police." Max saw the alarm on Tommy's face and hurried to make his voice reassuring. "It's nothing bad. He's just trying to trace him because of a legacy or something." He hoped this would appeal to the impecunious pro in Tommy Lang.

To his relief, Tommy seemed to relax. "I was on the bill with Charlie a few times. He could do all these voices. I started as a comedian but it was really Charlie that got me into doing the impressions. Mind you, my act isn't anything like his. I do all the usuals — Churchill, Attlee, George Formby — but Charlie did all these different characters. There was an Irish drunkard, a Frenchman, an Italian organ grinder. All of them had their own little story, they were monologues really. Some of them were a bit sentimental but others were really funny. There was a Welsh sheep farmer, a bit blue but very amusing."

And there was a British army general, thought Max. A bit of a cliché, like many of Haystack's characters. He didn't like the sound of the Italian organ grinder.

"Have you any idea where Charlie is now?" he asked.

Tommy shook his head sadly. "No, I haven't seen him for years. I thought he might be dead. I remember that bill and quite a few people on it are dead now. Raydini. He was a character. Dropped down dead at the Wood Green Empire. Poor old Lou Lenny, the drink got her in the end. Roman, he died a few years after the war. And Tony Mulholland. Did you hear about him?"

"Yes, I did."

"I didn't like Mulholland much but what a way to go. To be murdered like that. Makes you think, doesn't it?"

Max agreed that it did. "Charlie Haystack is still alive," he said. "I'm sure of it. Do you know where he might be living, where his family were from?"

"No. He was foreign. Czechoslovakian, Hungarian, something like that. I don't think he had any family here."

So Charlie Haystack was rootless, like so many pros. Like Max himself. And, if he really had left the stage, that made him harder to trace.

"I think he stayed with a family in Brighton before the war. Did he ever mention them? They were Roma, gypsies. Name of Barton. Or possibly Zabini."

Tommy looked slightly confused. "I don't think so. He did do a gypsy fortune-teller in his act though. It wasn't one of his best. He didn't suit drag. Too tall."

Had the gypsy woman been based on Madame Zabini? wondered Max. He tried — and failed — to imagine General Petre in a wig and hoop earrings.

"Well if he does get in touch by any chance," he said, "will you let me know?"

"Of course," said Tommy. "I'd love to see old Charlie again."

189

Edgar was having slightly better luck with his missing person. He had managed to telephone Ruby late on Monday night and they had arranged to meet that evening. He had thought that Ruby sounded a bit cool on the telephone but, with any luck, she would thaw out after a meal at Il Teatro, one of Max's pet Italian restaurants. He didn't allow himself to think that she might thaw out to the extent of accompanying him back to his flat, though he had changed the sheets that morning and even bought some flowers to mask the odd smell. He had slept with Ruby about five times (who was he kidding? exactly five times) in the last two years. Each occasion was etched on his soul but, try as he might, he couldn't see any pattern to them. Sometimes Ruby would suggest going back to his flat but, once there, appear surprised that he had any amorous intentions. Last summer she had even suggested that they spend the night together in a hotel ("Mr and Mrs Smith and all that"). The night, in a small hotel in Rye that creaked in the wind like a crow's nest, was one of the highlights of Edgar's life. At some point he had said, "Won't it be lovely when we are? Mrs and Mrs, I mean." "Yes," Ruby had said, "it'll be lovely."

These thoughts made it hard to concentrate on the day's work. Apart from asking Bob to check the electoral roll for a Charles Halász, Edgar didn't spend any more time on the General Petre mystery. Time enough for that when Max had spoken to his co-star, Tommy whatshisname. Instead Edgar worked steadily

190

all day, getting through the backlog of paperwork and ordering tasks for the week ahead. He found the fire brigade's report on the gypsy caravan: *Conflagration caused by ignition of petroleum-based liquid.* Translation: someone poured petrol on the caravan and set light to it. Was it really part of some Romany funeral tradition? Superintendent Hodges didn't want to spend any more time on the case but the fact remained that a woman had died and, just over a week later, evidence had been destroyed. You didn't need to have the gift of prophecy to find something sinister in the coincidence.

He dug out the original report on Doreen Barton's death. She had been reported missing when she failed to return home on the Tuesday night. Who had made the call? Edgar checked the log book. *P. Barton (son).* Edgar knew that Tol lived with his mother, grandmother and daughter in an admirably multi-generational household. Was Tol supporting them all from his wages as a chef? he wondered. But, no, the fortune-telling business had been "lucrative" according to Tol himself. Maybe that was why he was pushing his daughter into it now. Not that Astarte, sitting by the window gazing into her crystal ball, appeared to need much persuasion. Doreen's body had been found near Black Rock on Wednesday morning. According to the coastguard, this was where the tides would deposit a body that had fallen from the pier. But there was no break in the cast-iron railing by Madame Zabini's caravan. Had Doreen climbed over herself? The coroner sometimes avoided returning a verdict of suicide out of respect for the family but was this what

191

actually happened? Why would Doreen, who "loved life" according to her family, have jumped to her death? On the other hand, Doreen had been a small woman. It wouldn't have taken much force to have knocked her out and thrown her into the sea. But why?

Edgar put down the file and looked at the clock. Thank God. Lunchtime. He could run back to the flat and open some windows. Maybe even get some more flowers. It never hurt to be prepared.

By the end of the day Emma had had enough. She knew that the DI was meeting Ruby that evening. It was obvious, from his freshly ironed shirt to his rushing away for a long lunch break and coming back humming show tunes. "Tonight's the night with the showgirl, all right," said Bob, after encountering a manically cheerful Edgar adjusting his tie in the cloakroom.

"She's not a showgirl," said Emma. "She's got a name."

"Ruby," said Bob, rolling the R languorously. "Lovely Ruby. They're going to Il Teatro. The boss told me."

"I'm off," said Emma, closing her file.

"What? Miss Stays-late-every-night is actually going home at five?"

"I've got a lot of overtime owing," said Emma.

"A group of us are going to the Bath Arms at six," said Bob. "Why don't you come? Let your hair down a bit."

Emma realised that Bob was trying to be friendly and was rather touched. Nevertheless, the thought of going to the Bath Arms and playing pool with a gang of

192

noisy junior officers made her want to become a nun and take a vow of silence. At least, if she became a nun, no one could ever tell her to let her hair down. Of course, there was the slight problem of not really believing in God, but maybe some of the newer orders would be prepared to be flexible. At least she'd have no problem with the rules on celibacy.

"Thanks," she said. "Another time maybe. I'm a bit tired tonight."

She was tired, she thought, as she made her way through the Lanes towards the seafront. She wasn't sleeping well and, when she did manage to drop off, her dreams were full of gypsy caravans, plumed horses and playing cards. She had been so happy when the DI got back yesterday. At first he'd seemed rather preoccupied, not really listening to her, but then she'd recognised the photograph and there had been the excitement of interviewing the Zabinis, feeling as if they were making headway at last. And then, when they had the name, the heady pleasure of the trip to Mrs M's house, sitting with the DI and his best friend, drinking beer and talking, not just about the case, but about everything really: Brighton, the war, the coronation, variety, television shows, whether it was possible ever to be truly happy (Max had proved a surprisingly philosophical conversationalist). And then, today, when she'd come to work in her best skirt and her hair in a complicated French plait, the DI was completely preoccupied with thoughts of bloody Ruby, locking himself in his office for hours then dashing off to buy flowers — she'd seen the receipt on his desk. But she remembered Edgar's face when Max had mentioned Ruby last night. He hadn't looked happy to hear his fiancée's name. In fact, he'd looked rather shocked. And there had been something odd in Max's voice too. Maybe he didn't like Ruby? If so, it made her like Max even more.

Palace Pier was hotting up for the evening, music playing and lights flashing. Emma could still see the charred patch where Madame Zabini's caravan had stood. She decided to walk back along Madeira Drive, by the beach, rather than waiting for the bus on the coast road. Maybe the sea breeze would wake her up. The air inland had been rather heavy and thundery. But the seaside wasn't much better, there was an ominous yellow haze on the horizon and the beach smelt of seaweed and candyfloss. The sea was a dull pewter colour with dirty foam breaking lethargically against the pebbles. A train was trundling past on the Volks Railway but this too seemed to be moving almost in slow motion. A child on board let go of a balloon and it hovered motionless in the air, the child's screams echoing long after the train had moved on. Emma passed two promettes waiting for the lift up to Marine Parade. They looked as listless as she felt, their elaborate hairstyles drooping slightly and their heavy make-up running in the heat. At least she didn't have to spend her days parading along the seafront in a tight skirt and four-inch heels. As she got closer to Black Rock, the amusement arcades were left behind and there were only the arches on one side and the beach on the other. The swimming pool wasn't open yet — it

194

was too early in the season — and the diving boards, just visible over the fence, looked somehow sinister, like gibbets.

Emma stopped. Ahead of her was an area of bushes and stunted trees stretching up to the coast road and known as Duke's Mound. There were rumours that it had been mined in the war and it was still considered a slightly dangerous place, notorious for illicit sexual encounters. But it was a shortcut and, for some reason, Emma was suddenly anxious to be home. She looked back along the promenade. The train was almost at the pier now but the balloon was still floating above the crazy golf course, red against the white sky. Madeira Drive, crowded a few moments ago, was now almost empty. There was only a woman dressed in a green coat and a man taking two excitable pugs for a walk. The promettes had disappeared and even the seagulls were silent. Emma made her decision. She plunged into the bushes on Duke's Mound, breathing in the rank smell of privet and other, less identifiable, odours. After a few seconds she found a path and started to climb. She would be home in ten minutes. She encountered empty vodka bottles and a used condom or two. They really should be patrolling this area more regularly. Behind her a twig broke and she heard a rustle of leaves as if someone else were pushing their way through. She started to climb faster, slipping a little on the dry, stony ground. But the person behind was moving faster too and now Emma could hear them breathing. She began to run, fixing her eyes on the fence above and the houses beyond it. Only a few yards to go. Then the

195

world turned upside down and the cliffs and the sea changed places. Emma was falling into darkness and, high above her, the seagulls started to call again, as if they were trying to summon help.

CHAPTER
TWENTY-ONE

Edgar knew that it wasn't going to be easy. When he called at Ruby's digs she wasn't ready and he had to wait in the communal hall while the telephone rang constantly for Joan or Pamela or Elizabeth or Brenda. Just how many girls were living in this house? He must have counted at least ten in ten minutes, all of them sidling past him as if he were an axe murderer.

When Ruby finally appeared she was dressed in a tight-fitting red dress with a little black jacket. She looked beautiful but rather untouchable, like a gift-wrapped present. He kissed her anyway. Her cheek felt smooth and cold and her scent made his head swim.

It was a heavy, muggy evening. As they walked along the seafront to the restaurant, Edgar heard the first faint rumbles of thunder. With any luck, it would pour with rain and Ruby would have to shelter at his flat. He wouldn't bet on it though. She held his arm as they walked but he thought that was only because she was wearing high heels. Everything about her seemed remote tonight. She hadn't even asked him about America. Maybe she was upset because he hadn't brought her back any nylons.

"Are you excited about the TV show?" he asked. "Max says that it's a really big thing. Everyone will be watching after the coronation."

"I am excited," she said. "He's right. It's very important for me. Max doesn't seem to care though. All he does is moan about the old days of variety being gone for ever. As if they were good days! My mum says it was awful. Horrible digs, awful landladies, shows with hardly anyone in the audience, theatre bosses who kept jumping on you."

It was strange to hear Ruby complain about Max, just like any daughter finding her father annoying. It was odd, too, to think of Max being nostalgic for the old days. He always seemed ruthlessly unsentimental to Edgar. Interesting that Ruby's mother had no such nostalgia. Edgar had met Emerald once or twice and could well believe that, in her youth, she had had to fend off countless theatre managers.

"Do you know what you're going to do in your act?" he asked.

"I've got a good idea," she said, turning her head away with a little secret smile. "But I can't tell you, of course."

"Of course." Edgar wondered if she'd keep her act a secret even if they were married. It wasn't as if she could claim the confidentiality of the Magic Circle. Women weren't allowed in the Magic Circle.

"Do you know what Max is planning?" she asked.

"No," said Edgar. "He's as secretive as you. I do know that he went to see his cabinetmaker."

"That must mean he's planning a box trick," said Ruby. "It's a bit old hat, all that stuff, but I'm sure Max will do it well."

Edgar wondered what Max would make of this glowing accolade. Still, thinking about her act seemed to have cheered Ruby up. She nestled closer to him and said, "Will you come and see the show at the Empire?"

Edgar's heart sank. He knew his mother expected him to escort her to her street party. What time would that end? Would he be able to get away in time to watch Ruby's show? He had a feeling that his mother wouldn't think much of this as an excuse. Rose had met Ruby a few times now and, whilst she couldn't deny that her son's fiancée was both beautiful and charming, these weren't attributes that rated very highly with her. She wasn't like Lord Massingham, easily charmed by a pretty face. In fact, prettiness — like charm — was something slightly to be distrusted. "Ruby's very glamorous," she'd said after their first encounter and Edgar had known that it would be uphill from there. In retrospect, it had been a mistake for Ruby to have worn bright red lipstick.

"I'll come if I can," he said. "I've promised my mother I'll spend the day with her."

Ruby loosened her hold on his arm. "You don't want to let your mother down," she said.

I don't, thought Edgar. He knew that he would end up putting his mother before Ruby just because he felt guilty about loving her so much less.

"I'd really love to see your show," he said. "I bet you'll be the star." And that, too, was a frightening thought. Stars were beautiful but far away. Right now, he felt the need to anchor Ruby to the earth.

Ruby was definitely the star of Il Teatro though. Waiters scurried to take her coat, pull out her chair, offer her wine and olives on the house. Edgar felt invisible, dazzled by the light from the main attraction. Not that he minded. He liked being in the background; it was one of the reasons he had become a plain clothes policeman.

Ruby thawed out after a glass of wine and even asked him about his American trip. "I'd love to see New York," she said.

"It's an amazing place," said Edgar. "We'll go there one day."

"I'd like that." She smiled and Edgar felt his heart beginning to race. Being with Ruby sometimes brought on symptoms which he imagined were close to having a heart attack or a seizure. Once, lying in bed with her, he had felt himself leaving his body and looking down at their entwined figures on the sheets. It was as if they had fallen there from a great height and he remembered wondering if the pleasure had actually killed him. Thinking of this now, he felt absolutely desperate to make love to her.

"Do you have to rush home tonight?" he asked.

She looked at him through her lashes. "That depends . . ."

"On what?"

But he was doomed never to know her answer because, at that moment, the door was flung open and

200

Bob burst into the restaurant. He looked around wildly for a few moments before locating them.

"Boss!" Everyone was looking now. Bob stumbled over to their table, knocking down two chairs on his way.

"What on earth is it, Bob?"

"It's Emma. She's been attacked."

Edgar thrust some notes at the waiter and they left, the patrons still staring at them open-mouthed. Edgar dimly remembered offering to get Ruby a taxi home but, when they stood on the pavement outside, she was there beside him.

"Where is she?" he asked Bob.

"At the Royal Sussex. My friend Danny, who's a copper on night duty, he rang me from there. She was brought in about six o'clock."

"Do you know how she is?"

"No but he said it looked bad."

Edgar thought quickly. They were near the Theatre Royal and could try to hail a cab but it would probably be quickest to walk, cutting up behind the Pavilion.

"Let's go," he said.

He was amazed to see Ruby slipping off her shoes.

"What are you doing?"

"I can't run in these," she said. Edgar wanted to say something, to tell her how touched he was that she didn't resent the interruption to their evening, but there wasn't time. The three of them set off through the Pavilion Lawns, Edgar leading but Bob and Ruby close behind. It was only eight o'clock, still light, and

Brighton was as busy as ever; children roller-skating across the park and couples strolling hand-in-hand, looking up at the domes and minarets of George IV's fantasy building. Edgar hated them all. How could they be wandering about enjoying the summer night when Emma was in hospital, injured, perhaps . . . But he couldn't allow himself to think of that.

Edgar elbowed his way through the people patiently waiting for the lights at the bottom of Edward Street. Outside the law courts he saw a taxi and flagged it down.

"I'm off duty, mate."

"Police." Edgar waved his warrant card.

The cabbie looked sceptically at Ruby in her red dress but he allowed them to get in.

"Take us to the hospital," said Edgar. "Quickly."

It was only a few minutes in the car but it felt like an eternity to Edgar as he leant forward, willing the driver to go faster.

"Do you know what happened?" he asked Bob.

"No." Bob was sitting next to Ruby, looking very uncomfortable. "My mate just heard that a police-woman had come in and that she'd been attacked. Hit on the head."

"Do you know where she was when she was attacked?"

"Duke's Mound, Danny thought."

"Duke's Mound! What was she doing there?"

"It's on her way home. She must have been taking a shortcut."

Why on earth had sensible Emma taken a shortcut through such a notorious patch of ground? Edgar was surprised to find himself actually grinding his teeth.

The taxi came to a halt in front of the hospital and Edgar paid the driver. "Keep the change."

"Thank you, Sarge." It was said with exaggerated deference.

The Royal Sussex was a Victorian building, looming halfway up one of Brighton's steepest hills. Edgar had been there before, to interview victims and suspects, and he'd always admired the solidity of the place, the sweeping staircases, the panelling, the sense that being ill was a serious business. But now he found it oppressive and sinister. Having ascertained that Emma was on Martha Gunn Ward he set off up the stairs, two at a time, ignoring the receptionist's warning that visiting hours were over. Bob and Ruby followed him, Ruby still carrying her shoes in one hand.

At the doors of Martha Gunn Ward, their way was blocked by a fearsome vision in blue.

"You can't come in here. Visiting hours are over."

Edgar brandished his warrant card again. "I'm a detective inspector."

"And I'm the night matron." It sounded terrifying, like a nightmare.

"I have to see Emma Holmes, she's one of my officers."

"Miss Holmes's parents are with her now. And that's against regulations. I am not letting a single other person through these doors."

Edgar felt himself wilting. "Please," he said. "Is she going to be all right?"

If the night matron softened it wasn't apparent from her voice — or her stance — but she said, "She's not in danger. She's had a nasty bang on the head and has suffered mild concussion. We'll keep her in for a couple of days but there's no cause for alarm."

"Thank God." Edgar leant against the wall.

"Can you give her our love?" said Bob. "Say it's from Bob and the DI."

"I'll pass on your message," said the matron. And she shut the door.

Edgar, Bob and Ruby looked at each other. Edgar suddenly felt rather foolish. After the wild run through town and commandeering a cab, Emma wasn't in danger after all. He thought that he should apologise to Ruby but, when he looked at her, he saw that she wasn't upset. In fact, she smiled at him encouragingly.

"It's good news, Ed. She's going to be all right."

"I know," he said gratefully.

"Who could have attacked her though?" said Bob. He had his terrier face on and Edgar knew that he would worry away until he got an answer.

"I don't know," said Edgar, "but my hunch is that it's to do with the Zabini case."

"Those gypsies who burnt the caravan?"

"Yes." Edgar gave Bob a warning glance. "Let's talk tomorrow. I need to get Ruby home."

They started back down the stairs but stopped when the ward doors opened again. A man and a woman came out, both well-dressed and prosperous-looking,

204

even though the woman held a handkerchief to her eyes and the man looked choleric and angry.

Edgar approached them. "Mr and Mrs Holmes?"

"Yes," said the man. "Who are you?"

"I'm Detective Inspector Stephens."

"Oh," said the woman. "*You're* Inspector Stephens." She looked very like Emma but a glossier, more artificial, version, with coiffured hair and glittering earrings. Her voice, too, was pure cut-glass. It made Edgar realise how much Emma must have modified her own accent for their benefit.

"Yes," said Edgar. "We came to see Emma but the matron wouldn't let us in."

"She was a bit of a dragon." Mrs Holmes gave him a slight smile.

"How is Emma?" asked Edgar.

"A bit battered, poor darling," said Mrs Holmes, "but game as anything, you know Emma. Furious with herself that she didn't see it coming."

"Did she say anything about the attack?"

"Only that she thought it might have been a woman."

"A woman?"

"That's what she said but she was a bit woozy. I can't believe that a woman would have walloped her like that. You know, she was only saved because some dog walker came to her rescue."

Edgar would have to get a proper statement from Emma tomorrow and speak to the mysterious dog walker. He hoped that the duty policeman got a proper statement.

"Did the dog walker call the police?" he asked.

"Yes, and the ambulance too. He was a real good Samaritan. I must get his address and send some flowers."

Mrs Holmes was just the sort of woman who sent flowers to say thank you. In her powerful femininity she reminded Edgar slightly of Mrs M, a comparison he was sure she would not have relished.

Meanwhile Mr Holmes seemed to be building himself up to some sort of pronouncement. "I always said that she shouldn't have joined the police," he said. "Madness for a girl like Emma."

"But she loves the job, Archie," said Mrs Holmes. "You know that."

"And she's very good at it," said Edgar.

Bob suddenly stepped forward, his ears bright pink. "I'm Bob," he said. "I work with Emma and she's the best."

Mrs Holmes put her hand on his arm. "Delighted to meet you, Bob. Emma's spoken a lot about you."

Edgar thought that Bob might be in danger of exploding. He didn't know why, but he found Bob's sudden volubility rather irritating.

"We'll see Emma tomorrow," he said. "And don't worry, we'll find the person who did this."

"You'd better," said Archie Holmes, muttering something about paying his taxes.

Outside, Edgar finally managed to get rid of Bob and he turned to Ruby.

"Shall we have a late meal somewhere or do you want to go home?"

Ruby leant her head against his shoulder.

"Can we go back to your place?" she asked.

There were a hundred things that Edgar wanted to say but, in the end, he settled for simply, "Yes." He took her hand and they began to walk towards Hanover.

"It's quite steep," said Edgar. "I could get a cab."

"No, it's all right," said Ruby. "I'd like to walk. I'd better take my shoes off again though."

As they climbed the hill, the rain started to fall at last.

CHAPTER
TWENTY-TWO

"One minute I was walking up the path and the next minute I was hit on the head." Emma closed her eyes. "I'm sorry. I'm being a terrible witness."

"You're not," said Edgar. "It must have been an awful shock."

He had been shocked too when he'd rolled up at eleven o'clock, at the very start of visiting hours, to find Emma lying flat on her back with a bandage round her head. It wasn't just that she looked more bruised than he'd expected — "a bit battered," her mother had said. It was that she looked so dejected, lying there under the snowy white hospital sheet. She looked tiny, almost childlike, and he realised with a shock that Emma was quite a small woman. She seemed bigger at work somehow. If he'd thought about it he might have said that she and Bob were the same height, perhaps because he always thought of them as a twosome. With observational skills like that, he would make a terrible witness himself.

"I brought some flowers." He proffered a sad-looking bunch, bought at the stall outside. "And Bob sent a bar of chocolate."

Emma managed a smile. "I can't believe Bob gave away chocolate."

"Shows how shocked he was. We all were."

"Matron says you were here last night. I'm sorry she wouldn't let you see me."

"She was terrifying. Worse than Razor Eddie."

Emma smiled again at the mention of one of the most notorious local criminals. She put her hand up to her bandaged head.

"Does it hurt?"

"Not really."

Liar, thought Edgar. Aloud he said, "How long will you have to stay in here?"

"A couple of days, the doctor said, but I'll see if I can get out tomorrow. This place will drive me mad before long."

It was a small ward, quite pleasant, with big sash windows at one end. The patients had obviously been making bunting for the coronation and little red, white and blue flags were everywhere. But for someone as private as Emma, Edgar could see that it would be torture. The patients on Martha Gunn Ward were mostly well enough to sit up and chat. The two women opposite were swapping knitting patterns. Another woman called out "Hallo there" when Edgar arrived.

"You should try and rest though," said Edgar. "You've had a shock." He didn't think Emma looked well enough to leave. The doctor who'd examined her on admission said he thought she'd been hit on the head with a heavy object, "a stick or maybe even a truncheon". The other injuries had come from falling onto the stony ground. Luckily the attacker had only had time for one blow before the dog walker had called out for help.

Edgar asked Emma if she could remember anything about the attack. "Your mother says you thought your attacker was a woman."

"Yes," said Emma. "There was a woman walking along Madeira Drive. She was the only person in sight apart from the man with the two pugs on a lead. But, it was more than that. When I was knocked to the ground the . . . the assailant . . . was almost on top of me and I got a strong sense that it was a woman. She smelt like a woman, for one thing."

For a second Edgar had a heady, sensory memory of Ruby's sharp lemony scent. Last night had been a dream and, in a way, he felt as if he was still asleep. Even the grimness of the hospital and the shock of Emma's appearance hadn't woken him up entirely. Ruby had still been in bed when he left the flat that morning.

"The dog walker saved you," he said. "He heard you cry out and he raised the alarm. Then he ran to the flats opposite and called the police and the ambulance. He waited with you until the ambulance came. Nice man. I spoke to him this morning. He's called Arthur Donaldson and his dogs are Lancelot and Percival."

Emma laughed then looked as though it had hurt her. "Arthur, Lancelot and Percival," she said. "Where's Guinevere?"

"I dread to think," said Edgar. "Do you remember anything after you were hit on the head?"

"Not a thing. I woke up in the hospital with my mother crying and my father talking about complaining to his MP."

Having met Emma's parents, Edgar could imagine both reactions.

"Can you describe the woman you saw walking along Madeira Drive?" he asked.

Emma grimaced. "Not very well. She was tall with a green coat on, that's about all."

"A coat? It was hot yesterday evening."

"A summer coat. Like a jacket."

Edgar filed away the idea of a summer coat with other feminine mysteries.

"Anything else?" he said. "Anyone acting oddly?"

"No," said Emma. "Like you said, it was a really warm evening. Lots of people near the pier, promettes and so on, but when I got to Black Rock it was almost deserted."

"Why on earth did you go through Duke's Mound? Why didn't you stick to the road?" Some of Edgar's frustration must have crept into his voice because Emma blushed, the pink very noticeable on her pale, bruised face.

"It was stupid, I know, but I just wanted to get home quickly. And now look at me. My father said he's been waiting for something like this to happen ever since I joined the police."

"He said something like that to me. He worries about you. That's understandable."

A mutinous look came over Emma's face. Edgar was beginning to realise what it must have taken for a girl like her to have defied her parents and joined the police force. She may be small but she was tough, Emma.

"What are you going to do now?" she asked.

"I'm going to see the Zabinis. It's possible that this was a random attack but you were working on the Zabini case, you had just recognised the man in the picture, then you were attacked. It's a bit too much of a coincidence for me."

"I thought it must be to do with the case," said Emma. "The Charlie Haystack case. I don't know why, I just thought that the woman who attacked me must have had something to do with the Zabinis."

"Why?" said Edgar. "What was it about her?"

"I don't know." Emma tried to smile. "Maybe it was just the green coat."

"I'll have Bob out looking for women dressed in green," Edgar promised. "And I'll pay a surprise visit to the Zabinis. I don't know why one of them would have attacked you but it's still possible."

"Astarte will see you coming in her crystal ball."

Edgar laughed. "Now that would surprise me."

"What about Charlie Haystack? Did you find out any more about him?"

Edgar suppressed a smile. Emma was obviously not going to let being in hospital stop her following the case.

"Max was seeing someone who knew him," he said. "He was going to ring me yesterday but didn't. I'll telephone him today."

A shadow fell across the bed. Not Matron Nightmare but someone almost as intimidating: a nurse in striped uniform complete with starched cap and crackling apron.

"Emma needs to rest now," she told him.

"I'd better go." Edgar stood up. "Hope you feel better soon."

"Come back and tell me about Charlie Haystack," she said.

"I will." He didn't quite know how to say goodbye so he settled for a wave. Emma waved back, rather forlornly. As he walked away he could hear her asking the nurse for a pencil and notepad.

When Edgar got back to the station there was a note from one of the secretaries saying, "Mr Mephisto telephoned." No telephone number or anything helpful like that. But at least it might mean that Max had some news from his meeting with Tommy Lang yesterday. Edgar went into the CID room to find Bob half-hidden behind a pile of flowers and sweets. There was even a teddy bear and a tin of peaches.

"What's all this?"

"Presents for Emma. Even the cleaners sent some humbugs."

Edgar was beginning to realise that Emma was very popular at the station. When she'd first arrived, she had been subjected to a barrage of teasing about her name, her sex, her looks and her posh accent. Edgar hadn't noticed when the teasing had given way to genuine affection, prompted perhaps by the cool way that

213

Emma had handled all the attention. She was kind too, and thoughtful. He'd often seen her chatting to the cleaners and felt ashamed that he didn't even know their names.

"How was the girl wonder?" asked Bob.

"Not too bad. She's got lots of cuts and bruises but the doctor said that they were mainly from falling onto the ground. She's had a nasty bump on the head though, must be pretty sore."

"Danny said she was unconscious when she was brought in last night. He thought she might be dead. I thought . . ." He stopped, perhaps remembering his precipitate arrival at the restaurant last night.

"I know," said Edgar. "I thought the worst too. But it'll take more than a bump on the head to keep Emma down. Even at the hospital she was asking about the case."

"Which case?" said Bob. "The gypsies or the mysterious general?"

Edgar hadn't told Bob the whole story about General Petre but he realised he would have to do so now. With Emma out of action, Bob would have to be his right-hand man. Bob listened attentively to show that he was as keen as Emma.

"Blimey, boss," he said, when Edgar had finished. "Do you really think the general was the same person as this impressionist man?"

"Charlie Halász. Yes, I do. Did you check the electoral roll, by the way?"

"Yes I did. No one of that name registered. But if he was foreign he wouldn't be able to vote, would he?"

214

"Not unless he became a British citizen. There's no doubt it was him, though. I just don't know why he did it."

"Maybe he wanted you to investigate the death of your old colonel."

"But why make it so complicated? And why send me to America? He even got me a passport."

"At least you got to see America," said Bob. "And fly on a plane."

Bob's straightforward response was actually making Edgar feel a bit better about the whole thing. "And now there's a link with the Zabini family," he said. "Emma and I go round to their house asking about Halász and the next day Emma is attacked. I don't like that at all."

"Shall we go and see them?" asked Bob. He sounded eager to see the famous gypsy family. Edgar thought he must have resented being excluded from the investigation so far.

"Yes," said Edgar. "I've just got to make a telephone call first."

He should have thought of it earlier. If anyone would know about an old music hall act it would be Stan Parks, aka The Great Diablo. He rang the boarding house in Hastings where Diablo lived and, after an animated conversation with Queenie, the landlady, Diablo eventually came on the line, wheezing but full of bonhomie.

"Edgar, dear boy, how lovely to hear from you. How are you?"

"I'm all right. How are you?"

"Toddling along, dear boy, toddling along. Got a bit of a chest but Queenie looks after me nicely. I'm hoping to be well enough to do some panto this year."

Diablo was supposedly retired but he liked to do a panto every winter, specialising in the undemanding but showy parts like Baron Hardup in *Cinderella* or the Emperor of Peking. He had appeared in *Aladdin* with Max a few years ago. Apart from this sporadic income, Diablo didn't seem to have any visible means of support but Queenie seemed to have taken him under her wing. Edgar knew that Max sent him some money every month.

"You should come to Brighton for a weekend," said Edgar. "You can stay with Mrs M." He knew better than to invite Diablo to stay with him.

"Is Max still seeing Mrs M?"

"I think he is, yes."

"Who would have thought it? Max and Joyce Markham. Mind you, she's a good-looking woman. It's just that I never thought that Max would settle down with a seaside landlady."

"He's not exactly settled down," said Edgar, though this was pretty much what he had thought when he saw Max in Mrs M's sitting room on Monday.

"I wanted to ask you," he went on, "about a man called Charlie Haystack. Do you know him?"

"Charlie Haystack." An intake of breath as Diablo lit a cigarette — whatever else he did for his chest, he would never think of giving up smoking. "Man of a thousand voices. Yes, I was on the bill with him a couple of times. Had quite a clever act, monologues in

216

different voices, you know. Bit old-fashioned now though." Despite all evidence to the contrary, Diablo liked to think that he moved with the times.

"Have you any idea where he is now?"

"Not a clue. I heard he'd left the business. Why are you asking about old Charlie? Has he robbed a bank?"

"No, but when I saw him he was pretending to be a general."

"A general! Well, that's a turn-up for the books. I got the impression that Charlie wasn't that keen on the military. He was a refugee, you know. I think he was interned for some of the war."

"Do you know anyone who might still be in touch with him?"

"No, they're all dead that crowd. Roman, Raydini, Luigi Monte."

"Luigi Monte?"

"Had a juggling act. Got hit in the eye by a club at the Blackpool Tower."

Edgar thought of Emma. Had she been hit by a club? He felt no desire to laugh at the story of Luigi Monte.

"What's Max doing now?" Diablo was asking.

"He's just finished a run in London. He's doing a television show on the evening of the coronation."

"Oh, I heard about that," said Diablo. "That's Derek Conway, isn't it? I ran across him in my ENSA days. Nice fellow. Well, good for Max. The money's in television now, no doubt about it. I'd do a TV show like a shot if I was asked."

The thought of Diablo on television was truly awe-inspiring. But Edgar was touched, as ever, by the old magician's willingness to embrace the new.

"You must come to Brighton soon," he said.

"I will, dear boy, I will. Got to get this coronation over first. Queenie's got a houseful and she needs me to do little jobs about the place."

Leaving Edgar to wonder what on earth these could be, Diablo rang off cheerfully. Edgar telephoned the Strand Palace but was told that Mr Mephisto was out. Then he rang his flat, in the faint hope that Ruby might still be there. But the telephone rang on, unanswered.

Edgar and Bob went to the Grand Hotel, hoping to catch Tol off guard, Edgar didn't believe in the crystal ball but there was always the chance, if they waited until the evening, that the family would have had a chance to get their stories straight. After a slight argument with the maître d'hôtel they were shown to the kitchen where Tol, armed with a large filleting knife, was approaching a flat fish with murderous intent.

"What are you doing here?" was his greeting.

"They say they are the police," said the maître d', sounding unconvinced.

"We're investigating a serious assault that took place yesterday evening," said Edgar.

"And you think I had something to do with it?"

Interesting first assumption, thought Edgar. He didn't much like the way Tol was brandishing the knife though.

218

"What were you doing yesterday at five-thirty?" asked Edgar.

"I don't have to answer this, do I?" said Tol. He directed his question to the maître d', who shrugged.

"You don't have to answer," said Edgar, "but I'm asking myself why you wouldn't want to."

"I was probably walking home," said Tol. "I left here about five-fifteen. I usually go home for a bath and a rest before starting the evening shift at seven."

"Which way did you walk home?" asked Edgar. "Along the seafront?"

"Yes. It was a nice evening. Not like today." The rain, which had started last night, had continued unabated all day.

"Did you walk along Madeira Drive?"

"No." Tol put the knife down and stared at them. "I walked as far as the Palace Pier and then crossed over by the aquarium."

"What time did you get home?"

"Probably a bit after half past. What is this about?"

"Can anyone vouch for the time you got in?"

"My daughter, Astarte."

As if your daughter wouldn't lie for you, thought Edgar. He noted that Astarte seemed to spend a lot of time in the house. Didn't most nineteen-year-olds — he had asked her age when they last met — go out a lot, if not to work then to see their friends?

"What's this about?" Tol asked again. "I have a right to know."

"A woman's been attacked," said Edgar. "And we think there might be a link to your family."

"To *my* family? You're joking."

"We're not joking," said Bob. "We don't joke."

Tol laughed. "Where did you get this one, Inspector Stephens? What have you done with Emma? I liked Emma."

Edgar didn't answer and Tol looked from one policeman to the other until, finally, he got the message.

"I didn't like him," said Bob, "he's a slippery gyppo."

"But, if he did get in at five-thirty yesterday, he's got a pretty good alibi."

"Given by his daughter."

"Yes, that's true. I can see Astarte lying to protect her father."

"What's she like, the daughter?"

"Blonde and beautiful. Not your type."

Bob didn't smile. He could be surprisingly puritanical sometimes. They continued to plod through the rain, through the backstreets where the hotel kitchens spilled out in a chaos of rubbish bins and empty bottles. Edgar always thought that this contrast typified Brighton: the shiny hotel fronts looking out over the sea and the shambles at the back, dirty, dark and dangerous.

"But why?" said Bob. "Why would one of the Zabinis attack Emma?"

"I don't know," said Edgar. "Perhaps because she was getting close to the truth about Charlie Halász."

"But we don't know the truth about him," said Bob, annoyingly and unanswerably. They continued in silence.

Back at the station, Edgar's telephone was ringing. It was Max.

"Where were you this morning?"

"Working," said Edgar. "I do have other things to do as a policeman besides taking your calls."

"It's a tough life pounding the beat."

Edgar ignored this. "Did you find out anything about Charlie Haystack?"

"Not really," said Max. "Tommy had been on the bill with him a few times. Said the same as Mrs M really. That Haystack had an act where he put on different voices, became different characters. He was a refugee, a loner, no family. Tommy hadn't heard from him in years. He thought he must be dead."

"I rang Diablo," said Edgar. "He knew Charlie in the old days but hadn't heard from him for ages either."

"Bright idea to ask Diablo though," said Max. "He knows all the old acts. How is the old devil?"

"Says he's got a bad chest but seemed cheerful enough. I said he ought to come to Brighton for a weekend."

"Good idea. He could stay with Mrs M."

"That's what I said."

"Surprised you don't ask him to stay with you again."

"Once was enough." Edgar shuddered at the memory of the time, three years ago, when Diablo had briefly shared his flat. He said, "Diablo told me that most of Charlie's contemporaries are dead."

"That's what Tommy said, more or less."

"Did you ask about links to the Zabini family?"

"Yes. Tommy hadn't heard of them. One funny thing though. Haystack used to do an act where he impersonated an old gypsy woman. Maybe that was based on Madame Zabini?"

When Max had rung off, Edgar sat at his desk looking out at the basement view of feet hurrying past. It had been a frustrating day but he had learnt one thing from Max's visit to Tommy Lang: Charlie Haystack sometimes impersonated a woman. Could he have turned himself into a tall woman in a green summer coat, the same woman who had attacked Emma?

All day Emma had been wanting to be on her own. When everyone goes, she told herself, I can allow myself the luxury of one really good cry. But it seemed that they were never going to leave her alone. First there was the doctor, trailed by his team of learner white coats. He said that Emma had mild concussion, cuts and contusions. Obviously a fan of alliteration.

"Can I go home tomorrow?" Emma asked.

"Make it the day after," said the doctor. Addressing his students, "Sometimes serious brain damage manifests itself several days after the trauma." Turning back to Emma, "Nothing to worry about, my dear."

As if being threatened with brain damage wasn't enough, the woman opposite chose the moment after the consultant's departure to heave herself out of bed and pad over to Emma.

"Feeling blue, dearie?"

"I'm fine."

"You looked ever so ill when you got in last night. You must have come a real purler."

"Someone hit me on the head but I'm all right now."

"Someone hit you on the head? Why?"

It seemed a strange question to Emma. What was the required answer? Because I'm just the sort of person who invites random knocks on the head? Because I irritated them by asking one question too many?

"I don't know," she said. "The police are investigating."

"Ah, the police. Was that handsome young man who was here earlier a policeman then?"

"Yes."

"What a shame. I thought he might be your admirer."

"No," said Emma. "He's my boss."

Her neighbour only went back to her bed when lunch was served. Emma wasn't able to eat much stew and even the steamed pudding defeated her. Her head ached and she just wanted to close her eyes. But, as soon as afternoon visiting started, Emma's parents appeared, weighed down with books and fruit and a layer cake from Ada, the housekeeper.

"Ada says you must keep your strength up."

Emma was grateful for the cake and even more so for the books, but she couldn't help wishing that her parents would leave her alone to read quietly. They took up so much room on the ward, her mother in her full-skirted dress, her father standing to attention by the bed, glowering at all the nurses. And their voices were so loud and upper class ("Darling, just look at that extraordinary device. What's it for, do you imagine?"). Emma felt herself cringing into the mattress.

She had thought that Edgar might come back in the afternoon but her only other visitor was Bob who arrived bearing a cardboard box full of presents from the station.

"You've got too many flowers," Sister Adams informed her.

"Can you give them to other people then?" asked Emma.

"That's against regulations."

"I'll take them home for you, darling," said her mother. "They'll be there to welcome you. It was so kind of Bob to bring them."

Bob blushed scarlet.

They had an awkward four-way conversation. Bob told Emma that they were "proceeding with the investigation". Emma longed to ask more. Had they seen Tol Zabini? Had Max come up with an address for Charlie Haystack? But it was difficult with her parents there. She had the sense too that Bob was rather enjoying being the sole sergeant again. "I can't say any more," he said, on more than one occasion. Emma wanted to hit him.

After Bob left, Emma suggested that her parents didn't need to stay any longer. "It must be boring for you."

"I'm not bored," said her mother and, unfortunately, this seemed to be true. She wafted around the ward saying hallo to people and getting in the nurses' way.

224

Emma's father fumed about his daughter being on a public ward. "I wanted to get you a private room but they said that the nurses needed to keep you under observation. Ridiculous."

You're keeping me under observation, Emma wanted to say, but she didn't. She knew that, with her father, worry often manifested itself as belligerence.

Eventually visiting time ended and Sister Adams was chivvying people out of the double doors. "See you tomorrow, darling," her mother called from the door. Emma heard her saying, "Thank you *so* much," to the staff nurse, as if she were the doorman.

Emma hoped for respite but, as soon as she opened *Persuasion*, her favourite book, a motherly woman with a trolley was asking if she'd like a cup of tea; Distribution of tea and digestive biscuits seemed to take for ever and, as soon as the trolley squeaked away, supper started to come round. Emma toyed with her junket. Her head was aching worse than ever but she didn't want to draw attention to herself by asking for an aspirin. Her skin felt stretched and tender and she could feel her hair itching under the bandage. What must the DI have thought when he saw her looking so awful, with a black eye and her hair — her best feature — covered up? Well, it didn't matter what he thought. The night matron hadn't failed to report that the two policemen last night had been accompanied by a girl in a red dress who "looked like an actress". Emma tried to imagine the scene which had ended in Ruby turning up at the hospital, barefoot apparently, "her shoes in her hand". Maybe the DI had groaned when he'd heard the news. "I'm so sorry, darling. Emma's got herself into a spot of trouble. I'd better check up on her. It won't take long." And Ruby would have laughed, the throaty laugh that she'd often heard on the telephone. "Of course not, darling. It'll be quite amusing to pay a sick call."

"Not eating any more?" The motherly woman was back.

"No. Thank you. I'm just not hungry."

She hoped that she would be able to sleep but two nurses descended on her and started to make her bed. "The night sister is fussy about corners." They wouldn't even let Emma get up while they did it. It wasn't until the night nurses had taken over and the ward was in darkness, apart from a violet glow over the nurses' station, that Emma was able to shut her eyes and let the tears roll down her face.

CHAPTER
TWENTY-THREE

Edgar saw the lights from the hospital as he climbed the hill on his way home. He wondered what Emma was doing. He imagined her sitting up in bed with her pencil and writing pad, making notes about the case. She was a great one for paperwork, Emma. He wished he could have gone back to see her that afternoon but he had been busy and Bob was keen to go. Was Bob a bit sweet on Emma? Edgar remembered Bob's sudden declaration to Emma's mother — *she's the best* — and he had certainly seemed devastated at the thought of her being attacked. For some reason Edgar didn't like the thought. It wasn't a good idea for members of the same team to get romantically involved, he told himself. Not that Emma would ever be interested in Bob. Her ideal man was probably a lord with a private plane and RAF moustache. Meeting Emma's parents had made him realise just how different Emma's background was from his own. He tried to imagine his mother meeting Mr and Mrs Holmes. Rose would be distrustful of Mrs Holmes' charm and wary of Mr Holmes' bluster. "Posh people," she'd once said, in relation to Max, "are all very well in their place." But both Emma and Max seemed determined to get as far away from their allotted place as possible. Perhaps they were rather alike? They had certainly got on well the other night.

He stopped to look back over Brighton. The hill seemed to be getting steeper every day. Or maybe he was just unfit. He had lost a toe in the Norway campaign and sometimes that foot ached at the end of the day. God, he was turning into an old crock, the sort who complained about their war wound. He was only thirty-three but sometimes it felt as if he had lived several lifetimes. This was the great divide, he thought, between people who had fought in the war and people who had been too young to serve. Bob, for example, was twenty-four, but he often seemed like a schoolboy to Edgar. By the time Edgar was twenty-four he had fought in Norway, been injured, been seconded to the Magic Men and had his heart broken. He had only been twenty-five when the war ended but remembered feeling far too old to go back to university and finish his degree. He had joined the police because he had a vague feeling that it was up to him to make the world a better and safer place. And, all things considered, he didn't regret the decision.

It had been raining all day and the smudges on the horizon showed that it was raining out at sea as well. Lights were going on in the houses below, in the Regency terraces, in the fishermen's cottages, in the hotels and boarding houses. Somewhere in the town was the man — or woman — who had attacked Emma. Maybe the same person who had killed Madame Zabini and Colonel Cartwright. Was it Charlie Halász, aka Charlie Haystack? But why would Halász have drawn attention to himself in the first place by dressing up as a general and getting Max and Edgar involved?

After Max's telephone call, Edgar felt slightly less suspicious of Tol Barton. But, even so, he thought it was worth checking his alibi. When Bob was out visiting Emma, Edgar walked round to Marine Parade and, sure enough, Astarte was home, playing what looked like a complicated game of patience.

"Shall I read the cards for you?" she offered and Edgar saw that they were tarot cards: the hanged man, the moon, the tower. He'd seen tarot cards before but these seemed particularly vivid and disturbing.

"They're Aleister Crowley's Thoth Tarot," said Astarte. "Aleister used to live in Hastings. He and Grandma were good friends."

Doreen Barton certainly had some unusual friends, thought Edgar. He'd heard of Aleister Crowley; everyone in Brighton knew the name. Crowley was an author, painter, occultist and magician who — after a varied career in Egypt, Paris, Berlin and America — eventually ended his days in Hastings. He died in 1947, just after Edgar moved to Brighton, and, because Hastings City Council refused to let him be buried in the town, the funeral had taken place in Brighton. Edgar remembered the day well. It had been a snowy December morning and he and another policeman had provided what was known as "covert surveillance" — in other words they sat in their car outside the crematorium. Only a dozen people had attended and the atmosphere had seemed suitably subdued. This hadn't stopped the newspapers talking about a "Black

229

Mass" and making wild claims about pentagons, sacrifices and upside-down crosses. Crowley was also said to have cursed Hastings for its inhospitality which, having visited the town recently, Edgar could well believe. He wondered if Doreen had been one of the mourners at the funeral.

Edgar looked at the card that Astarte had just laid on the table. It showed a bearded man wearing a tall hat with a pentagon on his chest. A bull and an elephant twisted themselves around his body.

"What's that card?" he asked.

"It's the hierophant," said Astarte. "It symbolises rules, duty, authority, membership of a club. It's very significant that you should choose that card."

I didn't choose it, Edgar wanted to say, you did. But he didn't want to be drawn into a discussion of the mysteries of tarot reading.

"I want to ask you a question," he said.

"Ask away." Astarte laid another card beside the hierophant. It showed a two-headed woman pouring golden liquid into a goblet.

"What time did your father get in yesterday?"

Astarte looked up, surprised. For once her mermaid's eyes looked dark, pupils dilated.

"Why do you want to know?"

"Just answer the question, please."

Astarte placed another card on the table before replying. "The usual time."

"Which is?"

"About five-thirty or six."

"Which was it yesterday, five-thirty or six?"

Astarte looked at him, calm and seer-like again. "Five-thirty. I remember because I had the wireless on."

That gave Tol an alibi, thought Edgar. Emma was attacked at five-thirty. Arthur the dog walker had provided them with a very exact time. "Five-thirty pip emma," he'd said, not realising how appropriate this phrase was. Edgar couldn't help feeling, though, that Astarte had made a guess and — through good luck or mystical powers — ended up with the right time.

"Thank you," he said. "I'll see myself out."

"Goodbye," said Astarte. "Let me know if you change your mind about the reading. You've got a major decision to make, you know."

What did she mean? thought Edgar, as he set off up the hill again. He had decisions to make every day but Astarte made it sound as if there was one portentous choice to be made. Maybe that was just her fortune-telling manner, managing to make everything sound as if it were a matter of life or death. Despite the alibi, he still felt suspicious of the Zabini family.

As he reached the top of Albion Hill, his house came in sight. It was easy to spot because it was painted a particularly virulent shade of pink — "Cheerful," explained the landlady. Edgar had the ground-floor flat. It wasn't particularly nice or cosy but Edgar felt unusually warm towards the place today. Last night, with the rain falling and Ruby turning to him in the red glow of the one-bar fire, last night had been incredible. He hadn't been able to reach her today but, even so, for almost the first time since they met, he felt relaxed about their relationship. She must love him. After last night, she must.

He noticed with irritation that someone was waiting by his door. Was it one of the other lodgers who had got themselves locked out of the upstairs flats? He couldn't have said why but something about this visitor made him uneasy. It was a tall man with white hair, standing almost to attention under the streetlight.

As Edgar got nearer the figure turned. And Edgar found himself looking into the face of a man who did not exist.

CHAPTER
TWENTY-FOUR

"Can I come in?" asked Charlie Halász.

"Yes," said Edgar, fumbling for his key. He felt as though he needed to get the man inside before he disappeared in a puff of smoke.

He let them into his flat, turning on the light and trying not to notice the smell (not completely masked by Ruby's flowers). On the coffee table was a page torn from a notebook. It was blank apart from one perfect, red lipstick kiss. Edgar put the piece of paper in his pocket.

"How did you find me?" he asked Halász.

"It wasn't difficult. I'm a four-star general, after all."

Edgar didn't smile. Halász looked like General Petre but there was something different all the same. The face was more mobile, the movements less constrained. One hand was drumming nervously on a cigarette case. General Petre would never have fidgeted.

"Sit down," said Edgar. "I've got a few questions to ask you."

Halász sat on the sofa and took out a cigarette. "Do you mind if I smoke?"

"I'd rather you didn't." Petre hadn't been a smoker either.

"What shall I call you? Charlie Halász or Charlie Haystack?"

"Congratulations," said Halász. "You have been doing your detective work."

"I'm a detective," said Edgar, aware that this sounded like Halász's earlier comment about being a general. "I've also been halfway across the world because of a trick you played on me. I'm pretty keen to get some answers."

"Call me Charlie Haystack," said the man opposite, ignoring this. "That's the name I've been going by for ten years, British people being constitutionally incapable of pronouncing a foreign name."

It still felt odd to hear General Petre — that bastion of Britishness — speaking disparagingly about the country. Haystack's voice was not as patrician as the general's but it was still perfect, accentless English. Almost too perfect, in fact. There was something flat and uncomfortable about the tone, as if it was coming from a machine, one of those artificial intelligence machines that the Americans were said to be inventing, automatons that could walk and talk and think.

"All right, Mr Haystack," said Edgar. "Why did you do it? Why did you impersonate a member of the British army? That's a criminal offence, by the way."

Haystack smiled, as if the law was of no importance to him. "1 wanted you to investigate my friend's death," he said. "I knew that if I made it a bit more interesting — the playing card and so on — that you and Mephisto would take the bait."

234

Edgar was momentarily silenced. His first thought was that, not for the first time, Bob had been closest to the truth. "Maybe he wanted you to investigate the death of your old colonel," Bob had said. Could this really be what was behind the elaborate charade? And Max had been right too when he'd detected misdirection in the elaborately staged crime scene.

"'The playing card, the playbill," he said. "Was that you trying to make it interesting?"

"No, the playbill was there," said Haystack, "and the newspaper cutting. That's what made me think of you. Peter had told me all about the Magic Men. The playing card was my own addition. I knew Max would pick up on the connotations, the blood card and so on. I'd seen Tony perform that trick in Liverpool."

Like other criminals Edgar had known, Haystack sounded rather complacent as he recalled his own cleverness. Edgar decided to take advantage of the garrulous mood.

"How did you find out about the colonel's death in the first place?"

Haystack was silent for a moment and, glancing at him, Edgar realised that he was battling with emotion. Eventually he said, in the same even tone, "We'd arranged to meet but Peter didn't turn up. I went round to his flat, let myself in . . ."

"You had a key?"

Haystack waved the question away, "I let myself in and I found him, on the bed, just like I told you. The knife was still in his chest."

"Did you call the police?"

"Yes —" with a trace of a smile — "you'll find that the death was reported by one Charles Hastings. Don't know why I picked Hastings. I loathe the place."

"But when you took us there the next day . . ."

"That was easy. I had a key and I was dressed as a general. Those PC Plods, they were too busy saluting to ask for any identification. The car belonged to a friend of mine, he dressed up as the chauffeur."

"And the rest of it?" said Edgar. "The office, the passport and so on."

"Well, the office was easy," said Haystack. "I had the general's uniform for the act. It wasn't quite right actually but I didn't think you or Mephisto would notice. But, when I was wearing the uniform, it was easy to come and go. I went to the Whitehall office the day after Peter died. Just walked straight in, wearing the uniform, no one even asked my name. I managed to palm a set of keys fairly easily. I used to do a few magic tricks on the side and any magician can be a pickpocket. Just ask Mephisto. I asked you to come that first time when the offices were empty, just to be on the safe side, but it was easy enough in broad daylight too. Those secretaries are told never to address a superior directly. Typical of the British. All that deference to rank and no curiosity at all."

"But the passport? How did you manage that?"

Haystack smiled. "That was the easiest of the lot. I work in the passport office."

Edgar stared at him. "You're joking."

"No. I left show business after the war. Variety is dying. Your friend Mephisto will tell you that. And, after

236

what I'd seen and heard about, I didn't want to make people laugh any more. So I got a job at the ministry. It wasn't difficult. I'm fluent in three languages, after all."

"And the money? The American dollars?"

"That was my savings," said Haystack.

"But why?" Edgar almost shouted it. "What was the point of it all?"

Haystack leant back in his chair. He put his hands together and, for the first time, looked like an actor.

"I came to England in 1938," he said. "I could see the way the wind was blowing in Europe for Jews and for the Roma. Hungary was becoming a very nasty place, very nationalistic, lots of anti-Jewish laws and so on. So I came to England and I stayed with Doreen. Our families were distantly related but there was a network of safe houses for Roma refugees. Doreen was very good to me. Anyway, while I was staying with Doreen I got involved in a group. An anarchist group, I suppose you'd call it, but in those days anarchist didn't mean blowing things up. We believed in a Utopia, free from rules of any kind. After all, look where rules had got us. Nazi Germany and Fascist Italy."

He paused.

"Who else was in the group?" asked Edgar.

"There were a few other theatricals. Raydini, Roman and Renée. Some others I can't remember, a comedian, a dancer, two Italian jugglers. Oh, and Ptolemy, Doreen's son."

"Tol Barton?"

"Yes. He was young then but a real firebrand. He was in the army catering corps in the war and he grew to

237

hate them all, all the brass hats and handlebar moustaches. He wanted to overthrow society."

"Violently?"

"No!" This was said emphatically, violently even. "We weren't violent, that was the point. But, after the war, everything changed. Twenty-eight thousand Hungarian Roma were killed in the Nazi death camps. You can't fight evil like that by talking about love and peace. Our group disbanded but there were others who started to say we had to use violence, we had to do something really big so that people would notice us."

Edgar thought of Haystack, as General Petre, talking about the anarchist threat. He'd dismissed it then, partly because he thought it was the type of thing a character like the general would say. But the general was just that, a character.

"You talked about a threat to the coronation," he said. "Was that real?"

"Just before the war I was in a show with Tony Mulholland," said Haystack. "He was talking about all these mind-control techniques, how you could use them on a really big scale. That was why Peter wanted him in the Magic Men. I kept in touch with Tony after the war and I knew that he was talking to people in America, people who were working on that sort of thing. Then, Peter had that breakthrough . . ."

"That was true then?"

"Yes, of course it was true." Haystack sounded shocked. "He said he was onto a group who had plans to disrupt the coronation. Then, that night, he died . . ." He stopped and Edgar saw that there were

238

tears in his eyes. He wondered exactly what the relationship had been between Peter Cartwright, the upright army man, and Charlie Haystack, Hungarian gypsy and ex-variety entertainer.

"When he died" — Haystack had control of his voice again, in fact he seemed to have injected a note of General Petre steel — "there was the press cutting in his bedside cabinet with the telephone number written on it. I thought that William Hitchcock might be the link. I couldn't investigate by myself but then I thought of you. Peter had talked about you and Mephisto. He thought a lot of you."

Edgar felt absurdly pleased to hear this. He'd always thought of his army career as a complete failure — the disastrous Norway campaign followed by the ultimately futile Magic Men experiment — but to have had the admiration of a man like Colonel Cartwright . . .

"And then I read about Doreen's death. It was just a tiny piece in the *Evening Standard*. 'Gypsy Fortune Teller Falls to Her Death'. I thought there might be a link. That's why I sent that letter to Tol. I knew he'd show it to you and you'd make the connection."

Astarte had described the writer of the letter as a tall man "sad and angry in his heart". Edgar was beginning to think that she had hit the nail on the head.

"Doreen had a playbill with your name on it in her caravan," he said. "Did you know anything about that?"

Haystack shook his head. "That must have been for sentimental reasons. She was fond of me, dear old

239

Doreen. That's why I had to go to her funeral. I didn't reckon on your bright young sergeant recognising me."

"How did you know about that?"

"Tol told me."

"So he did know where to reach you."

"Of course he did. You couldn't expect him to tell the police though. Tol still hates all authority."

Edgar thought of Astarte saying of the hierophant card, "It symbolises rules, duty, authority, membership of a club." He wondered what her attitude to authority was. But the mention of Emma had reminded him of a more important concern.

"Where were you at five-thirty yesterday?" he asked.

Haystack didn't look surprised at the abrupt question. "I was still in London, at my flat. I only came down to Brighton today."

"Can anyone vouch for you?"

"The doorman saw me come in at about five. I stopped to talk to him. Why?"

"Emma, my sergeant, was attacked on the seafront."

Now Haystack did look shocked. "That's terrible."

"I know it is."

"I mean, this shows that someone knows exactly what's going on. They know that Emma identified me. We're all in danger."

This seemed, to Edgar, to be slightly jumping to conclusions. Emma could still have been the victim of a random madman (or woman). But Emma herself had thought that the attack was linked to the Zabinis and to Charlie Haystack, the man she had so brilliantly identified from the old playbill.

240

"Then you'd better tell me exactly what you know," said Edgar. "I don't believe that you're not in touch with any of your anarchist pals."

"I'm not." Haystack ran his hand through his hair which, freed from General Petre's brilliantine, stood up like a . . . well, like a haystack. "Raydini and Roman are dead. Tony's dead. There's only Bill Hitchcock . . ."

"He's dead too," said Edgar. "You'd have found out if you'd only stuck around for a few more days. Why didn't you, by the way?"

"It was too risky," said Haystack. "I knew I'd get rumbled sooner or later. Anyway, it didn't matter. Once you'd got the bit between your teeth, I knew you'd carry on with the investigation. That was all I cared about."

"Well, I found out that Bill Hitchcock was dead. Knocked down by a car. In fact, the same car probably tried to run me down when I was in Albany."

"So I was right," said Haystack. "They're everywhere."

This sounded a bit melodramatic to Edgar, forgetting this was exactly how he'd felt in America when the car with out-of-town plates bore down on him.

"The American police thought that Bill was a communist," he said.

"Americans see the red menace everywhere," said Haystack. "It's so simplistic. Two legs good, four legs bad. But I never knew the man, perhaps he was a raging communist. I only know that Peter had written his name before he died."

"He wrote something else too," said Edgar. He went to his desk and took out the completed cryptic crossword. "This was under Colonel Cartwright's bed. I finished it."

He was unprepared for the effect on Haystack. He took the paper as if it were a holy relic, brushing away tears with the back of his hand.

"One of Peter's crosswords. He loved cryptic crosswords. That was partly why I picked the name N.D. Petre. As a sort of tribute. It's an anagram of Peter too." He smiled rather mistily. "If I'd known you liked them too, perhaps I would have thought twice."

"Colonel Cartwright wasn't that hot on anagrams actually," said Edgar. "He was better at the codes."

"He worked at Bletchley Park for a while," said Haystack. "He knew about codes."

"It was the doodles that interested me," said Edgar. "Look how he wrote our names at the side of the page."

"It shows I was right," said Haystack. "He was thinking about the Magic Men."

"But why?" said Edgar. "Why was he thinking about us? Was it just the link with Tony?"

"I don't know," said Haystack. "Peter didn't have much time for Tony but I quite liked the boy. He was brash and arrogant but he was fun too. And that's how Peter and I met. He came to see Tony's act — scouting him out for the Magic Men — and I was on the bill."

This raised a lot of new questions for Edgar. He also realised that it was the first time he'd met someone who had actually liked Tony Mulholland.

242

"You must remember some other names from the anarchist group," he said. "You mentioned a comedian, a dancer and some Italians."

"The Italians were brothers. They went back to Italy, I think. The comedian was Tom something but I think he's dead now. The dancer was only a young girl. She was from an Italian family too. I think she went to live in America. I can't remember her name."

Edgar felt a cold hand on his heart. He remembered sitting round the table in Albany, talking about marriage, babies and the theatre. *Sometimes I want to wear the sequinned dress again, you know?*

"Was it Genevieve?" he asked.

CHAPTER
TWENTY-FIVE

"I still can't believe it," said Max.

They were sitting in the pub frequented by Tol, the Fortune of War, chosen by Charlie Haystack for their evening rendezvous. Haystack had declared himself anxious to meet Max and, after Edgar had telephoned Max with the news of Charlie Haystack's reappearance, the feeling was more than mutual. Max had travelled to Brighton earlier that day, visited his cabinetmaker and — Edgar was sure — Mrs M. Now they were sitting drinking in the dark, smoky pub, which was shaped like an upside-down boat. Outside the sea hissed against the shingle and the fishermen were dragging their boats up onto the beach. Edgar wondered whether it was significant that Haystack had chosen Tol's favourite drinking place for their meeting. There was no sign of Tol tonight. He had obviously been warned of their presence or, more likely, he was at work. It was nearly seven o'clock, the time specified by Haystack.

"It's pretty unbelievable," said Edgar. "From the way he tells it, he just strolled in dressed like a general and everyone believed he was one."

"Didn't I say that?" said Max. "Tell the audience something enough times and they come to believe it."

244

"Haystack said he used to do some magic on the side. That was why he was able to get hold of the keys to the office."

"Sleight of hand," said Max. "Any magician is a pickpocket."

"That's exactly what Haystack said."

"What sort of a man is he?" asked Max.

Edgar drank some beer, dark and smoky like the pub. "It's hard to tell," he said. "I got the impression that, when he's not acting a part, he's almost a blank. His voice is completely accentless but kind of featureless. Listening to him, you have no idea where he comes from and that's a bit disturbing. The only emotion in his voice was when he talked about Colonel Cartwright."

"What was the relationship between them? Do you think they were lovers?"

"It did occur to me," said Edgar. "Haystack had a key to his flat, they were certainly very close. Colonel Cartwright had told him all about the Magic Men. They actually met when Cartwright went to see Tony perform."

"God, that's an inauspicious start to any relationship."

"Haystack said that he quite liked Tony. He said he was fun."

"Clearly a man with original views."

"Of course Cartwright and Haystack could just have been good friends," said Edgar. "It's hard to imagine a man like Cartwright in a homosexual relationship."

"What, you think there are no homosexuals in the British army?"

"I know for a fact that's not true," said Edgar, remembering a rather uncomfortable train journey from Catterick at the start of the war. "Maybe it's just that Cartwright and Haystack are such an unlikely couple."

"Which makes it more likely to have been a love affair," said Max. "Opposites attract and so on."

Was Max thinking about his relationship with Mrs M? thought Edgar. But he wouldn't have called them opposites exactly. In some ways they were very alike.

"Did you check Haystack's story about finding the body?" asked Max.

"Yes," said Edgar. He'd rung Alan Deacon in London that morning and found that the body had been discovered by one Charles Hastings, a friend of the deceased. "I was surprised they didn't treat Haystack, Hastings, as a suspect but they were so caught up in this idea of a break-in gone wrong."

"And what about this dancer Haystack mentioned?" said Max. "The woman you met in America?"

Edgar had put a telephone call in to Mike Moretti that morning. He'd been told that Genevieve was in hospital "some complication with the pregnancy". He'd sounded worried to death and Edgar hadn't had the heart to probe further.

"I just can't believe she's involved," he said now to Max.

Max looked sceptical. "Except that she lived in the same town as Bill Hitchcock and knew him. She was there when you were nearly run over."

"She's eight months pregnant, for God's sake. I can't see her killing a man."

"You always were a sucker for a pretty face, Ed."

Edgar tried to think of an answer to this but, unfortunately, Max had quite a lot of historical evidence on his side. To change the subject, he looked at his watch. "Twenty past seven. Haystack's late."

"He's not coming," said Max.

Edgar looked at Max and knew that his friend was right.

"He's done another disappearing act," said Max, draining his whisky. "I don't suppose he left a forwarding address."

"No," said Edgar. He'd asked, of course, but Haystack had said, "I can't tell you. The fewer people know the better." Edgar reminded him that he was a policeman and that, strictly speaking, he should arrest Haystack for a number of offences, including impersonating an army officer, falsifying passport details and making a detective inspector look stupid. But Haystack had just smiled sadly as if he knew a bluff when he heard one. And now he'd done it again. Disappeared *and* made Edgar look stupid.

"Tol Barton," he said. "Charlie said that Tol knew his address."

"Is that the gypsy chap?" said Max. "Where are we going to find him?"

"At the Grand," said Edgar. "He's a chef."

"Let's give it another half an hour," said Max, "and then go and ask him. Another drink?"

The kitchens at the Grand were in full swing for the evening service. Plates appeared at the hatch and were spirited away by liveried waiters. Tol, his head covered in a white bandana which made him look more piratical than ever, talked whilst frantically chopping vegetables. Edgar wished that, one day, he could interview the man without him having a sharp knife in his hand.

"I didn't even know that Charlie was in Brighton," said Tol. "He certainly didn't come to see me."

"But you know his London address," said Edgar. "Charlie said that you did."

He had to step back as three plates of lobster went past him. Austerity obviously wasn't having much effect on the menu at the Grand. The maître d' was glaring at them from the doorway.

"Can I have the address?" said Edgar.

"Oh, for God's sake." Tol tore a piece off the Special True Blue Coronation Menu in front of him. "I can't remember the flat number."

"Thank you," said Edgar, pocketing the paper and backing out as what looked like a whole duck went past. In the lobby he found Max deep in conversation with a couple of women who were clearly fans.

"I can't believe you're really here," said one.

"I'm not," said Max, raising his hat and making his exit.

Outside, Edgar gave the address to Max. "It's probably better if you go and see him. This still isn't an official police inquiry."

248

"I'll certainly try," said Max, "but I have a feeling that the bird will have flown."

"But why turn up at my house and then disappear?"

"It sounds as if he's genuinely scared of this group."

"Yes," said Edgar. "He did seem frightened."

"Are you frightened?" asked Max, as they set off along the promenade. "That something might happen to disrupt the coronation, I mean."

"I still can't believe it," said Edgar. "What sort of extremists would blow up innocent people just to make a political point?"

"But Hitchcock did drop that clue. What was it? With hesitation. ER. Elizabeth Regina."

"Yes," said Edgar. "And Cartwright obviously thought he was onto something. I'll have to try to talk to Scotland Yard tomorrow. They'll think I'm mad but I've got to have a go. I'll speak to my friend Deacon too. Maybe he can keep a lookout. It's difficult though when we don't know what they've got planned. If it's a bomb it could be anywhere."

"But we know that someone killed Cartwright and probably the gypsy woman too. And someone attacked Emma. That's worth taking seriously."

"I am taking it seriously," said Edgar, rather nettled.

"How is Emma?"

"She's out of hospital. Bob went to visit today and they told him she'd insisted on discharging herself."

"Do you know what I think you should do?"

"I'm sure you're going to tell me."

"Visit Emma at home tomorrow. Take her some flowers and tell her about Haystack turning up. She must be going mad wondering what's going on. And she's a bright girl, she might have some ideas."

"I haven't got time to be visiting people," said Edgar. He knew Max was right but he felt irritated all the same. Why was Max suddenly the expert on Emma?

"Go after work," said Max. "Make time. And now, let's get something to eat. My friend Aldo's got a nice little bistro near here."

Much later, travelling back to London on the midnight train, Max thought that he'd done his best. If Edgar really couldn't see that Emma was in love with him, then he had only himself to blame. Except it wouldn't be only Edgar who was hurt if he made a disastrous marriage to Ruby. There was Emma, whom Max had liked very much, and there was Ruby herself. Ruby might say she wasn't ready for marriage but she was clearly more deeply involved with Edgar than she'd led him to believe. He'd rung Ruby's digs late on Tuesday evening to be told that she was out "with her boyfriend". "Can you ask her to ring Max when she gets in?" he'd asked the nameless housemate. But Ruby hadn't rung him until Wednesday afternoon which either meant that she was annoyed with him or that she'd spent the night with Edgar. Judging from her dreamy manner, it was the latter. It wasn't that he disapproved exactly . . . Damn it, he did disapprove, he just knew he hadn't any right to. And his own hypocritical, paternal feelings aside, he didn't think the pair were well matched. Edgar might be besotted with Ruby but he was clearly far better suited to clever, competent Emma. She was a very attractive girl, too, Emma. It was just that Edgar didn't seem to have noticed it.

He lit a cigarette. The rich meal he'd eaten at Aldo's was churning unpleasantly in his stomach. He felt disturbed by the whole evening. He didn't like the mysterious Charlie Haystack turning up and then disappearing again. "He's playing games with us," Edgar said and Max had to agree that the old impressionist seemed to be controlling the game. It was an unpleasant feeling, being the stooge. And he was also feeling rather unsettled about his relationship with Mrs M. Not that she was making any demands on him. That was one of the things he liked about Joyce. She was always pleased to see him but never asked when his next visit was going to be. It was more that he felt that the status quo was becoming unsatisfactory. At best, he was taking advantage of her. At worst, he was falling in love.

Max often told himself that he'd never been in love. He'd had intense love affairs, of course. He'd loved Emerald, that long ago summer in Worthing. He'd loved Trixie, a German accordion player with hair like a Rhine maiden. After the war, he'd tried to find out what happened to Trixie and was told that she'd died of dysentery in postwar Berlin. "Though starvation was probably a better word for it," said the Red Cross official who had given him the news. He'd once fallen madly in love with the wife of a theatre impresario and, after the impresario had come home unexpectedly early one afternoon, had had to get out of town in a hurry, leaving his stage clothes and effects at the theatre. But he had never loved any woman enough to imagine a future with them in the way that Edgar — poor fool — was doing with Ruby.

Did he love Joyce? He enjoyed her company. She was attractive, clever, funny and wonderful in bed. But he didn't really miss her when they were apart or worry that she might be seeing another man. When they were together, though, there was no doubt that he felt something which he had never felt in the company of any other human being — he felt at home. After his mother died Max had never once thought of his father's house as home. And, as an adult, he had never had a permanent address. His life consisted of theatrical digs and hotels, a different bed every week. A summer season felt like a lifetime. During the war there had been various army camps, a way of life that he had secretly rather enjoyed. The longest he had ever stayed in one place was the two years in Inverness with the Magic Men. No wonder that had driven him nearly mad. Was he ready to settle down in Brighton with Joyce, or should he buy a mansion flat in Kensington, a bit like the late Colonel Cartwright, and live a life of solitary overindulgence?

As the train passed Battersea Dogs' Home he wondered if he should get a dog. Then he thought of Alfie and his almost insufferable cuteness. Dogs were too dependent. Joyce had a handsome black and white cat whose elegance and *savoir faire* Max rather admired. But he was thinking about Joyce again. The train crossed the dark river and pulled into Victoria

Station. There were only a few other passengers on board, one of them a woman in a rather good fur coat who gave him a distinctly predatory look. In the old days he might have followed up on this but now he just concentrated on getting to the taxi rank as quickly as possible. He was getting old, there was no doubt about it.

CHAPTER
TWENTY-SIX

Charlie Haystack lived at the top of Kensington Church Street, a mere ten minutes' walk from Colonel Cartwright's flat but some distance away in desirable residence terms. The block where Haystack lived was almost at Notting Hill Gate, where the large dwellings now housed multiple families, many of them Caribbean immigrants. Max enjoyed seeing the Caribbean faces on the street — he always identified strongly with immigrants — and the new shops that were springing up seemed full of interesting colours and smells, so welcome after grey wartime austerity. But the woman in the shop where he asked for directions told him that the area had "come down" and there was no doubt who she blamed for it. "They're not like us, are they?" Max wished he could find a way to disassociate himself from the "us"; after all, he had often been described as having a "touch of the tar brush" about him. The best he could do was raise his hat and say, "And so much the better for them, madam." He doubted whether she got the inference.

Haystack's mansion block was still old-school enough to have a doorman, though, and Max was grateful for it. After the offer of a cigarette and the

254

subtle, sleight-of-hand passing of a coin, the doorman was quite happy to tell Max about Mr Halász. He pronounced it Harlarge.

"Nice gentleman. Always ready to chat. When he found out I was from Dublin he was ever so interested. I think he must have Irish blood himself. He can do the accent like a native."

Max was sure that this was true. He wondered if the doorman had helped perfect Haystack's stage Irishman act.

"Have you ever seen him on stage?" he asked.

"On stage?" The doorman looked quite shocked. "He's not an actor. He's got a job at the ministry. In fact, I think he may be in the forces. I've seen him in uniform a couple of times."

"Does he have many visitors?"

"No. He keeps himself to himself. There was a man used to call, looked like a military man himself, but he hasn't been around for a while."

"When did you last see Mr Halász?"

"Now that would be the day before yesterday. I remember because he told me that he might be going away for a few days."

"Do you remember what time you saw him?"

"About five," said the doorman, rather too promptly for Max's liking. "I remember because I go off duty at five and Ronnie was a bit late relieving me. But I was glad to get to see Mr Halász."

I bet Charlie was glad to see you too, thought Max. Ronnie might not have been nearly such a good witness.

"Have you any idea when Mr Halász will be back?"

"Well he only said that he'd be away for a few days. I should think he'll be back soon. The post's piling up." He gestured towards the pigeonholes behind him. Max's fingers itched to go through Haystack's mail. As Haystack rightly commented, any magician is a pickpocket.

"I'll tell him you were asking after him," said the doorman. "What name shall I say?"

"Mulholland," said Max. "Tony Mulholland." That would give Haystack something to think about anyway.

Edgar was having a frustrating morning trying to convince Scotland Yard that he wasn't a lunatic. "We're getting a lot of crank calls," said a man who introduced himself (without apparent irony) as Hills of the Yard. "We've got men on every street corner." But a policeman on the street corner couldn't do anything about a bomb, thought Edgar. Especially as he had no idea where such a device might be hidden.

"I know this sounds crazy," he said, "but a man I spoke to in America, he said something about televisions sending subliminal messages."

"I wouldn't be surprised," laughed Hills. "Half the world's got a television now. My wife's insisted that we buy one to watch the coronation. She's invited all the neighbours round to watch. Thank God I'm on duty."

Alan Deacon wasn't much more help. "No one's going to disrupt the coronation. Everyone loves the Queen."

256

Not everyone, thought Edgar. He was willing to bet that Tol Barton, for one, wasn't a fan.

"But this anarchist group, I'm sure they're behind at least two deaths. Isn't that worth taking seriously?"

"I'd take them seriously if you had at least one name for me. Otherwise it's all just fairy tales."

The only name Edgar had was Charlie Halász and he gave it to Deacon, along with the address. He doubted whether the police would find Halász at the Kensington Church Street flat. Max had already reported his conversation with the doorman. Edgar had also rung the passport office to be told that Mr Halász was on leave. So Charlie Haystack had gone to ground again. It was, as Max said yesterday, like looking for a needle in a Haystack. But, even if Charlie Haystack could be found, Edgar didn't think that he knew anything about the plot, if there was one. It was just an idea, put together from a jumble of coincidences. Haystack's fear, though, had been real enough.

"I'll send a man round," said Deacon. "But there's really nothing else I can do. We'll be flat out policing street parties on Tuesday."

That reminded Edgar that he was due at his mother's house in Esher on Tuesday, to watch the coronation on her newly acquired television and to attend the street party afterwards. He wished he had the excuse of work but Hodges, an ardent monarchist, had given everyone in CID the day off. Brighton would have to exist with a skeleton police service.

He sent Bob to talk to Arthur Donaldson, the dog walker who had saved Emma. But Donaldson, though eager to help, had nothing to add to the story that he had already told Edgar. "I heard a woman cry out and I rushed into the bushes. Lancelot and Percival were barking. When I got there I saw the young lady lying on the ground with blood coming from her head. I left the boys to keep guard and I ran across the road to Sussex Square. I rang the first bell I could see and called the police and ambulance." Reading this, in Bob's round schoolboy hand, made Edgar think again that Donaldson deserved some sort of good citizen award. The dogs too, though it was doubtful how much protection could be given by two distinctly overweight pugs. He resolved to look into the award all the same.

Edgar thought about Bill Hitchcock and his fascination with televisions. Could he really have been experimenting with sending messages via the television screen? Edgar had finally finished "How Psychiatric Measures can be Applied to Market Research" and, whilst he still only understood about one word in a hundred, he had been able to grasp the fact that the writer thought that you could use psychiatric techniques — "tells" like blinking or fidgeting — to help you to sell things. And, as he had learnt, selling things was what lay at the heart of America. He tried to find out a bit more about the author of the article, James Vicary. It was difficult because the Brighton library had nothing under V for Vicary or even T for television. He wished now that he'd given this job to Emma, who was wonderful at research. But he had finally found Vicary in a book about advertising. James Vicary was a market researcher in Michigan who claimed that, if you flashed up a message onto the screen — "Eat popcorn", say — during a movie, the movie-goers would all buy popcorn in the interval. The words would appear and disappear so quickly that the viewer would hardly be aware of them but their message would get through all the same. Vicary called this "subliminal advertising". One detail that Edgar found fascinating was that Vicary used to be a snake charmer, "Detroit's youngest snake charmer" according to the *Detroit News*. Snake charmers, mesmerists, hypnotists, they all wanted the same thing: to control another living being. Was this why Bill Hitchcock had made Velma Edwards sing and dance, why Tony Mulholland had enjoyed saying "I know what you're thinking"? Bill Hitchcock had been fascinated by televisions and obviously saw the small screen as a potential means of controlling thousands, millions, of minds. But what was the message that Hitchcock had wanted to broadcast?

By afternoon he felt that he'd done enough thinking about Bill Hitchcock and Charlie Haystack. He had tried to warn people of a threat that was nebulous and vague even in his own mind. There was a Friday feeling about the station, helped by the excitement of the holiday next week. Secretaries were putting up bunting that reminded Edgar of Martha Gunn Ward. There were plans afoot for a Bartholomew Square street party on Tuesday. Edgar thought that it would probably be jollier than his mother's celebration in Esher. At least in Brighton you were never too far away from a decent pub. Edgar sent Bob home early and, at five o'clock, called into the flower shop where he was now quite a familiar figure. Armed with a bunch of brightly coloured blooms (he had agonised over this; roses were too romantic and lilies too funereal, so he settled for stocks) he set out for Roedean.

He took the route that Emma had taken on Tuesday. Then it had been warm and Emma had reported that the beach had been full of tourists. But today the weather was very different, the rain that started that night still showed no sign of stopping. Edgar plodded on with his head down, water running off the brim of his hat. The beach and the promenade were deserted, deckchairs flapping in the wind, cafes already shutting for the night. An ice cream van trundled mournfully past playing "I've Got a Lovely Bunch of Coconuts". There was no way anyone was going to be out walking today, but Edgar was determined at least to reach Duke's Mound. He got there at last, conscious that one of his shoes had sprung a leak. He looked up at the path between the dripping bushes. Could someone have been hiding there on Tuesday evening, lying in wait for Emma? Except that this wasn't her normal route home. She usually walked along the coast road or caught the bus. Did that leave the woman in a green coat? Could this mysterious personage have been Haystack or even Tol in disguise? Haystack's alibi depended on a doorman who, from Max's account, could easily be bought. Tol depended on his daughter, not a woman who struck Edgar as incorruptible. Could the attacker have been Astarte herself? But she was a slight girl and the doctor said that Emma had been hit

260

with some force. And why would Astarte attack Emma in the first place? By now Edgar was distinctly wet around the edges. He didn't want to turn up at Emma's house looking like a complete derelict. He took the steps up to the coast road and waited for the bus.

The first surprise was that the door was opened by a servant. At first he'd thought that the elderly woman was Emma's grandmother but when he'd asked for Emma, she'd said, "Miss Emma can't see anyone today" and looked as if she was about to shut the door in his face. Did anyone still have servants in 1953? He was always reading that those days were gone for good. It reminded him of Velma Edwards and her maid, Charlene: "Miss Velma is resting."

"It's Detective Inspector Stephens, from the police station," he said, as ingratiatingly as possible. "I won't stay long." He proffered the flowers as a sign of his good intentions.

The maid looked undecided but then a voice called, "Who is it, Ada?" and Sybil Holmes floated onto the scene.

"Inspector Stephens! Do come in. Has Ada been keeping you on the mat?"

"You said yourself that Emma needed to rest today. She shouldn't be out of hospital by rights." Whatever her status in the house, Ada was evidently a woman of strong opinions.

"I'm sure she'll want to see Inspector Stephens. Come this way, Inspector. Ada will take your hat and coat."

Relinquishing his sodden outer garments, Edgar followed Emma's mother into the house.

Sybil pushed open the door of a room so large that Edgar couldn't at first see Emma. Then he spotted her, sitting on a window seat with her knees drawn up. The views — across the golf course and out to sea — were probably spectacular on a fine day but today the sea and the sky were both the same steely unrelenting grey, as grey as the rain sluicing against the windows. No wonder Emma looked rather tired and washed out herself. But she coloured when she saw him and jumped up. She was wearing three-quarter length trousers and a white jumper and looked much younger than usual. Her hair was in a ponytail and he could see the graze on her forehead where she had fallen.

"How are you?" he said. "These are for you." Remembering the flowers.

"I'll take them, darling," said Sybil. "Can I get you anything, Inspector Stephens? Tea? Coffee? Martini? Can I tempt you to a cocktail?"

"No, thank you very much. And do call me Edgar."

"I'll just put these in water." Edgar could see Emma relaxing as soon as her mother left the room. She had also winced at the mention of cocktails. For his part, Edgar thought that Sybil Holmes was charming. He often wished he had someone to offer him a martini when he came home from work in the evening.

They sat on one of the two sofas either side of a marble, art deco fireplace. The house was twenties' hacienda style with white walls and a green tiled roof, and Gothic touches — leaded light windows and exposed beams. It was not exactly cosy but it was certainly luxurious. As well as the sofas, the sitting room also boasted an oak drinks cabinet, a grand piano and a vast radiogram. This reminded Edgar of something.

"Have you got a television set?" he asked.

"There's one in Daddy's study. Mummy thinks it's so ugly that she's made little curtains for it."

Edgar thought of the three sets fighting for space in Bill Hitchcock's sitting room. He saw them now as rather sinister objects, snake oil salesmen planning to ensnare innocent viewers. He told Emma about the reappearance of Charlie Haystack.

"I can't believe it," she said. "I can't believe he just turned up at your door like that."

"It was incredible. The strangest thing was that he still looked just like the general. I found myself treating him like a general and not like a conman."

"Is that what he is, a conman?"

"It's part of what he is," said Edgar. "He certainly conned Max and me. But he does seem to genuinely believe in this conspiracy. He's convinced that Colonel Cartwright was murdered because he'd discovered something. He thinks this group is going to do something to disrupt the coronation."

"What?"

"I don't know. That's the frustrating thing. But Haystack used to belong to an anarchist group. He said that they were against violence but that there were other groups who wanted to bring down society by

263

whatever means possible. You're always hearing about anarchists making bombs, aren't you?"

"It can be a peaceful philosophy," said Emma, frowning as she always did when she was thinking. "Didn't Kant define anarchy as 'law and freedom without force'?"

"I've no idea," said Edgar. Though he had studied PPE at Oxford for two terms.

"I read that the rebels in the Spanish Civil War were anarchists at first," said Emma. "Stalin refused to help them unless they had leaders and a hierarchy."

"Apparently Bill Hitchcock used to be a communist," said Edgar. "But he became disillusioned by Stalin."

"And Haystack thought that Hitchcock was linked with these anarchists?"

"He didn't know. The only clue was the newspaper cutting by Colonel Cartwright's bed. The one mentioning a woman fainting at Bill Hitchcock's show. That's why he hit on the idea of getting me to go to America to investigate. He could get me a passport because he works, quite legitimately, in the passport office."

"Why didn't he go himself? He could have just pretended to be a policeman in the same way that he pretended to be a general."

"That did occur to me," said Edgar. "I think it was because Cartwright had talked to him about the Magic Men, the group Max and I were involved with in the war. It probably gave him an inflated idea of our capabilities."

He was aware that he'd never told Emma anything about the Magic Men and he hoped that she wouldn't ask any questions now. It wasn't that he was ashamed of the Magic Men, exactly. It was more that those days seemed so impossibly far away. How to explain to Emma, who was a child when the war started, about those desperate days when it seemed that defeat was imminent and about the strange surreal time in Inverness when Max and his show-business friends tried to defeat Hitler by the deployment of stage magic? To his relief, Emma said only, "What about when you were in America? Were there any signs that Hitchcock was involved in anything shady?"

Edgar told her about O'Grady and O'Flynn and their idea of Hitchcock as a dangerous red. He told her about the hit-and-run driver who nearly killed him and about Velma Edwards and Genevieve Moretti. He even told her about the subliminal advertising and Detroit's youngest snake charmer. He realised that this was the most that he had talked about his American trip to anyone, even Max. Telling the story out loud gave it shape in his mind too. He wondered why Colonel Cartwright had chosen that particular newspaper story.

"If someone killed Bill Hitchcock then there must be something to this plot," said Emma. "Someone killed Madame Zabini too, I'm sure of it. From the way people talked about her at the funeral, she was the last person to have killed herself."

"And someone attacked you," said Edgar. Emma's black eye was greenish now but her pale skin still showed the cuts and grazes from her fall on Duke's Mound. "Can you remember anything else about that?"

"No," said Emma. "I keep thinking about it though. I can't sleep because I . . ." She stopped and Edgar thought that she sounded as if she was about to cry. But, when she spoke again, her voice was back to normal, calm and slightly brisk.

"What have we got?" she asked him, rhetorically he assumed. "Let's make a list." Edgar suppressed a smile as Emma fetched her notebook from the window ledge where it had evidently been sitting beside her.

She wrote:

Charlie Halász, aka Charlie Haystack
Bill Hitchcock
Tony Mulholland and the others on the playbill
Tol Barton

"And Velma Edwards," said Edgar, "and Genevieve Moretti. It's never a good idea to forget the women. Max told me that once."

"Then we should add Astarte Zabini," said Emma, "and Isobel Zabini too. Maybe neither of them were strong enough to attack me but they could certainly have ordered someone else to do it. The funeral was full of uncles and cousins. Any of them could have done it."

"I'll talk to the Zabinis again," said Edgar. "Tol must remember something about the anarchist group. Though whether he'll tell me is another matter."

"I could try," said Emma, flushing slightly. "I think he quite liked me."

"He did," said Edgar. "He told Bob that he did."

"I bet Bob loved that."

"He looked very jealous," Edgar assured her. Then he said, rather hesitantly, "We could go to see Tol on Monday. I was going to tell you to take the day off. After all, you'll have Tuesday off for the coronation."

"I don't want another day off," said Emma, with some heat. "I'm coming into work whatever happens."

Edgar imagined that this idea would meet with some opposition at home but, knowing Emma, he had no doubt at all that she would turn up for work on Monday.

CHAPTER
TWENTY-SEVEN

There were times when Emma thought that the weekend would never end. Her parents, horrified at the thought of her going back to work, continued to fuss and treat her like an invalid. As for Ada, she seemed to take it as a personal affront if Emma's feet ever touched the floor. "Put your feet up, Miss Emma," was her constant refrain. Emma spent Saturday and Sunday reading and making notes about the case. At least her convalescence meant she could escape the dinner party her mother had planned for Saturday. Instead she sat in her room listening to the laughter and clinking glasses and feeling like Mrs Rochester. To add to the gloom, the rain continued intermittently all weekend and, by Monday, not even the most optimistic newspapers were predicting that the sun would shine on the new Queen.

It had been strange seeing the DI here, in the house. She had worked so hard, over the last two years, to keep her home and work life separate that it seemed wrong, somehow, to see him walking into the sitting room, tall, sandy-haired, slightly rumpled, and to hear her mother offering him a cocktail as if he were just another caller, as if he were a *guest*. She'd been embarrassed because she was wearing Capri pants and hadn't washed her hair. But, of course, the DI had hardly looked at her. He'd simply called round to see how she was and to keep her up to date with the case. And she was grateful, she really was. She'd fetched her notebook, like a good little sergeant, to show that she knew that it was work and nothing else. And she was fascinated by the latest development, Charlie Haystack turning up out of the blue. If the DI thought she was going to stay home for another day and let Bob have all the fun, well he had another think coming.

Her father insisted on driving her into the station so she was there early. The DI was already at his desk, reading what looked like a book about advertising.

"Oh hallo," he said, looking up. "How are you?"

"I'm fine," said Emma firmly, averting her eyes from the photograph of Ruby that was flashing its starlet smile from the desk.

"Are you sure you're OK?" said Bob, when he turned up. "The DI and I could have coped without you for another day."

"I'm fine." Emma's patience was wearing thin by this time. "And you don't seem to be solving the case very fast without me."

She persuaded DI Stephens to let her see Tol on her own. "I think I might get more out of him," she said. She arranged to meet Tol at Marine Parade at ten. "I don't need to be in work until midday," he told her. Bob tried to come with her but only because he wanted to see the inside of the Zabinis' house. As Emma walked from Bartholomew Square in the drizzle it felt as if she was free for the first time in days. At that moment it didn't matter that Edgar was engaged to Ruby and had her picture on his desk. She was doing her job, walking through town in the rain when everyone else was imprisoned in their house or office. She felt, if not deliriously happy, then steadily content.

The feeling lasted right until the moment when Tol opened the door, dark and saturnine in his chefs trousers and a blue jumper.

"Is it still raining?" he said, watching Emma shake out her umbrella.

"Yes," she said, "they say it'll definitely rain tomorrow too."

"Good," said Tol. "I'm a republican myself."

For the first time, he led her through to the back of the house, into the kitchen. "Astarte's doing a reading upstairs," he explained.

"Is she taking over your mother's business already?" asked Emma. "What about the caravan?"

"We'll get her a new caravan," said Tol. "I've got a carpenter working on an exact replica. But the business won't wait for that. Astarte's got a backlog of clients. You'd be surprised how desperate people are to consult a medium."

It was impossible to tell from his tone whether he thought these people were fools or not. Emma had no idea whether he even believed in his daughter's mediumistic abilities. She suspected that, for Tol, the whole thing was a commercial venture. Build Astarte a caravan and let her carry on with the lucrative family business. She wondered whether a gypsy fortune-teller earned more than a chef.

270

The kitchen was a large, dark room. The architects of the Marine Parade terrace had evidently concentrated their decorative talents on the front rooms with their corniced ceilings and sea views. They probably expected the kitchens to be occupied by servants and had subsequently wasted no time on making them agreeable spaces. The windows looked out into a yard where, on a day like today, not a ray of natural light could be seen. The room itself, with its old-fashioned range and wooden surfaces, could have come from another century. Tol waved Emma to a chair at the table.

"Do you want some tea?" he asked. "Astarte gets this herbal stuff sent by a slow boat from China."

"No, thank you very much," said Emma. She wouldn't trust Astarte's tea not to contain some oriental hallucinogenic drug.

"How are you?" asked Tol. "I was sorry to hear what happened."

Emma was surprised. Tol sounded genuinely sympathetic and his strange, turquoise eyes looked almost kind.

"I'm fine," she said, for what felt like the hundredth time that morning. "It was just cuts and bruises really."

"Astarte can find you some cream for that eye. An old gypsy remedy. It really works."

Unconsciously Emma raised her hand to her face. She felt the same about Astarte's remedies as she did about her tea. Her mother would say that gypsies knew about black eyes because the men were always hitting the women.

271

"I've got some cream," she said, "from the doctor." Tol smiled but said nothing. Emma decided to dive straight in.

"I wanted to ask you about the anarchist group that you belonged to during the war," she said.

To her surprise, Tol threw back his head and laughed. "The anarchist group that I belonged to. You make it sound like the bloody boy scouts."

Emma told herself not to rise. "You don't deny that you were part of such a group then?"

Tol stopped laughing. "No, I don't deny it. I was in the catering corps. If you want to get a deep and enduring dislike for the human race, try feeding them for a while."

"Is that what made you an anarchist? A deep and enduring dislike for the human race?"

"Partly," said Tol. "I hate rules and regulations and the army's full of that. Why should I salute some bastard just because he's got a bit of material sewn on his shoulder? How come, if you went to the right school, you became an officer automatically but if you're working class you're stuck as a private for ever, however brave or intelligent you are? I'd have volunteered for the RAF if they'd have let me fly one of their bloody planes. But no, it was all these Pilot Officer Prune types with their moustaches and their 'prangs' and 'whizzos'. It made me sick."

Tol sounded like a child, thought Emma. "I'd have played their game if they'd let me be in charge." Nevertheless, she'd met a few ex-RAF types at her parents' house and she had no difficulty in recognising the species.

"Tell me about the group," she said. "I know Charles Halász was a member."

"There you go again," said Tol. "Members, rules. Next thing you'll be asking me if we had little badges." Then, taking pity on her, "There were a group of Roma refugees that used to meet at Mum's house before the war. Charlie was one of them and there were a few other music hall performers, most of them foreign like Charlie, Roman and Renée Szolnoki and Pieter Raydini. Even I was on the stage briefly."

"You were? What did you do?"

"I had a knife-throwing act." Tol laughed. "I wasn't very good. One night I nearly took my partner's eye out. I couldn't go onto a stage after that so I turned my talents with a knife into chopping food. But my point is that these people weren't anarchists, they were just dreamers. They talked about the brotherhood of nations, no more war, all that codswallop. Charlie and Roman were briefly interned on the Isle of Wight. That might have hardened them up a bit. Roman was treated pretty badly and died soon afterwards. I don't know what the rest of them did, I lost contact with them during the war. I knew Charlie had kept in touch with Mum though. He was very fond of her."

"Were you involved with any other anarchist groups?" asked Emma. "After the war, perhaps?"

This time Tol paused before answering. And, uncharacteristically, he started to fiddle with a cigarette case that had been left on the table.

"I did join a group in London for a while," he said. "They were much more serious. They talked about doing something really big to make an impact."

"What sort of thing?" asked Emma.

"You know." Tol fixed her with that strange stare again. "Blowing up some big national event."

"Like the coronation?"

"Exactly like the coronation."

"Who was in the group, this serious group?" asked Emma. Then, when Tol hesitated, "You must tell me. People's lives could be in danger."

"I'm not holding back on you, Emma," said Tol. "We used aliases. I don't think I knew anyone's real name. But there were some pretty high-up people in the group. Politicians, policemen, civil servants."

"Colonel Cartwright, Charlie's friend who died, he thought he'd discovered a plot to disrupt the coronation. Do you know anything about that?"

"No." Tol held her gaze. "But it sounds just the sort of thing this group would do. I stopped going to meetings after a while. It was too rich for my blood. Now I'm an armchair anarchist."

Emma matched him stare for stare. Was Tol telling the truth? Was he really living a blameless life in Brighton, chef, caring father, gypsy businessman? Or was he still in touch with his old anarchist friends? He'd known where Charlie Haystack lived but hadn't told them until the DI had leant on him a bit. Emma didn't think that he was above holding things back from the police.

It seemed important to keep the eye contact but, just when Emma thought she would have to blink, she heard voices in the hall and the front door opening and shutting. Then Astarte wafted into the kitchen. She was evidently wearing her fortune-teller's costume, a long blue robe embroidered with runic symbols. It didn't take away from her ethereal beauty but it did make her look as if she was in fancy dress.

"All right?" said Tol, sounding completely normal.

"Fine," said Astarte. She opened her palm to show her father the note that was in it. He grunted approval.

"Tea anyone?" said Astarte, getting a red tin out of the larder.

"Emma doesn't trust your tea," said Tol. Though Emma hadn't said as much, this was close enough to the truth to make her blush.

"You should let me read the cards for you." Astarte looked at Emma. "I know there's a question you want to ask."

"I want answers to a lot of questions," said Emma.

Max had now heard the old adage about a bad dress rehearsal meaning a good first night rather too many times for comfort. Of course, a traditional dress rehearsal only had to cope with missed cues, ill-fitting costumes and stagehands who had overindulged in the pub at lunchtime. The dress rehearsal for a television show seemed to involve endless pauses while the technicians moved cameras about and long consultations between Derek Conroy and an individual called the Lighting Engineer. Max soon gave up and sat in the stalls with Sofija, one of the Bulgarian contortionists whom he'd employed to be his assistant. Sofija stretched her long legs onto the chair in front and offered Max some chewing gum.

"I'm giving up smoking," she said. "This helps."

"No thank you." Max remembered American troops in the war, their jaws working continually as they masticated their gum. He thought it made them look like cattle, buffalo most likely. He swore then that he'd never chew gum. Or give up smoking.

Ruby, wearing a red silk dress with a bustle, swished down the aisle to join them.

"What are they doing now?" she asked.

"Sorting out their uppers and their downers," said Max. "Something like that anyway."

"It's so boring," said Ruby. "We haven't got halfway through the first half yet."

Ruby was the next act on. Max wondered if she was nervous. If so, she didn't show it. He felt very proud of his daughter and, for a moment, wished that everyone in the theatre knew the truth about their relationship.

"You do magic, yes?" asked Sofija.

"Yes," said Ruby. "It's not the same as Max's magic though."

"Max is a master magician," said Sofija.

"It's as good," said Ruby, lifting her chin. "It's just different."

"Hi, beautiful." Both Ruby and Sofija looked round but Max had recognised the voice and was hoping that it would go away.

No such luck. "Hallo, Maxie — Sorry, Max. How are my favourite clients today?"

"We're fine, Joe," said Max. "How are you?"

"Busy, Max, busy. The showbiz world doesn't run itself, you know." Joe sat in the row in front and placed his soft-brimmed hat on his knees. Did he really believe that he alone turned the wheels of the entertainment world? Max had an uneasy feeling that this was exactly what Joe Passolini did believe.

"How's the dress rehearsal?"

"Boring," said Sofija, yawning dramatically. Max saw Joe's eyes focus on the rise and fall of the acrobat's chest.

"Joe Passolini." He extended a hand. "You must be an actress with a face like that."

Max hadn't noticed Joe looking at her face but Sofija didn't seem to mind. She gave Joe the benefit of her heavy-lidded stare.

"I act, yes," she said. "I also sing and dance and do acrobatics. Today I am Max's assistant."

"Are you, now? Well Max certainly knows how to pick 'em. If you're ever in need of an agent." He handed over his card.

"Thanks," said Sofija, tossing her hair, but Max saw her carefully tuck the card into the top of her basque. He knew that Joe had noticed too.

"Have you been on yet, Ruby?" Joe seemed to think he was in danger of ignoring his other favourite client and, indeed, Ruby was looking a little cross. Or maybe she was just nervous.

"I'm up next," she said.

"Then I'm just in time." Joe settled back in his seat.

"Ruby!" Derek shouted from the stage. "We're ready for you now."

Ruby got up and smoothed her skirts. Ignoring Joe's "Break a leg, beautiful", she walked to the front and climbed onto the stage from what used to be the orchestra pit. The pit was now full of cameras and one camera on a movable platform followed Ruby as she walked across the stage. She didn't seem nervous now, thought Max, with another surge of pride. Ruby waited until the spotlight was shining on her and Derek called out "Action!" before she smiled, straight into the one eye of the camera lens.

"Hallo. I'm Ruby French and I'd like to do some magic for you."

As she spoke Ruby spread out the fan in her hand. One twist and the fan became a mirror. Ruby then turned round (Max winced, brought up in the tradition that you never turned your back on the audience) and held up the mirror so that it reflected her vivid little face: black hair piled up at the back, red lips, smoky eyes. As she held up the mirror it showed something else. An evil face, white with devilish brows, the wicked witch from *Snow White*. Next to Max, Sofija gasped and, from the row in front, Joe gave a bark of laughter. Then Ruby put down the hand mirror and turned as the stagehands wheeled a full-size mirror onto the set.

It was a clever act. It played with the whole "They Do It With Mirrors" idea — the Agatha Christie novel of the same name had come out the year before. Ruby looked at herself in the mirror, just as if she was at her dressing table at home except, of course, that the audience and the TV cameras were watching her too. Reflection upon reflection, like the Hall of Mirrors at a fun fair. There was also a kind of Alice in Wonderland feel as Ruby stepped into the mirror at one point and came out dressed in completely different clothes, a white dress that would show up well on the black and white screen. Max, watching more critically than he could admit even to himself, thought that the magic was fairly simple. It was a real mirror only part of the time, sometimes it reflected the person standing behind it — stagehands dressed respectively as the wicked witch, a fairy and the handsome prince. It worked because Ruby looked so enchantingly pretty and because, in her alternating red and white dress, she seemed both innocent and knowing, both architect and victim of the trick. When she finished there was an unprecedented round of applause from the technical crew. Ruby curtsied and blew a kiss to Max.

"Does she love you?" asked Sofija.

"She's my daughter," said Max, suddenly not caring if Sofija knew the truth.

"That's what they all say," said Sofija, not believing it for a minute.

All this made Max slightly nervous for his own rehearsal. His moment didn't come until late in the afternoon, after the Fantinis had swooped through the rafters not once but three times so that Derek could get the camera angles right. Max, watching the Italians climb the ropes muttering Neapolitan swearwords under their breath, thought that the viewing public would never have the true experience of watching the acrobats. From where Max sat there was always the chance that Marco or his sons would lose their footing and fall into the seats below. But, live or not, the television would only show the finished act and the viewers would always know that it ended well, that Marco would catch Pietro's outstretched hands as they flew through the air. There was no jeopardy, not of the genuine fear felt by audiences in the early days of variety. Max had once seen a fire-eater catch light on stage, sustaining third degree burns. Television viewers would never know entertainment like that.

The auditorium seemed very full as Max made his way onto the stage. Rather to his surprise, Joe was still there, now sitting next to Ruby and whispering things that seemed to make her laugh a good deal. As Max watched, Reenie, Derek's wife, came to join them. She too said something to Ruby that made her smile and blush. Tommy Lang was sitting behind them, as anxious-looking as ever. Next to Tommy sat Jim Jones, Reggie the dummy on his knee. Max could hear the deep contralto laugh of Leonora Lorenzo and the Russian voices of Olga and Natasha. The pros were out in force, all right. Were they willing him on or were they secretly hoping that tonight would be the night when it would all go wrong, when the great Max Mephisto would take off his top hat to find it completely devoid of rabbits? Max thought he knew the answer to that one.

Max climbed onto the stage, trying to forget his fellow performers, the cameras, the extra lights and

Derek Conroy watching from the dress circle balcony. The orchestra, from their cramped quarters in the front rows of the stalls, played the "Danse Macabre" and he was off. It was a fairly simple routine. Some sleight-of-hand tricks at first and then the main event. The stagehands wheeled on the cabinet made to look like three television sets piled on top of each other. Then Sofija stepped inside and, through the glass screens, the audience could see her face, torso and legs. With much flourishing Max pulled out the middle set and, though it was halfway across the stage, the screen still showed Sofia's trim gymnast's stomach. The other sets showed, of course, her smiling face and shapely legs. It was a trick that depended on the girl. Not just Sofija but Emiliya and Ivana, her sisters who were inside the other boxes. Otherwise it was a fairly standard illusion, lots of theatre from Max but mainly relying on a clever cabinet and some very supple contortionists. Still, he got a very generous round from the auditorium, and even the crew clapped, so Max hoped that it would also impress the television viewers tomorrow.

Derek Conroy came down from the box to congratulate him.

"Just what we need to close the show. Fantastic stuff."

"Thank you."

"I think we've got a real winner here."

"I hope so."

"Your Ruby, she's a bit of a star too, isn't she?"

"She certainly is."

281

"It's a pity we can't put you together, a father and daughter act."

Max looked down towards the back rows of the stalls where Ruby was still laughing with Joe. Reggie, the ventriloquist's dummy, was watching them with a rather lascivious expression on his face.

"I think Ruby will make it to the top without me," said Max.

It felt a bit like sour grapes but it was almost certainly the truth.

Edgar rang Mike Moretti at two p.m., when he calculated that it would be nine a.m. in Albany. Mike answered immediately.

"Moretti TV repairs."

"Mike. It's Edgar. From England."

"Oh." Mike did not sound particularly friendly. Maybe he was wondering why Edgar was telephoning him again.

"How's Genevieve?"

"She's home from hospital. The doctors say she needs to rest. But the baby's OK."

"I'm really glad to hear that," said Edgar. "I just wanted to ask you a question."

"About Genevieve?"

"Well, partly about her. When she was in England before the war, did Genevieve know a woman called Doreen Barton? She may have known her as Madame Zabini."

"Auntie Doreen? Yes, she was the old dear that Genevieve stayed with. Nice old thing."

282

"Did Genevieve say anything about anyone else staying with Doreen, perhaps being part of a political group?"

Mike laughed. Either it was genuine amusement or Mike was a better actor than he appeared. "Politics? Genny? Do me a favour."

"Can I ask you something about Velma Edwards?"

"I hardly know her but shoot."

"You mentioned that Bill Hitchcock had made Mrs Edwards sing a song when she was hypnotised. Do you remember the song? I think you said it was about a Christmas tree."

"I couldn't quite hear the words but I think it was the Tannenbaum song. You know the one." Mike sang a few bars of "O Christmas Tree".

"Thanks," said Edgar. "Give Genevieve my best. Hope all goes well."

"Thanks," said Mike. "I'll tell her you rang."

Edgar was still humming the song when he put the receiver down. "O Christmas Tree" or, possibly, "The Red Flag", the communist party anthem. Which words had Velma sung and what was the message that Bill was trying to convey to her and to the wider world? That Velma Edwards, ex-burlesque star and pillar of the community, was also a communist? He wondered again why Colonel Cartwright had kept the newspaper cutting. Was it for the mesmerist or for the victim? And who had sent it to him? Could it have been Bill Hitchcock himself?

Bob knocked on the door. "We're having a whip-round for beer tomorrow," he said. "Do you want to contribute?" Edgar put in half a crown. "Have a good time," he said.

"Aren't you coming?"

"No, I'm going to my mother's in Esher."

"Emma's not coming either. She says she's going horse riding. *Horse riding*." Bob sounded quite disgusted. Edgar couldn't image Emma riding, but then he couldn't exactly imagine her sitting down to watch the coronation either. He was ashamed of hoping for an emergency in Brighton that would prevent him having to make the journey to Surrey. He'd also told Ruby that he'd be at the Empire, Shepherd's Bush, that evening, for *Those Were the Days*. "Don't the audience have to be in costume?" he'd asked. "Oh, they'll give you a scarf or something," said Ruby. "Promise you'll be there." And Edgar had promised.

"It'll be a good show," said Bob. "We're all going to wear Union Jack hats."

"It sounds a lot of fun," said Edgar hollowly.

CHAPTER
TWENTY-EIGHT

Coronation Day, 2 June 1953

Edgar arrived in Esher at ten o'clock. His mother greeted him at the door. "You're late. I was worried it would start without you."

"No, I'm exactly on time," said Edgar. "I said I'd be here at ten." Even as he said this, he knew it was a wasted effort. In Rose's eyes visitors were always late, unless they were inconveniently early, of course.

"Television started at nine-thirty," said Rose. "I've got a good signal now."

The television was in the sitting room, facing the sofa and the armchair. It seemed odd to see this little box as the focal point of the room. Previously all the chairs had pointed towards the electric fire and the radiogram. The bulbous little screen showed a cubist pattern of lines and squares which Edgar recognised as the test card.

"Coverage starts at ten-fifteen," said Rose. "I've got the *Radio Times* here." She pointed to the coffee table which also bore a selection of plates containing strange, frivolous food: cheese and pineapple chunks, melon squares, salmon mousse.

"Marguerite Patten was on the television last night," said Rose, "telling us how to prepare tasty snacks to eat while we're watching. They're making a special chicken dish for the street party. It's called Coronation Chicken."

Television, Edgar soon learnt, was Rose's new oracle. Since she had bought the set she had watched it almost constantly and it was now the source of all wisdom, not just about the coronation, but also about history, politics, household tips and how to turn those leftovers into a nourishing meal for all the family. Edgar was torn between irritation and pleasure that his mother seemed finally to have a new interest in her life beyond visiting the "incurables" and disagreeing with her friend Millie White.

"The mousse is delicious," he said untruthfully. It had an odd, rather metallic, aftertaste. "What time's the street party?"

"It's at three o'clock," said Rose, "to give us time to watch the ceremony at the abbey. There are trestle tables all the way up the High Street. They've been setting it up since eight o'clock."

"It's a shame about the rain," said Edgar.

"Oh, Jack Armstrong on the television said it would clear up by the afternoon," said Rose.

"I'll have to leave at about six," said Edgar. "Ruby is appearing in a show at the Empire and I promised I'd be there."

He had expected Rose to be angry. No, he had expected her to be disappointed, often her default position with regard to her children. Jonathan had

286

disappointed her by dying in the war, Lucy by marrying and moving to Herefordshire, Edgar by becoming a policeman. But, even as Rose's face fell into sad lines, something happened to smooth them out again. She smiled, and her eyes almost sparkled.

"The show at the Empire, is it on television?"

"Yes. It's called *Those Were the Days*."

"I thought so. It's in the *Radio Times*." Rose found the relevant page. "Old time music hall. Your friend Max Mephisto is in it."

"That's right."

"I'll watch it," said Rose. "Maybe I'll see you in the audience."

Edgar didn't think that this was in the least likely but he saw no point in damping Rose's unexpected cheerful attitude.

"Maybe you will," he said. "If I see a camera I'll wave at it."

Emma had been telling the truth about the horse riding. Her old schoolfriend Vera had two horses in livery near Rottingdean, and they had planned to spend the day riding and avoiding the coronation. Emma faced some routine opposition from her parents but, as her mother claimed to find the coronation depressing ("That poor girl, condemned to a lifetime of terrible clothes"), they hadn't planned anything special for the day. Emma knew that, sometime during the morning, Sybil would pull back the curtains on the little television and watch the ceremony, but she was prepared to go along with the fantasy that her parents would spend the day "doing little chores around the house". They would be alone as Ada was visiting her sister in Streatham to watch her television and attend a street party.

"I'm sure there'll be parties in Brighton," said Sybil. "There's an Old Time Ball at the Palais."

Emma shuddered. "There's a party at the police station. That's why I'm going riding."

"Well, be careful," said her mother. "Make sure you wear a hard hat. The last thing you want to do is hurt your head again."

And it had been lovely to get out of town, to walk up to the stables at the top of Steyning Road, to tack up the horses in the straw-scented stables, smelling the leather and hearing the chink of harness and remembering childhood riding lessons ("Legs, girl, legs! Where's your impulsion?"). Vera was mounted on a rather showy bay mare called Tempest but Emma was given a much quieter horse, a skewbald cob called Toby. She loved Toby already, the way his mane stood up in a crest, the way he sighed patiently when she got on board, the way he immediately started eating the hanging basket in the stable yard.

"Show him who's boss," said Vera, as she opened the gate with much curvetting and mane-tossing from Tempest.

Emma thought that it was already obvious who was boss. But she suggested to Toby that they follow his stablemate into the twitten. Maybe, instead of becoming a nun, she should become one of those leathery horsewomen, wearing breeches every day and

288

talking about martingales and strangles. She wondered what the DI was doing. He said he was visiting his mother in Esher. At least he wasn't spending the day with Ruby, but Bob had told her that Ruby was appearing in a TV show that evening. "She's becoming a star," said Bob, clearly besotted with Ruby after one evening in her company. Edgar would either be watching his fiancée on television or in the audience, clapping and cheering, possibly throwing roses. She sighed and pulled Toby's head up from the grass verge.

"Gee up," she said, kicking him on. Toby's ears flickered but he consented to plod along the lane. It was raining quite heavily now and Emma's thighs were already aching. Becoming a horsewoman, like becoming a nun, was obviously harder than it first appeared.

Max was not quite sure how he came to be in a church. He only knew that, as the day went on, he found himself assailed by the coronation on all sides. He had thought that he'd be safe at the Strand Palace but, after breakfast, the waiters started setting up a screen in the lounge and Old Alphonse at the piano was plinking his way through "Land of Hope and Glory". Max set off along the Strand determined to find a patriotism-free zone. He had various friends around the city but he had a nasty feeling that all of them — even Juan the Spanish communist — would be watching the television today. Ed was watching with his mother in Esher, and Ruby was watching in Brighton with Emerald and her stepfather, even though she had to catch the train to London later in the afternoon. Mrs M wouldn't be watching — she didn't own a set for one thing — but she'd be looking after her guests. The lodging house was full all week.

All the theatres and cinemas, seemed to be showing special screenings of the coronation. As Max passed the Odeon on Leicester Square the queues were already stretching into Cranbourn Street, despite the rain which had been falling steadily all morning. From pubs, bars and coffee shops he could hear the same trumpet music blasting out. Even Bertorelli's wasn't immune, with Union Jack bunting outside and the same sonorous music within. Eventually he found himself in Soho Square. Here, at least, the atmosphere was debauched rather than patriotic. A group of sailors and good time girls were drinking in the square. As he walked past, one of the girls performed the flying splits with an agility that made him think that she must have been on the boards once. "Hallo, handsome," shouted another. Max wished that he could disappear into a dark pub, drink whisky and think about the evening's show. But he couldn't trust any of the pubs — even in Soho — not to be showing the bloody coronation. So instead, almost without knowing it, he found himself heading towards a sign for St Patrick's Roman Catholic church. Here, at least, there wouldn't be a television set.

Inside, the scent of candles and incense was like balm. Max sat at the back and wondered if he dared light a cigarette. He had a far-off memory of being in a church like this with his mother. The voices in the background sounded musical and foreign. Was it in

Italy or just a Catholic church in England? The language could have been Latin rather than Italian. Maybe this was why he found churches so soothing. Once he had dimly associated the Virgin Mary with his own mother. Now they were both just memories. He had started doing card tricks after his mother died. She'd taught him to play cards, using an Italian pack that were rather like tarot cards: the staves, the cups, the swords, the golden *denari*. He remembered playing a game called *scopa* during long wet afternoons at his father's country house. Surely his mother had been bored and depressed too? Maybe that was why she had spent so much time with her infant son. Why hadn't she been content with that, just the two of them playing cards on the window seat? But no, she had to get pregnant again, dying in childbirth alongside his baby sister. Max took the pack of cards out of his pocket. Hearts, clubs, diamonds, spades. Cards had been his escape, his refuge. Also, he'd known that his father was distrustful of any game of chance or skill — his idea of sport was blasting defenceless birds with a twelve-bore shotgun. For Max, being able to turn the queen of hearts into the king of clubs had been a way of bending the world to his will. He still remembered the look of resentful bewilderment on his father's face as he tried to work out exactly what had happened to the card he had carefully chosen (he always went for the nine of clubs; an odd choice). Max never tired of seeing that expression.

"Are you all right, my son?"

Max swiftly palmed the cards. He turned to see a slim, dark man in a clerical collar smiling down at him.

"I'm fine, thank you, Father."

"The peace is very welcome, isn't it?" said the priest.

"Yes," said Max. "The outside world is rather overexcited today."

"It is indeed. But there's no harm in excitement, after all."

Was this true? thought Max. Wasn't excitement just another word for hysteria? He could imagine the crowds outside turning nasty, given the chance and a lot more drinking.

"I'm just a bit too old for that sort of excitement," he said.

"We're all children to Him," said the priest, pointing to the high altar. "Stay as long as you want. I'll be in the parish house if you need me."

"Thank you," said Max but the priest had already gone. Afterwards he wondered if he'd imagined him.

The television coverage started at ten-fifteen precisely. A young woman in an evening dress and pearls appeared on the screen to tell them that today was not just a day of general rejoicing but an occasion of deep significance for the British people.

"That's Sylvia Peters," said Rose. "Isn't she lovely?"

"For the first time in history," said Sylvia solemnly, "through the medium of television, the ancient and noble rite of the coronation service will be witnessed by millions of Her Majesty's subjects."

Edgar thought about those millions. Did the crowds include one person who was there not to celebrate but to make a devastating political statement, to blow up innocent people to show their hatred of the new Queen and of the old order? Or would there be a subliminal message on the screen ordering the masses to rise up in revolt? He wondered what Rose would say if he told her what he was thinking. The screen changed to show Buckingham Palace and the departure of the carriages. The Queen, they were informed, was travelling in the Gold State Coach.

"Isn't it wonderful?" said Rose. "Such pageantry."

"Wonderful," said Edgar.

After that it all rather merged into one: the coaches, the madly cheering crowds, Westminster Abbey, the small woman in the long fur-trimmed robes, the phrase "west of the organ screen" which meant, apparently, that most of the action was happening where the audience couldn't see it, the cries of "Vivat Regina". At just after two, the cameras left the abbey and Rose went to repair her face. Edgar sat in front of the television, eating pineapple chunks and wondering if that was it. Did this mean that the great anarchist atrocity was not going to happen after all? Was this what the coronation would mean to generations to come? Crowds, rain, gold carriages, street parties? He hoped so, he really did.

The rain had stopped by the time that they walked to the High Street but a cold wind was blowing and it felt more like March than June. This didn't seem to affect the spirits of the party-goers though. Children sat at the long table, many of them in fancy dress, wearing hats and blowing penny whistles. Millie White greeted them cheerfully, kissing Edgar and telling him that he was more handsome than ever. Then Rose and Millie, together with some other Women's Institute members, busied themselves handing out sausage rolls and egg sandwiches. Edgar felt rather spare until Millie introduced him to the mayor, a stout man wearing his chains of office and a party hat.

"A policeman, eh? Well, you can judge the fancy dress competition."

Edgar thought that this might be one of his most dangerous assignments to date. He was amused to see that many of the children had come dressed as televisions. He supposed it was an easy costume to make, just a cardboard box with some squiggles on it, but it was strange that this object had come to represent the wonder of the new Elizabethan age. But the vicar gave him a bottle of beer and Millie White brought him a paper plate with some Coronation Chicken sandwiches. The sandwiches tasted rather odd — they seemed to include curry powder and raisins as well as cold chicken — but nevertheless Edgar felt his spirits rise. It was mid-afternoon and no one had been killed yet. He thought that he might be about to enjoy the coronation after all.

Max was back at the Strand Palace by two. It was just as well that he didn't mind walking because there was no chance of a taxi, or even a bus. The roads were all full of people, crowds who had watched the coronation in various bars and were now just milling about looking for the next distraction. Oxford Circus had been closed off because the return procession was due to pass that way and eager spectators were packed onto the pavements, waving their little flags and generally enjoying the discomfort. Max took a labyrinthine route, trying to avoid places where there was the slightest chance of hearing people sing "Rule Britannia".

Back at the hotel the lounge was still full of guests watching the big screen. Max asked for some sandwiches and a pot of coffee to be brought up to his room. Waiting for these to be delivered, he smoked a cigarette and played a game of patience. If this comes out, the show will be a success. It came out but only because Max knew how to deal the cards. The sandwiches and coffee arrived, handed over by a harassed-looking bellboy. Max tipped him and sat at the table by the window looking down on the Strand. The street was quite empty, perhaps because everyone was inside watching the television. It would be a different matter when the broadcast was over at five. Max had to be at the Empire by five. He hoped Ruby would get there in time. The train from Brighton would probably be fine but she might have trouble getting transport from Victoria to Shepherd's Bush. He wondered whether he should try to pick her up on his way but that would be hard to coordinate. Besides, she might resent the interference. He'd already gone as far as he dared by booking her a room at the hotel for tonight.

He felt better after eating. In fact, he dropped off to sleep for a while, a practice he deplored. When he woke it was four o'clock. He had a bath and dressed in his usual stage clothes — his top hat and tails were at the theatre. Then he went downstairs to wait for his taxi. He hoped to God that the driver would know a route to West London that avoided the crowds.

"Mr Mephisto?" It was the commissionaire. "Your car's here."

Thank goodness the driver had the sense to arrive early.

"Is it a black cab?" he asked.

"No." The commissionaire sounded quite impressed. "It's a limousine. Sent from the theatre."

Max was impressed. Derek Conroy really knew how to treat his performers. Perhaps he'd even arranged a car for Ruby. He told the commissionaire to cancel his taxi.

The black limousine was waiting at the front. The uniformed chauffeur opened the door for him and Max got in, thinking that his day had suddenly got a whole lot better.

"Do you know a good route to Shepherd's Bush?" he asked the driver. "A lot of the roads in the West End are closed."

"Don't worry, Max," said the driver. "I know the way."

The use of his first name was odd. Max looked up and saw the driver watching him in the mirror. The voice had been strangely familiar but it was not until they were halfway along Victoria Embankment that he recognised Charlie Halász.

CHAPTER
TWENTY-NINE

"What the hell are you playing at?" said Max.

Charlie seemed to be finding something amusing. "You're all just the same. You never really look at the chauffeur, or the waiter or the bellboy. It was the same when I was a general. You just see the uniform and nothing else. This is the same car that took you to Peter Cartwright's flat. The same chauffeur's uniform too. I must say, I'd have thought better of you, Max."

"I'm sorry to disappoint you," said Max. "But what are you doing and where are you taking me?" He wondered whether he should jump out when the car reached the lights but, when he tried the handle, it was locked. The discreet chauffeur had opened the door for him and then, presumably, locked it. And Charlie was right, Max hadn't looked at his face once.

"I'm taking you to the theatre," said Charlie, "so that you can delight and enthral the crowds. That's what you do, isn't it?"

"I try my best," said Max. "You were in the business yourself once, weren't you?"

"I had some small successes," said Charlie, sounding modest. Max wasn't fooled though. There was nothing old pros liked better than talking about their acts. And Charlie was a pro to his fingertips.

"Tommy Lang said you were an impressionist." He knew this would annoy Haystack.

"Lang! He only became an impressionist to copy me. He was a comedian before that and a mighty poor one too. No, I was an *actor*. I didn't just do voices; I became different characters. Paddy O'Reilly, Monsieur Botte de Foin, Old Mario, Evans the sheep, General Petre DSO."

As Charlie said each name, the voice changed. It was rather disconcerting, like a car changing gears — he was doing that too, rather jerkily, as they progressed along the Embankment. General Petre's name came out with a bark and, just for a second, Max saw the patrician old soldier in the driving mirror. He had been completely taken in at the time and the thought annoyed him now.

"Your Italian accent wants some work," he said. "I'd like to know what game you're playing now."

"Not a game," said Charlie, "a warning." He was speaking in his own voice now which, as Edgar had observed, was rather flat and colourless. "I want you to be on your guard at the theatre tonight."

"Why?" said Max. "You'll have to do better than that."

They were setting up the fireworks on Victoria Embankment. Tonight's display was going to be the greatest blaze since the Great Fire of London. Two policemen walked past, exchanging a few words with the men putting up the barriers. Max wondered what they'd do if he wound down the window and shouted that he was being kidnapped.

"In the group," said Charlie at last, "we had a system, a way of communicating, through the small ads in the *Evening Standard*. In yesterday's paper there was an advertisement that said, *Tomorrow's show at the Empire will go with a bang*. So, be on your guard."

"Christ, what can I do if some lunatic anarchists decide to blow the place up? You need to tell the police."

"If I go to the police, they'll kill me."

"Who?"

"The same people who killed Peter. I don't know who they are but I know they'll kill me. They did for that mind reader in America, didn't they?"

"Well, what can I do then?"

"You can keep a lookout. You're a clever fellow, that's what Peter used to say. And your friend Stephens will be there too, won't he? His girlfriend's in the show."

His girlfriend, my daughter, thought Max. For the first time he began to hope that Ruby wouldn't get to the theatre on time.

"You put too much faith in us," he said. "You always have. You've got to give us some more to go on. I may be a magician but there are limits to my powers."

"I don't know any more," said Charlie. "I didn't even know that the group was still in existence until Peter . . . until Peter was murdered. I've no idea who's in it now. The people I knew are all dead. Tol was involved with the London group but they all used aliases. I'd be surprised if even he knew their names."

Max thought furiously as the car took him towards west London. Should he speak to Edgar and get the theatre closed? But what had they got to go on? A few words in the personal ads in the *Evening Standard*. He tried to imagine Derek's face if he told him that the show couldn't go on. "Millions will be watching," he'd said. It would take more than a bomb to stop the BBC's music hall extravaganza.

They were heading along Chelsea Embankment now, making good time.

"Good route," said Max.

"It's the Knowledge, gov," said Charlie, switching to Cockney cab driver persona. "East to west, Embankment's best."

They continued in silence.

It had been a fantastic day. Emma had forgotten the thrill of galloping over the Downs, the wind in your hair, the horse's power beneath you. All right, Toby had got tired of galloping after a few strides and settled for a rolling canter, but that was very pleasant too and much less alarming than Tempest's wild disappearance over the horizon. When they caught up, Tempest was standing by the next gate, pawing the ground. Vera was looking rather wind-swept but she still had some words of advice.

"You should kick him on," she said. "Toby can go faster than that. He takes advantage."

"It was fast enough for me," said Emma, patting Toby's shoulder. "It was wonderful. I love this horse."

"You can come and ride him any time," said Vera, persuading the snorting, sidling Tempest to walk into the gate and open it. "I've got my work cut out with two of them."

"I'd like that," said Emma.

They stopped after a while and ate their sandwiches in a barn, sheltering from the wind and sleeting rain. They took off the horses' saddles and let them drink from the cattle trough. Vera told Emma about her boring job as a secretary and the married man she was seeing.

"He doesn't even lie and say his wife doesn't understand him. He says they're very happy together."

"That makes him honest," said Emma, "but it doesn't make him very nice."

"I know," said Vera, passing Emma the thermos. "I wonder if I'm only seeing him to make the office less dull. Maybe if I had an exciting job like yours. I bet you're too busy for romance."

"That's right," said Emma. She had never told any of her friends about her feelings for Edgar and she wasn't about to start now.

The rain had stopped when they set off again. They had another canter along the edge of a field and Emma pointed out the craters left by Second World War bombs.

"Pilots would jettison them on the Downs, away from the town."

"I wish we'd stayed in Brighton during the war," said Vera. "To think of all those lovely sailors billeted in the school."

"I loved being evacuated," said Emma. "It was the first time I'd been away from home." It was the truth too. Emma thought of those years when the school had been evacuated to the Lake District as the happiest of her life.

It was mid-afternoon when they turned for home. They walked side by side through the lanes, Toby occasionally stopping to shred the leaves off a low-lying branch. The horses speeded up when they recognised the path back to the stables and even Toby broke into a rather spritely trot. Up, down, up, down. Emma struggled to get into the rhythm of it. Tempest was going even faster, skidding slightly on the wet ground. Tempest clattered round the corner first and Emma heard Vera give a cry of surprise; As Toby rounded the bend Emma saw Tempest on her hind legs, objecting to the sudden appearance of a tall, dark-haired man.

"It's all right," said the man, taking hold of Tempest's bridle. "Calm down, nag."

"Thank you." Vera dismounted. "She doesn't like men very much, that's all. Did you want to see me?"

"It's Emma I wanted," said Tol. "Hallo, Emma. I like your circus horse."

"He's called Toby," said Emma. "What do you want?"

"We need to go to London immediately," said Tol. "I think your DI might be in danger."

Edgar left the street party at five. His mother seemed quite happy to see him go. She and Millie were helping to clear up and afterwards Millie was coming back to watch *Those Were the Days* at Rose's house.

"We'll look out for you," said Millie.

"It'll be easy," said Edgar. "I'll be the only one not in costume."

The word costume reminded him of the fancy dress competition. He hadn't made himself popular by choosing a little girl who had come dressed as a playing card, the queen of hearts. "Rather poor taste for a child," sniffed Rose. But Edgar had liked the costume, a simple cardboard square front and back. It reminded him of *Alice in Wonderland* and also of Max describing a card trick. What was it called? Oh yes, the Whispering Queen. *The queen is going to whisper to me, tell me what to do.*

For once, Rose didn't make him feel guilty when he left.

"Thank you for coming," she said. "We had a nice day, didn't we?"

"We did," said Edgar, kissing her on the cheek. "I'll see you again soon."

"Give me a cuddle," said Millie, with the exuberance that often made Rose roll her eyes and talk about lack of breeding. "Rose is lucky to have such a good-looking son."

Was it just cussedness, thought Edgar, as he headed towards the Kingston bypass, that he felt slightly aggrieved that Rose hadn't been sad to see him go? Of course it was good that Rose had her old friend Millie and her new friend, the television set. It would make visits so much easier in. the future. Maybe he should get a set at the flat? He wondered if Ruby would like it. Thinking of Ruby made him drive faster. In a few hours, he would be seeing her.

"What do you mean?" asked Emma, standing by the gate with Toby's reins in her hand. "What do you mean, he's in danger?"

"He's going to this show at the Empire tonight, isn't he? Well, I think something bad might be about to happen. We need to warn him."

"What do you mean, something bad?"

"I'll explain in the car. Can you give the horse to your friend?"

"I'll take him." Vera took the reins, her eyes round and her suspicions about Emma's job confirmed. "You go. It sounds important."

So Emma got into the front seat of Tol's car, the same car that Adam had driven at the funeral.

"How did you know where to find me?" she asked.

"I called in at the station. I thought DI Stephens might be at work but there was a right old shindig going on, coppers in funny hats all over the place. I saw the other sergeant and he told me where you were. He told me where the boss was too."

Thanks, Bob, thought Emma. But it was unlike him to be so free with information. Maybe Tol had hypnotised him. Maybe he had hypnotised her, otherwise what was she doing, sitting in this stranger's car and heading along the Falmer Road towards London?

304

"What is this bad thing that's about to happen?" she asked.

"You remember the anarchist group that you were asking about? They communicate through the small ads in the *Evening Standard*. There was something in yesterday's paper that makes me think that they're going to try something at the Empire. *Tomorrow's show at the Empire will go with a bang.* I only saw it when I went in to do the lunchtime service. The hotel gets the London papers a day late."

"Have you told anyone? The London police?"

"I tried to but they treated me like a nutcase. I tried to get hold of Charlie too but God knows where he is. I thought you were my best bet."

Despite everything, Emma felt rather pleased to hear this. Emma to the rescue. But then she thought, what if the group have already planted the bomb? What if the whole place blows up taking Max, Ruby and the rest of the cast with it? Taking Edgar with it.

She leant forward. "How long will it take to get there?"

"It's nearly four o'clock now," said Tol. "We should be in London by six. The show starts at seven-thirty,"

It was only when they were on the London Road that Emma realised that she would be turning up at the theatre in breeches and mud-splashed boots.

Charlie pulled up smoothly in front of the Empire. Max saw the two huge generators outside, required to run the lights and the cameras. How easy would it be to rig them up so they exploded? He had a feeling that it would be only too possible. He had often used small explosives in his act and, in the war, he had once blown up a whole makeshift town using a remote control device. Who had been the sparks who had worked with him in Egypt? Frankie something, a taciturn Scotsman. Well, he could do with a bit of Frankie's expertise now.

The audience were already queuing, a bizarre sight in their bustles and top hats. Max scanned along the line for Edgar but, of course, he wouldn't be there yet if he was driving from Esher.

"Well, goodbye, Max," said Charlie. "Break a leg."

"You're not coming in then?"

"Not this time, no."

"Well, you'd better get out and open the door for me," said Max.

Some of the crowd looked round in time to see a uniformed chauffeur hold the door open for Max Mephisto. They may also have seen Max lean forward and whisper something in the chauffeur's ear. "Coward," said Max. Then, with a wave towards the queue, Max disappeared through the stage door.

He found Derek Conroy fussing with the lighting rig. The director looked nervous and Max caught a definite whiff of alcohol.

"Max! Glad you made it early. I've been worried about all the road closures."

"That might not be all that you've got to worry about."

"What do you mean?"

Max led the director towards a dark corner of the wings. "Derek, someone has told me that there might be an attack on the theatre tonight."

"An attack? What sort of attack?"

"A bomb, something like that. Have you had any threats, heard any rumours?"

"No." Derek Conroy shook his head. "Why would anyone want to bomb a TV show?"

"For the publicity," said Max. "Is it possible to search the audience as they come in?"

"What? All two thousand of them? You must be joking!"

"Can we get some police reinforcements here then? Even the sight of a policeman might put these people off."

"I'll see what I can do but the police will be busy with all the coronation celebrations."

"Well, can you try? I really think it's important."

It was too dark for Max to see Derek's expression but he could sense his fear and indecision. He tried to make his voice reassuring, perhaps to include a touch of Bill Hitchcock's mesmerism. "Just ring them. Please."

He thought that the director was going to ask another question but then there was a shout of "Derek!" from the stage and, with a muttered "Sorry", Derek Conway hurried away.

Max stood in the dark of the wings. Should he start looking for suspicious boxes? The trouble was that there were so many electrical leads lying about, any one of them could be connected to a device. An infernal machine, that's what they used to call bombs, before everyone got so used to them in the war. He'd read somewhere that you could train dogs to sniff out explosives. Typical, just when he'd got rid of Alfie.

A movement in the back of the wings made him jump.

"Who is it?"

"It's me." Max caught a glimpse of a white shirt and pale face with dark hair. Then he saw a strange triangular shape, wide shoulders, tapered trousers.

"Joe! What are you doing here?"

There was a pause and then Joe said, "Looking for you, me old china."

Then why not look in my dressing room, thought Max. Aloud he said, "Have you seen Ruby?"

"No, not everyone's here yet. I've just seen Papa Fantini and the impressionist. Sofija's here too."

That was a relief. In the worry about the bomb, Max had almost forgotten about the girls. He noticed that Joe had remembered Sofija's name. Had she fished his card from her corset and telephoned him?

"It's going to be a full house," said Passolini. "I've just seen them queuing up outside, all in their Victorian clobber. I tell you, this show's going to be the biggest thing ever."

In other circumstances, Max would have been delighted to know that the theatre was full. Every actor longs to see the "Full House" boards up by the box office. Tonight, though, he would have been happier if a freak hailstorm had kept everyone away. He wondered if he should ask Joe to keep a lookout for anything suspicious. But maybe the fewer people who knew about the threat the better.

"I'm going to my dressing room," he said. "Let me know when Ruby arrives."

The traffic was fine until they reached the Great West Road. Then there was a diversion and they found themselves stuck somewhere in Chiswick, Tol leaning forward over the wheel and swearing, Emma trying to follow the route on an old A-Z found in the glove compartment.

"Left here. No, the road's closed. Right. No, that's the wrong way."

Tol cursed, grinding gears. "You've got lousy road sense for a policewoman."

"Actually," said Emma with dignity, "I passed the police driving course with a score of a hundred per cent. Go right at this roundabout. No, there's another street party going on."

"Bloody street parties," said Tol. "Bread and circuses. Keep the peasants amused."

"Just concentrate on driving," said Emma, "and save the Marxist stuff for later."

To her surprise, Tol laughed. "I like you, Emma," he said. "You're wasted on the police force."

"What should I be doing? Telling fortunes on the pier?"

"You could do worse. There's big money in fortune-telling."

"You're very keen on money for a Marxist."

"I keep telling you I'm not a Marxist, I'm an anarchist."

"Hammersmith Bridge Road!" shouted Emma. "Go that way."

Ignoring the hooting behind him, Tol veered across two lines of traffic and took the corner on two wheels. Emma shut her eyes.

When she opened them again they were bowling serenely along an almost empty road.

"Almost there," said Tol with a grin.

Emma looked at her watch. It was almost seven. Would there be time to warn the DI and stop the show? Was it even possible? She wondered what her parents would think when she didn't turn up for supper. She could hear her mother's voice: "And you just got into a strange man's car? Without even brushing your hair? Really, darling, what a way to behave."

"Can we go any faster?" she asked Tol.

Tol pressed the accelerator and they shot forward onto Shepherd's Bush Road, startling a family coming home from a street party wearing paper crowns and carrying Union Jacks.

Edgar had also been held up by road closures and street parties. It was seven o'clock by the time he reached Shepherd's Bush. He parked the car in a backstreet and made his way to the theatre. The audience were still filing in and Edgar felt self-conscious all over again about being the only person not in Victorian costume. As he stood on the pavement wondering if he'd look more Old Time if he turned his collar up, he heard a voice calling, "Ed!"

It was Ruby, running down the road with her coat open and her hair flying. He caught her in his arms.

"Nightmare," she panted. "I've had to run all the way from High Street Kensington."

"It's lovely to see you."

"You too but I must dash. Derek told us to be here at six and I'm on in the first half." She kissed him on the cheek and vanished into the unobtrusive little door which Edgar knew must be the stage entrance.

He was still standing there, slightly dazed, when he heard another voice shouting his name. Only this time it was, "DI Stephens!"

The whole day had been so bizarre somehow that it almost seemed natural that Emma should be running along Shepherd's Bush Green dressed in riding clothes and followed by Tol Barton.

"Emma. What are you doing here?"

Emma stopped, catching her breath. Her hair was loose and her cheeks were flushed. She looked like an entirely different person. It was Tol, arriving a second or two later at a slower pace, who spoke first, "DI Stephens," he said, "I think there could be a bomb threat to the show tonight."

"What?" When the Queen had finally made her way back to Buckingham Palace, Edgar had breathed a sigh of relief. Nothing bad was going to happen after all. But here was Tol Barton, looking more serious than he had ever seen him, talking about bomb threats.

"Tol came to tell me," said Emma, "and so we drove up to London to warn you. He's tried to tell the police but they won't take it seriously."

"But how do you . . ." Edgar was beginning when another player appeared on the scene. Max, dressed in old-fashioned tails and carrying a top hat.

"Ed. Ruby told me you'd arrived. Have you heard?" He took in Emma's outfit for the first time. "Did you ride here, Sergeant Holmes?"

Emma brushed this aside. "How do you know about it?" she asked Max.

"Charlie Haystack," said Max. Tol gave an exclamation. Max turned to him, eyebrows raised.

"Max, this is Tol Barton," said Emma. "He was a member of the group."

"I see," said Max.

"I don't," said Edgar.

"It was a lineage ad in the *Evening Standard*," said Max. "*Tomorrow's show at the Empire will go with a bang.* It's how the group communicate with each other. As I'm sure our friend here could tell us."

"Look, I didn't have to come here —" Tol began angrily.

Edgar raised his hand. "Is this a real threat?" he said. He turned to Tol. "Do you believe it's possible that such a thing could happen?"

"Yes, I do," said Tol.

"Charlie believed it too," said Max. "So much so that he refused to come into the building."

"Then we have to stop the show," said Edgar.

CHAPTER
THIRTY

Edgar found the director, Derek Conroy, in the wings delivering last minute instructions to two dancers in Russian costume.

"I'm Detective Inspector Edgar Stephens. Can I have a word?"

"What is it? The show's about to start."

Edgar drew the director aside. "You may have to stop the show. I've had intelligence that there may be a bomb in the theatre."

Derek Conway stared at him. Edgar could see the sweat on his forehead and smell the alcohol in his breath. Behind them the girls in their Cossack costumes continued limbering up, oblivious to the two men and their whispered conversation.

"Is this the thing that Max was talking about? What's going on?"

Edgar told him about the advertisement in the *Evening Standard*. Conroy's eyes looked about to pop out of his head.

"We've got a television audience of millions. *Millions*. I'm not going to empty the theatre because of a few lines in the *Evening Standard*."

"It might be real. We can't take the chance."

"Look." Conroy pushed his face close to Edgar's. "Unless you get someone from Scotland Yard here in the next ten minutes the show's going on."

But, when Edgar managed to commandeer a telephone, he couldn't get through to Inspector Hills or anyone else at Scotland Yard. Finally, in desperation, he rushed out into the street and came back with a uniformed policeman who had been cycling home to Ladbroke Grove.

"We'll just have to keep watch," he told the bemused officer. "What's your name?"

"PC Syd Finch, sir."

"All right, PC Finch, you and I take the stalls. Watch out for anything, *anything*, suspicious. Someone reaching for their bag, someone looking nervous, sweating, ill at ease. Do you understand?"

PC Finch nodded, looking like there was a whole lot that he didn't understand. But Edgar had showed him his warrant card and was a superior officer so his job was clearly to stand still and look solid. He did that now.

"Sergeant Holmes." Finch looked surprised to see the girl in riding clothes referred to in this way. "You take the Royal Circle. Tol, you go to the Upper Circle."

"There aren't many people up there," said Tol. "Most of the seats are taken up with lights and such like."

"Could be a good place to hide then," said Edgar. "And, remember, keep your eyes open for anyone you might recognise."

An usherette approached nervously and asked them to take their seats. Edgar flashed his card. "Police," he said. "Security." The girl backed away. The audience were obviously all enjoying themselves hugely. Being in costume seemed to have taken away all their inhibitions and there was much laughter and shouted badinage. "God save Queen Elizabeth!" shouted someone and there was a ragged chorus of "God Save the Queen." It still sounded odd to hear Queen instead of King.

Edgar walked slowly backwards from Row C. The first two rows were taken up by the orchestra. Looking across the auditorium he could see PC Finch doing the same. "It's the laughing policeman," shouted one wag. The trouble was that Edgar had no idea who or what he was looking for. Could the assassin be the large woman in plum velvet whose hat was obscuring the view of at least five seats behind her? Or could it be the thin fellow in black, like a Dickensian undertaker? What about the young lady in blue whose hair colour was distinctly modern? Or the young man beside her? He looked nervous but that could be the effect of his high collar which was clearly much too tight.

Edgar had reached Row J when the lights were dimmed and the audience gasped in anticipation. He could see the light of Finch's torch and wished he'd brought a torch or a truncheon or something else useful. But then the stage lights went on and they were so dazzling that Edgar couldn't see anything else. He stumbled and almost fell.

"Get out of the way," hissed a voice behind him. It was a cameraman with a tripod. Obediently Edgar

315

stepped back and now he was in complete darkness. The orchestra, sounding very close and rather discordant, launched into the overture and the heavy red curtains started to rise.

The show had begun.

Ruby, waiting backstage, knew that this was her moment. All the other audiences, drab faces in drab seaside theatres, paled into insignificance beside this. In just a few minutes she would be beamed into thousands of people's homes. Millions, according to Derek. But what if she didn't get it right? The other day she hadn't managed the quick change into her white dress and had stepped back through the frame with her stays showing. She'd die if that happened to her on stage. What if the stagehand didn't slide the glass away in time so that the audience would just see her white, scared face and not the illusions behind the screen? "If you just look cute," Joe Passolini had said, "it won't matter if the trick goes wrong." But Ruby knew that it did matter. She was the daughter of the great Max Mephisto. She had to get it right.

Olga and Natasha were doing the Cossack routine now. The audience were cheering. They were easily pleased because the girls were average dancers at best. It always annoyed Ruby that Olga was always half a beat behind Natasha. But the audience were clapping as if they were from the Bolshoi Ballet. The curtains closed and a sound behind her made her jump. Then she had to stifle a scream because she was looking into a pair of eyes so menacing, so unblinking, that they seemed to belong to a creature from hell itself.

"Break a leg," she whispered to Jim Jones, the ventriloquist.

"Thanks, duckie." He had a surprisingly high voice. Except when he was being Reggie, of course.

The curtains swept open again. Jim shouldered his monstrous dummy and marched onto the stage.

Even with everything else that he had to worry about, Edgar still found time to feel nervous for Ruby. He had only appeared on stage once, playing Donalbain in a school production of Macbeth. As he remembered it the character only had a few lines but he had been terrified waiting to go on, his palms sweating and his mind alternately blank and full of unhelpful thoughts. What must Ruby be feeling, about to face this packed house and the lights and the cameras? The ventriloquist was clever but it was the sort of act where you longed for it to stop. Despite this, Edgar found himself half hoping that Jim Jones would go on for ever so that Ruby would never have to face the audience. But, all too soon, Jim was drinking a glass of milk while Reggie sang the national anthem. Applause, curtain call.

Then. "Hallo. I'm Ruby French and I'd like to do some magic for you."

She looked so beautiful in her red dress, the full skirts turning her waist to nothingness, that all thoughts of bombs fled from Edgar's mind. And it seemed that the audience too were falling in love with Ruby. They cheered her every move and she seemed to blossom

317

with their attention. When she stepped into the mirror there were gasps and cheers. When she appeared wearing the white dress there were whoops and wolf whistles. It's like a wedding dress, thought Edgar. Would he ever be worthy of marrying this magical creature?

Ruby was like Max, she was totally at home on stage. It was a simple act really, just Ruby and the mirror, but it worked because she was so lovely and assured. When she took her final curtsy she was cheered to the rafters. A star is born, thought Edgar to himself. He was surprised to find that there were tears in his eyes.

Ruby knew that it had gone well. As she came off, Stew Stewart, who was waiting in the wings, kissed her on the cheek.

"Go back. They're still cheering for you."

"Mr Conroy said only one curtain call per act."

"You're a pro." He squeezed her arm and prepared himself for his entrance.

Derek Conroy hugged her. "You little star. You'll be the hit of the night."

"Thank you." Now that it was over she felt quite calm. In fact, she felt as if she could easily do it all over again. This, as Max could have told her, was a common symptom of Applause Syndrome or Doctor Theatre. She half thought that someone else would come up and congratulate her but no one did and the stagehands were busy getting the wires and pulleys ready for the Fantinis before the interval. Rather disappointed, Ruby walked back to her dressing room. She'd have to stay in costume for the final curtain but she could do with loosening her corsets for a few hours. How on earth did Victorian girls manage? By fainting a lot, she supposed.

The trouble was, it was hard to reach the laces on her own. Maybe Olga or Natasha would pop in but they were probably with the Bulgarians somewhere, chatting about the good old days in Siberia. Or was that Russia? She was a bit hazy about geography, she'd admit. She wondered whether Ed would come to congratulate her. But he would be worried about doing the right thing. He'd never leave his seat and come to look for her in the mysterious world of backstage. What was he thinking as he sat there in the stalls? He'd seen her on stage before, of course, but tonight was something different. After tonight he would realise that she could never leave the business. Once he had talked as if, when they were married, the theatre would be in her past. But, when she looked into the future — like that old gypsy woman that Ed was telling her about — she saw herself being a star, not married to Ed. She loved him, she really did. She just couldn't see herself married to him, living in that grotty flat, buying food in the market, having — horrors! — children. If only he could be happy with this; seeing her occasionally, going to bed with her occasionally, watching her on stage.

Ruby put on some powder and tidied her hair. Her corsets really were tight, the bones stuck into her when she sat down. If Ed did come, she would ask him to untie her. Hell, she'd even ask Max or that creepy ventriloquist. She struggled for a few minutes and was relieved to hear a tap on the door.

319

"Come in."

"I just wanted to say well done."

It was Reenie, Derek's wife.

"Thank goodness you're here," said Ruby. "Can you undo these laces for me?"

In the interval everyone was still talking about Ruby. Edgar, Emma, Tol and PC Finch met in the foyer and all around them they heard the words, "the girl in the red dress". Edgar wanted to tell everyone that he was engaged to this amazing creature but there were more serious matters to attend to first. While people were out of their seats there was a chance for a proper search of the theatre. Finch and his torch went up to the Upper Circle, Tol took the dress circle and Emma and Edgar the stalls.

"I thought your . . . I thought Ruby was really good," said Emma as they waited for a couple of magnificently dressed women to swish past.

"Thank you," said Edgar though he didn't really know why he was accepting praise on Ruby's behalf. Her talents were nothing to do with him, after all.

The search revealed nothing beyond some outraged looks as Edgar and Emma pushed their way along the rows. "Sorry, sorry, police, sorry, nothing to worry about."

The orchestra were taking their seats again and were not pleased to see Edgar and Emma opening cases and disturbing their beloved instruments.

"Sorry," said Edgar, knocking over a music stand. "Police search."

320

"Why are the police searching in my violin case?"

"Everything all right?" This was Derek Conroy, watching anxiously from the aisle.

"We need to look everywhere," said Edgar.

"Well, don't disturb the musicians, there's a good chap. You've no idea what the musicians' union is like."

"I'm sorry," said Edgar, "but I am taking the threat seriously."

"But nothing will go wrong now." Edgar could see that Derek was buoyed up by the success of the first half. "It's all going splendidly. Max tells me that you're stepping out with Ruby, by the way. Wasn't she wonderful?"

Edgar agreed that she was. Beside him, Emma said nothing.

"Can you give Ruby my congratulations," said Edgar, "and explain why I couldn't come backstage? Don't alarm her. Just say it was police business." He had an uneasy feeling that Ruby wouldn't think much of police business getting in the way of her acclaim.

"Oh she's fine," said Derek. "Reenie, my wife, is with her now."

Edgar was about to say something else, to convey another, more conciliatory, message, but the bell sounded for the second half and Derek hurried away. Still looking disgruntled, the musicians started tuning up.

Max could hear the music from his dressing room. They sounded very ragged, he thought. Maybe the acoustics in the stalls weren't as good as in the pit. He wanted to go out front and talk to Edgar, to see if he'd managed to get to the bottom of the bomb mystery. But, if he went outside now, he'd be mobbed by the crowd. It didn't do his own mystery any good to be seen hobnobbing with the audience in the interval. Besides, the show hadn't stopped so he presumed that either all was well or Edgar hadn't been able to get hold of anyone in Scotland Yard. Well, there was nothing he could do about it now. Unless the bomb blew up earlier in the second half, he'd have to go on and perform.

He would have liked to go to Ruby's dressing room and congratulate her but he was afraid that, if he saw her, he would tell her about the bomb threat. What would Ruby do if he asked her to leave the theatre now and not come back for her curtain call? He had a feeling that he knew the answer to that one. The trouble was that he hadn't brought Ruby up so he had no authority with her. Mind you, he didn't think that Ruby would obey anyone unquestioningly. Especially not tonight. Tonight she knew she was a star and should be treated accordingly. How well she had worked out there. He'd watched from stage left so as not to make her nervous and, seeing Ruby on the stage, he had felt that rare pleasure that transcends family bias or jealousy. Tonight was the start of a great career. There was no doubt about that.

He could hear the orchestra playing the introduction to Leonora's first number, "My Own True Love". Leonora liked them big and obvious, with lots of swooping strings. He hummed along, putting the finishing touches to his make-up. He assumed that

322

everyone else would be in their dressing rooms or in the wings so was surprised to hear a timid tap on the door.

"Come in."

It was Tommy Lang, looking, in dinner jacket and greasepaint, somehow even older than he had looked sitting in his own front room.

"Can I have a word, Max?"

"Of course, but aren't you on next? Pearl will be looking for you if you're not in the wings."

"It'll only take a second."

Looking at Tommy more closely, Max thought that the impressionist looked ill. He was sweating under his make-up and the black dye on his hair was running at the edges. He hoped that Lang wasn't about to throw up all over the place.

"I wanted to know if you'd heard about the bomb?"

Max stared. Lang put a shaking hand up to his forehead. He looked as if he might be about to faint.

"I'd heard," said Max. "The question is how did you know?"

"I'm one of them," said Lang. "Or at least I used to be. I saw the ad in the *Evening Standard*."

Who knew so many people read the small ads, thought Max.

"And did you believe it?" he asked.

"I didn't," said Lang miserably, "but I do now."

Before Max could speak, the door opened again and Pearl stood there with her clipboard.

"Tommy!" she said. "I've been looking for you everywhere. You're on in five minutes." As she propelled him away, Lang managed one last terrified look over his shoulder at Max, like a French aristocrat on his way to the guillotine.

"I'm so glad it's you," said Ruby. "I thought it might be one of the men and I couldn't really ask one of them to undo my stays." Though she would have dope so and with very little embarrassment too.

She thought it was odd that Reenie didn't answer. And she thought it was odder still when she turned round to see that the director's wife was pointing a gun at her.

Where did she get that? thought Ruby. There wasn't a Wild West act in the show. Maybe it was from the props cupboard. She opened her mouth to ask but somehow the words wouldn't come. She found herself backing away until she was pressed against the dressing table.

"There's a bomb in the theatre," said Reenie. "In about half an hour it'll blow up and blast us all to kingdom come. Now, I don't intend to be here when that happens. I'm getting out and I'm taking you with me. You're my insurance, you see."

"A bomb?" said Ruby. "Why? How?"

"It's a statement," said Reenie, as if explaining a magic trick to a child. "A political statement. Now they'll take notice of us. Two million people will be watching this show and they'll see the great Max Mephisto blown up before their eyes."

"Max . . ." Ruby felt her own eyes fill with tears. She couldn't quite comprehend that she was in danger but the thought that Max might die . . . She could understand that, all right.

"Yes, your father," said Reenie. "Sorry and all that. But the bigger the star, the bigger the statement. That's why I persuaded Derek to have him in the show. Joe Passolini helped, of course, but he insisted on having you too. I wasn't sure at first but it's worked out rather well. You made a hit tonight. People will notice when you go missing. You'll give me bargaining power."

"Joe . . ." Ruby was just picking out the odd word because the whole thing seemed so mad. "Is Joe involved?"

"Oh, he doesn't know about the bomb," said Reenie. "But Joe's father was interned with my first husband, my *real* husband. Joe's always happy to help."

"Edgar's here," said Ruby. "He'll stop you."

"Edgar?" said Reenie, admiring herself in the mirror behind Ruby. "Oh, the policeman. He's got no chance, I'm afraid. He'll never find the bomb. Besides, he's only got a girl and some clueless constable with him. It's hardly Scotland Yard's finest."

A girl. That must mean Emma. Despite everything, despite the gun at her head, Ruby could still feel annoyed that Emma was there. It was meant to be her evening, after all. Then she thought, It doesn't matter. We're all going to die. The thought gave her a cool courage. She had just performed magic tricks in front of millions. She wasn't going to be outsmarted by a middle-aged woman who dyed her hair orange.

"We'll wait until the second half starts," said Reenie, "and then we'll get out. I've got a car waiting."

Ruby reached backwards, feeling for a hat pin.

The first half had ended with the Fantinis performing terrifying tricks on trapezes, so the second half was rather an anticlimax at first. The opening act was a large woman who sang emotional songs with lots of hand-wringing and vibrato. The people in the crowd who liked this sort of thing enjoyed it immensely but Edgar thought that his ears might be about to bleed. Then it was Tommy Lang, the impressionist who had known Charlie Haystack. Edgar was mildly interested in Lang — had he known any other members of the group? — but the man turned out to be a complete disaster. He stumbled on stage looking absolutely terrified and mumbled his way through a series of impressions that, if it hadn't been for the props, could have been almost anyone. Lang himself seemed confused: "Here's Winnie . . . no it's Charlie Chaplin . . ." He looked into the wings as if hoping to find inspiration there. The audience, desperate to enjoy everything, fidgeted uncomfortably in their seats. Fob watches were consulted and fans fluttered. Lang was almost saved by his last impression, George Formby. Not because it was particularly good but because the audience could sing along to the last number, "When I'm Cleaning Windows". This at least allowed the applause to cover Lang's exit. He didn't come back for a curtain call.

But this didn't matter. As soon as Lang had left the stage and George Formby was just an unpleasant memory, the atmosphere started to build. From his vantage point stage right, Edgar could hear the words "Max Mephisto" being whispered all around as people checked their programmes to be sure that, yes, Max was on next. But first Olga and Natasha had a brief spot, dancing a sub-Swan Lake number with blue lights and lots of feathery effects. The dancers got a sporting round of applause but, as soon as the curtains swept shut, the chanting started. "We want Max, we want Max, we want Max." Edgar felt absurdly proud of his friend. He looked across at Emma to see what she was making of it all.

But Emma was gone.

Max heard the chanting as he waited in the wings. All thoughts of Tommy Lang, even of the bomb, had vanished. Carefully Max performed his last minute routine, checking sleeves and pockets for props, touching the silver Madonna in his breast pocket, walking in a slow anticlockwise circle. Then the "Danse Macabre" started, the curtains flew up and he stepped onto the stage, the applause rising to a crescendo.

Ruby found the pin. Reenie was listening to the show being relayed over the loudspeakers.

"Tommy Lang. Max will be on soon."

"Look!" shouted Ruby with her very best shocked expression. Reenie turned and Ruby lunged with the pin. She knocked the gun from Reenie's hand but fell over in the process and, hampered by her long skirts, was unable to get up in time. Reenie, on hands and knees, grabbed the gun and crawled over to Ruby. She put the gun to Ruby's forehead, pressing it so hard that Ruby could feel the indentations on the muzzle.

"You little bitch," she panted. "I ought to kill you right now."

Ruby could see the woman's eyes, blue with red veins on the whites, mascara smudged. Reenie was breathing into her face, wine and garlic and something sweet like a herbal cigarette. Say something, Ruby told herself, try to make contact. Remind her that you're a person too. You're young enough to be her daughter. Make her feel sorry for you.

"Please don't kill me," was all she managed.

Reenie got to her feet, still levelling the gun at Ruby. "I'm not going to kill you. Yet." There was a burst of applause from the loudspeaker followed, a few minutes later, by the "Danse Macabre".

"Max's music," said Reenie. "Come on. Get up. We haven't got much time."

For what? thought Ruby. Reenie kicked open the door and motioned for Ruby to go first.

"Remember I'm right behind you."

It sounded like a music hall song. Look behind you I'll be there, following you around. Ruby suppressed a mad desire to laugh. She prayed that they'd see someone, anyone, outside.

But the corridor was empty.

328

Max felt himself working well. The doves flew from his sleeves and, when he descended into the audience, waves of laughter and applause greeted his discovery of pearls in evening bags, eggs in ears (crack and a tiny mechanical dove flew out), even a crown on the head of a passable blonde in Row G. Now it was the time for the main event.

"You'll have heard tell," he said, "of a magic cabinet that shows moving pictures." Laughter. "Some of you will have even seen such a cabinet. Well, tonight I have not one, not two, but three of these wonders."

A clash of cymbals and Sofija walked on stage pushing the cabinet made of three televisions. The audience were in the mood to applaud anything, but Sofija, in her basque and feathers, got an extremely warm reception. She pranced and preened a bit — she was a little too fond of centre stage for Max's liking — and manoeuvred the cabinet to its mark.

Some more patter about the miracle of television and some more twirling from Sofija. Then Max turned back to the movable camera on its trolley. This, so Derek was always reminding them, was their window to the wider world. The camera was a large aluminium tube with four lenses at the front — it moved rather disconcertingly on a wheeled mechanism. On top was a square black box that Max had never noticed before. A drum roll started in the background. Max continued to stare at the little black box with its flickering red light.

He knew that he was looking at an infernal machine.

CHAPTER
THIRTY-ONE

Reenie pushed Ruby towards a back staircase. She stumbled and almost fell again in her stupid long skirts. She was crying now, as she walked. Was the theatre about to blow up? Would Max and Edgar be killed? Oh, and everyone else. Tommy Lang, Jim Jones, Olga and Natasha, the Bulgarians, that annoying policewoman, the two thousand people in the audience. It couldn't be true. It just couldn't.

At the bottom of the steps was a fire door. Reenie told Ruby to push it open. She did so and found herself in a small courtyard. She was amazed to see that it wasn't dark yet, just a soft grey twilight. At the courtyard gate was a car with a man in the driving seat.

"Get in," said Reenie, gesturing with the gun.

Now was her moment. But what could she do? And, even if she could overpower Reenie, how could she stop the bomb? As she stood hesitating, holding up her skirt like a deb, a voice shouted, "Stop!"

Ruby and Reenie both looked round. A figure was standing on a fire escape halfway up the building.

It was the annoying policewoman.

Max moved slowly and carefully. He knew that there was no point in shouting for help and, in any case, the last thing he wanted to do was frighten the audience into a stampede. He lifted the box from the top of the camera and put it on the little table that held his props. He thought he should say something to alert Edgar, at least, about the danger.

"Aha. An infernal machine." He twirled an imaginary moustache. "Just let me defuse the wretched thing."

The audience laughed. They, at least, were going along with it.

The box opened easily. Inside were three wires attached to a crude-looking timer. Two minutes. One minute, fifty-nine seconds.

What had Frankie, the electrician, told him all those years ago in Egypt? Look for the fuse. One cut should do it — he always kept a penknife in his pocket — but which fuse and which wire? He could see Sofija looking at him. Two minutes didn't seem a lot of time to defuse a bomb but it was an eternity in the theatre. He nodded at Sofija and she obediently twirled across the stage, hopefully taking the audiences' eyes with her.

The wires were red, green and brown. Red for danger. Could it really be as simple as that? Concentrate, he told himself. It's just like mending Mrs M's clock. One minute, fifty-eight seconds. Glancing into the wings he saw Edgar standing there holding, of all things, a fire extinguisher.

"I'll just make a cut," Max informed the audience.

Reenie fired the gun. Ruby ran towards the doorway. She expected to feel a bullet in her back any second but what actually happened was that a man appeared on the balcony beside Emma. He threw something that glinted in the half-light. Ruby heard Reenie give a cry of surprise or pain.

"Mum!" shouted a man. The driver of the car?

In the doorway, Ruby turned round. Reenie was lying on the floor with a knife sticking out of her shoulder. The gun was on the ground but luckily the car driver was concentrating only on Reenie. Ruby knew that she should run and get it but somehow her legs wouldn't move. As she watched though, Emma came galloping down the fire escape and picked up the gun. Then she shouted up to the man, "Get an ambulance!"

Ruby edged forward. Emma was kneeling on the ground beside Reenie, holding her jumper over the wound.

"Reenie Conroy," Emma was saying, "you are under arrest for the murders of Peter Cartwright and Doreen Barton and the attempted murder of Ruby French. Do you understand the charge?"

Reenie laughed, even though her blood was turning the white jumper red. "Don't you understand? It's all useless. This place is going to blow up in a few minutes." She turned to the driver who was hovering, rather uselessly, in the background. "Lazlo, get in the car. Get as far away as you can."

"I'm not leaving you, Mum."

"We're all going to die then." Reenie closed her eyes and smiled beatifically.

Max leant over the box. Red for danger, green for go, brown for? Thirty seconds, said the timer. He looked up and caught Edgar's eye. An unspoken message passed between them. Then Max cut the brown wire.

The timer stopped. Max passed the box to Edgar with a ceremonial bow. Then he turned to the audience, "My lovely assistant is now going to take her place in the cabinet."

There was a bucket of water in the wings and Edgar put the infernal machine into it. He believed that Max had made the thing safe but, all the same, he wanted to get it out of the building as quickly as possible. He headed for the fire door just as Tol came bursting through it.

"Ambulance," he panted.

"What?"

"Outside," said Tol. "Emma. The other girl. Woman with a gun."

Without another word, Edgar pushed past him, still carrying the bucket.

Outside he found Ruby, in her red dress, kneeling on the floor beside a woman who was bleeding heavily from a shoulder wound. Emma, dressed only in a thin shirt and breeches, was reading a scared-looking man his rights.

"Hallo, boss," she said without looking round. "Reenie here tried to kill Ruby but I don't think she's going anywhere now. I've told Tol to call an ambulance."

"I'll be back in a minute," said Edgar. He ran across the road to Shepherd's Bush Green and put the bucket in the middle of the grass. He was delighted to see PC Finch running towards him. That boy would go far.

"I've called for the UXB squad, sir, like you said."

"Well done, Finch. Now, guard that bucket with your life. Don't let any of the public near it."

"Is that it, sir?"

"Yes, but I don't think it'll go off."

With those encouraging words he headed back to the theatre.

The little group in the courtyard now included Tol, who had put his jacket round Emma's shoulders. "The ambulance is on its way," he informed Edgar.

"What happened to this woman?"

"I threw a knife at her," said Tol. He turned to Emma. "I told you that I had a knife-throwing act once."

"But you said you weren't very good," said Emma. "I was surprised."

"I've been practising."

Edgar thought that he should stamp his authority on the proceedings.

"Will someone tell me what's been going on?"

Ruby got to her feet and came to take Edgar's arm. Her hair had come out of its bun and was hanging in tendrils around her face. Her eyes were bright and Edgar thought that she had never looked prettier.

334

"*She* pulled a gun on me," said Ruby, pointing to Reenie, "and *she* rescued me."

Emma looked modest. "I only just realised in time."

"But how did you realise? What did you realise?"

"Roman and Renée, the singers who headlined the bill in 1939. The playbill that Madame Zabini had in her caravan. Well, Reenie was Renée. When Derek Conroy mentioned his wife I thought there was something about the name. Then it came to me halfway through the second half and I went to find her. I took Tol with me because I thought he'd recognise her."

Reenie looked at Tol for the first time. "Hallo, Ptolemy," she said. "You've changed."

"So have you, Renée."

Emma carried on. "I went to Ruby's dressing room but they weren't there. Then I heard voices outside and went onto the fire escape. Reenie was pointing a gun at Ruby, trying to force her into the car."

"She was trying to get away," said Ruby. "Oh God, she said there was a bomb in the theatre."

"There was," said Edgar. "Max defused it. It's on Shepherd's Bush Green now."

Emma started to laugh. "Max defused it? How?"

"As part of his act," said Edgar. "The audience lapped it up."

When the ambulance arrived, the crew found a woman in a Victorian dress and a woman in riding clothes accompanied by two men, all four of them weak from laughter. Another woman lay on the ground clutching a jumper to a bleeding flesh wound. A third man stood watching, as if he didn't understand what was going on.

"And who can blame him," said the ambulance driver, as they set off for the hospital.

They were held up for several minutes outside the BBC Television Theatre, formerly the Empire, as the crowds streamed out, full of praise for Max Mephisto and his amazing trick with a magic cabinet and an infernal machine.

CHAPTER
THIRTY-TWO

It was Edgar who accompanied Reenie to hospital. He had asked Ruby if she wanted to come too, thinking that she might be shaken or hurt, but not a bit of it.

"If I go back now," she said, "I might be in time for the curtain call." And she had picked up her skirts and headed back to the theatre, followed by Emma and Tol. So Edgar got in the ambulance accompanied by the man who introduced himself as Reenie's son Lazlo. He had no way of knowing whether Lazlo was involved in the plot but thought he shouldn't let him get too far out of sight. He left PC Finch in charge of the bomb. The young policeman would certainly have something to report to his superiors on Monday.

At the hospital he found himself waiting with Lazlo while the nurses tended Reenie's knife wound. The young man seemed strangely passive, sitting staring straight ahead with his hands hanging.

"Am I under arrest?" he asked.

"You'll be charged as an accessory to the crime," said Edgar. "Did you know that your mother had planted a bomb in the theatre?"

"No!" The shock seemed genuine. Two bright patches appeared on Lazlo's pale cheeks.

"What did you think was happening? You must have suspected something."

"Mum just told me to meet her at the theatre. I didn't know what was going on."

Could this be true? Lazlo did seem rather slow on the uptake but he told Edgar that he was a saxophonist and, in Edgar's experience, musicians tended to be rather clever. Could he be putting it on? They were a theatrical family, after all. Lazlo, he learnt, was the son of Reenie's first husband, Roman, the singer. Before he could ask any more though, Derek Conroy burst into the waiting room.

"What's happened to Reenie? That policewoman told me that she'd been arrested."

"She's under arrest for murder," said Edgar, and Lazlo jumped up to catch his stepfather as he fell.

Ruby was in time for her curtain call. Tol and Emma watched from the wings as she stepped forward to meet the thunderous waves of applause. Ruby had a smudge on her cheek and her dress was slightly torn at the back but she curtsied and smiled with complete composure. "Bravo!" shouted a voice from the dress circle.

"She's a star, that one," said Tol.

"Yes," said Emma. She thought that this was probably true and, if Edgar wanted to marry this gorgeous creature, maybe she should be happy for him.

"She's not half the woman you are though," said Tol, still with his eyes on the stage.

"You haven't the faintest idea what I'm like," said Emma.

"Maybe I have second sight," said Tol, "like my mother."

The entire cast lined up for a final curtain call. Emma saw Max stretching out his arms to include his fellow performers. He also seemed completely unaffected by the events of the night. But, then, he was Ruby's father and maybe this too was inherited.

As the performers came off stage though, Max caught Emma's arm. "Where's Edgar? What happened?"

"He's accompanying a suspect to the hospital," said Emma. "We'll need to take a statement from you. From Ruby too."

"Ruby?" Max looked over to where Ruby was being congratulated by a young man in a preposterous wide-shouldered suit. "What's Ruby got to do with it?"

Ruby heard her name and came over to her father. "Have you heard?" she said. "Reenie tried to kill me. Emma rescued me and this gentleman too." She dimpled prettily at Tol.

"I think we'd better go to my dressing room," said Max.

Edgar sat at Reenie Conroy's bedside. She was pale but quite composed, her bandaged arm lying stiffly by her side. Derek Conroy held her other hand, tears flowing freely down his face. He had almost fainted in the waiting room and now looked far worse than his wife. Lazlo hovered in the background.

"I killed Cartwright," Reenie was saying. "Doreen told me that he'd got wind of the coronation plot. He'd seen the ads in the *Evening Standard* and worked something out. Apparently he told Doreen that he'd 'cracked the code'. Cartwright went down to see Doreen in Brighton. He was asking about people who had been on the bill with me and Roman. He'd even taken a playbill with him. So I went round to his flat in Kensington. He opened the door and I stabbed him. It was quite easy. I dragged him into his bedroom and made it look as if there had been a fight in the sitting room. I wasn't sorry. I hate the British military. The way they treated Roman in the war. They killed him really. He was never the same after he left the camp."

"What about William Hitchcock, Wild Bill Hitchcock?" said Edgar. "Did you have anything to do with his death?"

"No, that was Velma. Velma Edwards. She was another member of the group, though more of a communist than an anarchist. Hitchcock had been in touch with Cartwright, he'd sent him some cutting about Velma. Hitchcock told Velma as much. So she had him killed. Or she got her husband to do it. I'm not sure which." She made it sound as if Benson Edwards had been helping out with the household chores.

"What about Doreen Barton? You must have killed her first."

"I was sorry about Doreen," said Reenie, "because she was good to Roman and me in the old days. But she knew too much. She was never in the group but she knew everything that was going on. Everyone confided in Doreen. She wrote me a letter telling me that

340

Cartwright had been to see her. She said that we should talk. Talk! Talking was all we did in the old days. Talking doesn't get you anywhere. So I went down to Brighton and waited until Doreen left the caravan. Then I threw her into the sea. It wasn't difficult, she was quite a small woman and, of course, she wasn't expecting it." Beside her, Derek made a sound somewhere between a sob and a groan.

"And my sergeant, Emma Holmes, were you behind that attack too?"

"Yes. She was asking too many questions. It was Tommy Lang who told me about her. Your friend, Max Mephisto, had been to see him. Max told Tommy that the Brighton police were interested in people who'd worked with Charlie Haystack. So I went down to Brighton and followed your sergeant home from work. I had a cosh in my handbag and hit her over the head with it."

"Did you mean to kill her?"

"No, just to put her out of action for a bit." But Edgar wasn't sure that he believed this. He didn't think that Reenie would lose any sleep over Emma, any more than she had over Colonel Cartwright. Wasn't Emma, too, part of the hated British establishment?

"And the bomb in the theatre? Who was involved with that?"

"I made the bomb myself. It was something I learnt in the old days. Then I put the final advertisement in the paper. Just so that everyone would know that we were back."

"What did Lazlo know?" Edgar looked at the young man in the background, who was gazing at his mother in a kind of dumb misery.

"Lazlo knew nothing. He's a good boy. He's his father all over again. My Roman. My real husband."

Derek Conroy started to weep in earnest.

CHAPTER
THIRTY-THREE

"And Derek really had no idea?" said Max.

"Apparently not," said Edgar. "He told me that he'd loved Reenie from the first moment that he saw her, before the war."

"Well she was a good-looking woman once," said Tol. "I remember being quite dazzled by her myself."

They were in the bar of the Strand Palace Hotel. When Edgar finally left the hospital he had spent an hour with Scotland Yard, who were now treating him very seriously indeed. The UXB Unit had confirmed that the infernal machine was a bomb, home-made but no less deadly for that. "It would certainly have blown the place up," said a cheerful lieutenant. "How did you know what to do with it?"

"It wasn't me," said Edgar, "it was a magician."

He'd arranged to meet Max back at the hotel but he was surprised to find not only Ruby (now dressed in a jumper and slacks) but also Emma and Tol, all of them stuck into what looked like a very good bottle of brandy.

"There was no point trying to get back to Brighton tonight," said Emma, "We're staying here. It's full up but I'm staying with Ruby and Tol's sharing with Max."

Edgar felt like a child excluded in the playground. Emma was giggling with Ruby, the two of them suddenly the best of friends. Even Tol and Max seemed to have reached an understanding, based on variety circuit memories and an appreciation of good brandy.

"No, you share with Max," said Tol. "I don't like hotels. They make me think of the Grand. Also, I know what goes on in the kitchens."

"Where will you go?" asked Emma.

"I'm going to find Charlie Haystack," said Tol. "I think he's got some explaining to do."

Max pushed the brandy bottle towards Edgar. "I don't think Charlie knew about Reenie though," he said. "He was pretty scared when he drove me to the theatre. I think he would have said if he knew who was behind it."

"Why did Reenie put that ad in the paper?" said Emma. "Surely she knew that would put the other members onto the scent?"

"She had kept up the tradition of putting ads in the paper," said Edgar. "I think she wanted people to think that the group was still operating."

"Sheer bravado," said Tol. "I don't think the group exists any more. It was just her and Lazlo."

Edgar thought that Tol was a bit quick to pin everything on Reenie and her son. If he were in charge of the Scotland Yard investigation, he would take good care to find out if there were any other members lurking out there. Sleepers, it seemed, could sleep for a long time but still be deadly when awoken.

344

"Lazlo seemed harmless to me," said Max. "He's a jazz musician, for God's sake. But what about Tommy Lang? He'd seen the advertisement in the paper. He told me as much. He was terrified."

"You should have seen him on stage," said Edgar. "Lang was obviously still slightly involved. He told Reenie that you'd visited him, Max, and that the police were investigating Charlie Haystack. That's why she attacked you, Emma."

"I'm sorry," said Max to Emma. "I shouldn't have mentioned the police."

She waved this away. "I knew it was a woman who had attacked me," she said. "Reenie was the woman in the green coat."

"She said that she just wanted to put you out of action for a while," said Edgar. "But I think she would have killed you if Arthur, Lancelot and Percival hadn't turned up."

"She'd have had a fight on her hands," said Emma. Edgar didn't remind Emma that she had been unconscious at the time. Tol was looking at her in admiration. "You're a tough cookie, Emma," he said.

"How did Cartwright first find out about the group?" said Max.

"Colonel Cartwright told Charlie that he was onto a group who had plans to disrupt the coronation," said Edgar. "I think he must have worked it out from the ads in the *Evening Standard*. He told Doreen that he'd cracked the code and Colonel Cartwright was pretty hot on codes. I wondered why he had kept that unfinished crossword but I'm pretty sure that the small ads were on the back of it. Bill Hitchcock got the *Evening Standard* sent to him in America too. His wife said so."

"That figures," said Max. "Hitchcock was probably quoting one of the messages to me, all that 'with hesitation' stuff."

"Cartwright made the connection with the theatricals," said Edgar, "maybe because of his link with Charlie Haystack and with Tony Mulholland. That's why he went down to see Doreen in Brighton. He must have had a few of the playbills and he took one with him when he visited Doreen, which explains why it was found in her caravan. Doreen made the mistake of writing to Reenie and telling her about Cartwright's visit. That sealed her death warrant. Reenie went down to Brighton and killed her. Then she killed Cartwright."

"The evil bitch," said Tol. "Mum was really good to Reenie and Roman."

"I'm sorry," said Edgar. "It sounds as if she was good to everyone."

"But who killed Bill Hitchcock?" said Max. "That couldn't have been Reenie too, on a quick visit to America?"

"No," said Edgar. "Reenie said that it was Velma Edwards. Bill Hitchcock sent Colonel Cartwright that news cutting, about the woman fainting at his show. We just didn't realise the significance of it. We thought Hitchcock was the important person in the story but really it was the woman, Velma Edwards. She'd been a burlesque dancer and, apparently, a communist. Hitchcock hypnotised her and made her sing 'The Red

346

Flag'. So Velma killed him. She tried to kill me too. Or she got her husband's heavies to do it for her. I telephoned the Albany police and they're going to investigate. I don't know if they'll find any proof but that's what I think happened."

"It's the women," said Ruby. "You thought it was the men behind it but it was the women all along." Ruby hadn't been contributing much to the conversation, just listening with her eyes wide. Edgar thought that she seemed stunned by the evening's events, or maybe it was just the effects of the brandy. Emerald would certainly not like to see her daughter drinking spirits.

"Never forget the women," said Emma to Edgar. "That's what you told me once."

"It's good advice," said Max. He gave Edgar rather a sharp look as he said it. Edgar wondered what he was getting at.

"We did overlook Reenie," said Edgar. "Roman and Renée, that was what was on the playbill. Equal billing. But we only thought about Roman and he was dead."

"I should have known she was married to a Hungarian when she served goulash for dinner," said Max. "And she played Bartók too."

"It's fitting really," said Edgar. "We've got a queen now. The women are in charge. We might even have a woman prime minister one day."

A loud bang made them all jump. Edgar thought of the Blitz. When he'd been in the convalescent hospital he'd been able to hear the bombs dropping on London. He looked at Max and knew that he was having similar memories.

"What the hell was that?" said Max.

It was Emma who answered. "It's fireworks. They're letting off fireworks for the coronation."

"I wish we could see them," said Ruby.

"We can," said Max. "I know a way up onto the roof. We'll have the best view in London."

Max led the way up two staircases until the opulent carpets gave way to matting and then to bare boards. There was not a soul in sight. It seemed that everyone was still in bars and restaurants celebrating. Eventually, on a top floor landing, Max pushed open a door. They climbed a short flight of metal stairs and then they were on the roof.

"How did you know about this?" asked Edgar.

"I've stayed here a lot," said Max. "I've got to know the housekeeper quite well."

Edgar didn't think he wanted to know the circumstances in which Max and the housekeeper had ventured onto the roof. It wasn't the place you'd choose for a romantic liaison, a flat space covered in pigeon droppings with a terracotta stone balustrade around the outside. But the view was amazing, across the Strand to the river and, beyond that, Waterloo Bridge and the lights of the capital. To their left they could even see Tower Bridge, lit up like a mirage.

Ruby slipped her hand into Edgar's. "I'm not very keen on heights," she said.

"It's all right," said Edgar, though his legs felt slightly wobbly. "We're quite safe as long as we don't go near the edge."

348

"Look!" said Emma.

The night was suddenly split open. Shooting stars blazed and fell, illuminating, just for a second, the ancient buildings and monuments. Big Ben, the Houses of Parliament, bridges, cathedrals, terraced houses, towers. All of London was here, thought Edgar, somewhat dizzily. All those people, all those lives. The stars bloomed and burnt and then darkness fell again.

"Is that it?" said Emma.

"I think there'll be some more," said Tol, smiling down at her. Emma still had his jacket clasped around her shoulders. Edgar noticed, with displeasure, that Tol had stayed close to Emma all evening, offering her his hand to climb the last step, occasionally talking to her in a low tone which made it impossible for Edgar to catch his words (though he tried). Emma couldn't be interested in Tol, surely? He was at least twenty years older than her, for one thing. "I think he likes me," Emma had said. But what if she liked him back?

The last fireworks lit up the river, its sinuous twists and turns through the city. Wasn't there some reference in the Old Testament to a river of fire? thought Edgar. There was something almost apocalyptic about the spectacle. He'd heard RAF pilots say that, when they'd seen the Blitz from the air, they had thought that the world was ending.

"The new Elizabethan age," said Max, with only a trace of mockery in his voice. "What will it bring?"

"Peace and goodwill to all men," said Edgar, responding in kind;

"And women," said Emma. And she smiled at him while, behind her, the sky exploded again.

Epilogue

Two months later

Edgar walked along Brighton seafront towards Hove, enjoying the sun on his face after a day in the underground CID offices. It was seven o'clock in the evening but the air had stayed warm and the beaches were still crowded. The bad weather that had greeted Elizabeth II's coronation had not lasted long into her reign. Brighton had never known such a busy summer.

He was on his way to pick up Ruby and then they were going to Mrs M's for supper. She had also invited Emma. "I've taken quite a fancy to that pretty sergeant of yours," she told Edgar when he popped in for a drink last week. "You're not the only one," said Max, one of his irritatingly gnomic remarks. Once again, Edgar was struck by how comfortable Max seemed in Mrs M's house: opening doors, pouring drinks, stroking the cat. To Edgar's knowledge, Max had been staying at Mrs M's for the whole of August, which almost constituted a permanent address for him.

Diablo was also staying at Mrs M's. He had booked himself in for a week as soon as a garbled account of the events at the BBC Television Theatre had made their way into the papers. "It seems you've been having some fun without me, dear boy," he said over the telephone to Edgar. "And now I want to hear *all* about it."

The seventh member of the dinner party was Charlie Haystack. Not the company Edgar would have chosen but Haystack had virtually invited himself. After all that had happened, he had the cheek to contact Mrs M and ask if he could stay for a couple of weeks. "I've been feeling a bit under the weather," he told her. "Some sea air will do me good." Mrs M had agreed, on the proviso that no Irish or French accents were involved. "I don't do the voices any more," Mrs M reported Charlie as saying. "I'm going straight."

Going straight. It was odd, thought Edgar as he strolled between the piers, listening to the shouts of laughter coming from the carousels and the helter-skelter, theatricals used the same phrase about leaving the stage as criminals did about abandoning a life of crime. Would Charlie ever really turn his back on either pursuit? Edgar still wasn't convinced that Charlie hadn't known anything about Reenie's plans. He must have had an idea, surely, which was why he had been too frightened to go inside the Empire that night.

But Charlie Haystack hadn't been charged with any crime. He could go back to his job in the passport office without anyone knowing that he had once, briefly, been a four-star general. But Edgar thought that Charlie had been deeply shaken by the metamorphosis of Renée Szolnoki, songstress, into Reenie Conroy, murderess. And Reenie had killed Peter Cartwright, the man Charlie had loved. This was something Reenie hadn't foreseen, thought Edgar, that her old comrade, Charlie Haystack, had loved the British military man and would seek to avenge his death.

Tol Barton had also escaped charges for throwing a knife at Reenie. "You saved Ruby's life," said Edgar. "I'm not going to press charges. But it might be an idea to lose the knife."

"I can't lose the knife," said Tol. "I'm a chef, remember." But Emma — who remained rather too friendly with the Barton family — reported that Tol was thinking of leaving the Grand and starting one of the coffee shops that were becoming all the rage in Brighton. "Astarte's going to run the fortune-telling business upstairs," said Emma. "I think it'll be really successful."

Edgar had reached Hove now, the cheery brashness of Brighton giving way to the smooth, creamy terraces. Last week he'd looked at a flat in Hove, second floor with a balcony, two bedrooms, sitting rpom, modern bathroom and kitchen. He would put down a deposit on it, he thought, and move from the insalubrious pink house on Albion Hill. Strange that the thought of leaving it now made him feel slightly sad. But the Hove place was more suitable for a married couple. Ruby seemed to have dropped her resistance to setting a date and they were planning to be married next spring.

"Maybe we'll come to the wedding," said Mike Moretti when they'd spoken on the telephone last week. "Genny would love to see Brighton again." Mike was in high spirits, Genevieve having given birth to a healthy baby girl the week before. "We're calling her Hope," said Mike, "a bit corny but Genny liked the idea." It was from Mike that Edgar had learnt that O'Grady and O'Flynn had traced the driver of the hit-and-run car, who was in the process of "singing like a canary" and had implicated Velma and Benson Edwards in Bill Hitchcock's death. "To think of Velma killing a man because he made her sing a commie song," said Mike. "Mind you, Genny always said she was as hard as nails, even in the old days." Edgar thought of the charming woman in the pale blue mansion. "Why, if you lived here I could fix you up with a nice girl in a second." As Max had said, it was never a good idea to underestimate women.

Reenie's case Was due to come to trial in the autumn. Derek Conroy had remained loyal to his wife, paying for expensive lawyers and attending every hearing. This despite Reenie saying openly that it was Roman who had been the love of her life. "My real husband," she'd said, that night in the hospital.

Derek at least had the consolation of seeing *Those Were the Days* attract a record TV audience. It was going to be a regular series — Victorian costumes, the lot — and the BBC Television Theatre was going to be adapted to house more lights and more cameras. Max and Ruby had been offered their own show, *Magician and Daughter*. Joe Passolini, whom Edgar had now met, was enthusiastic. "It'll make you a star," he told Ruby over a lunch in Brighton where he had simultaneously patronised and ignored Edgar. But Max

354

was reluctant. "I'm not sure I want to be a television star," he told Edgar, not doubting for one minute that he was going to be a huge success, of course. "Going into people's homes every night, I might as well become a burglar and have done with it." Thinking of his mother and her blossoming love affair with the screen, Edgar thought that Max had no idea just how much people seemed to want to be burgled.

Ruby, on the other hand, was extremely keen to be on television. "It'll be so much easier than touring, darling," she said to Edgar. "It'll be just like having a regular job." Edgar doubted that. He was not sure how much he liked the idea of his wife breaking and entering every sitting room in the land. "You'll be a household name," said Joe, but Edgar still hadn't worked out if this was a threat or a promise.

He was nearly at Ruby's flat. They'd have to hurry if they wanted to be at Mrs M's for seven-thirty. But he had no doubt at all that Ruby would make him wait. Would she make him wait at the altar? A tiny puff of air, not big enough to be called a cloud, floated across the evening sky.

Emma was hurrying too, but in the opposite direction. She had a call to make before supper and didn't want to be late. Apart from anything else, she was longing to meet the mysterious Charlie Haystack, to say nothing of The Great Diablo. She had been looking forward to this evening all week. Even the fact that Ruby would be there couldn't ruin it for her. After the events of June the second, Emma had become quite fond of Ruby. She remembered Ruby flying across the courtyard in her red dress as Reenie pointed a gun at her. She didn't lack courage, Ruby; she hadn't been about to get into the car without a fight. She'd even attacked Reenie with a hat pin, she told Emma later. That night, after the fireworks, they'd sat on Ruby's bed at the Strand Palace, chatting like schoolgirls. Ruby told Emma about her childhood, about her longing to go into show business in the face of her mother's opposition. "I wanted to be a magician long before I knew about Max." Until that evening Emma hadn't realised that Max was Ruby's father. What did Max think about his daughter marrying his best friend? Was Emma right to have detected a slight disapproval on Max's side? At any rate, Ruby hadn't wanted to talk about Edgar that night. "I want to be a star," she'd said. "That's all I want." Having seen Ruby on stage, Emma was pretty sure that she'd get her wish.

At the Palace Pier she stopped and looked along Madeira Drive, now full of tourists as it had been on the day she was attacked. The train was still chugging along the Volks Railway and the vendors were still shouting about ice cream and candyfloss. The promettes were making their way through the crowds, kissing babies and dispensing sticks of rock. All was right with the world.

Emma crossed the coast road by the Aquarium. The houses in Marine Parade looked their best in the sunshine. Her parents talked about getting a second home in Spain but, really, on days like this, Brighton was almost perfect. Emma hadn't protested about the

Spanish house though. She was saving her ammunition for the day when she told her parents that she wanted to move into a bedsit.

Emma rang the bell of number eighty-seven. After a few minutes, Astarte opened the door.

"Is your dad in?"

"No, he's at work."

Emma followed Astarte up the stairs to the front room. She remembered the first time she'd been in the house, Astarte and Isobel sitting on the sofa like the dowager queen and the young princess. She thought of the funeral, the long room with the flowers and the gypsy violinists playing. Uncle Lucian drinking from his silver flask. "In my day we had real Romany funerals. They would last all day, music and singing and story-telling. Then, in the evening, we'd burn the dead person's caravan." Tol said that it was Lucian who had burnt Madame Zabini's caravan. But there was no proof and it didn't look as if the case would ever come to court. Emma didn't know what Lucian thought about the coffee shop idea but she doubted that Tol would care much about the old man's opinion either way. She remembered Lucian telling her that Tol had almost blinded his wife. That had been the knife-throwing act, of course. "Sally didn't hold it against me but I couldn't go on after that," Tol told her. He'd given up the act and married Sally. Then Astarte was born and they were happy for a while. But Sally died of cancer two years later. "I really did love Sally," said Tol. Emma believed him. She also believed that Tol didn't plan to remain a widower all his life.

Astarte sat at the table by the window. The balcony doors were open and the soft breeze blew her hair as she shuffled the cards. She was dressed in ordinary clothes but she still looked pretty witchy all the same, thought Emma. She remembered the strange, eerie song that Astarte had sung in the church. *Sleep well, my love, sleep while the night sky weaves its spell.*

"Cut the cards," said Astarte, "and think of your question. Just keep that one question in your mind all the time."

Emma sat opposite and cut the cards. Astarte took the deck back and shuffled them again. Then, slowly, carefully, she laid out five cards in a cross shape, one at the top, then three below, then one at the bottom. One by one, she turned the cards over. Emma could see shapes and colours but she had no idea what any of the cards meant. There was a woman, maybe that was a good sign? But there was also a skeleton, which looked less promising. She wished she'd done a bit of research first. It wasn't like her to be at such a disadvantage.

Astarte looked at Emma. Her blue-green eyes were surprisingly kind.

"He's not going to leave her," she said. "Get on with the rest of your life."

Acknowledgements

All the people and events in this book are imaginary. The places, on the other hand, are mostly real. There was a police station in Bartholomew Square until the 1960s and Marine Parade, Madeira Drive, St John the Baptist Church and Duke's Mound are all to be found in Brighton. In fact, this book includes two addresses where I lived as a child: Abbott's Court in Kensington Square and Marine Parade. I also used to go riding in Rottingdean. Incidentally, Rottingdean was the setting for my first completed novel, written when I was eleven. The hero of that novel was Edgar Stephens.

The town of Albany in America also exists. I was lucky enough to visit when I attended the Bouchercon crimewriting convention in 2013. The Shangri-La is imaginary, though, as are all the inhabitants mentioned in the book. James Vicary was a real person and he was indeed Detroit's youngest snake charmer. He was also the first person to experiment with subliminal advertising. Vicary's famous "Eat popcorn" experiment did not take place until 1957but I thought it was conceivable that Bill Hitchcock might have heard of him. "How Psychiatric Measures can be Applied to

Market Research" is an actual article and was published in 1951.

The Empire, Shepherd's Bush, also exists and for details of its transformation into the BBC Television Theatre I'm indebted to Martin Kempton's wonderful website "An incomplete history of London's television studios". I think Max would enjoy the fact that the theatre is now the Empire again and is operating as a music venue. *Those Were the Days* obviously also owes a debt to *The Good Old Days* which also first appeared on television in 1953. I need hardly say that my show and the circumstances of its first night are entirely imaginary.

All my books must include grateful thanks to my wonderful editor, Jane Wood, and agent, Rebecca Carter. Thanks to everyone at Quercus and Janklow and Nesbit for working so hard on my behalf. Thanks also to my American agent, Kirby Kim, and to Naomi Gibbs, Katrina Kruse and Michelle Bonanno-Triant from Houghton Mifflin Harcourt. Thank you all for embracing this new cast of characters.

Love and thanks always to my husband, Andrew, and to our children, Alex and Juliet. This book is for Mandy Merron and Heather Williams, my dear friends from university days.

Elly Griffiths, 2016